MADE IN HAWAII

STORIES

GUERNICA WORLD EDITIONS 46

MADE IN HAWAII

STORIES

Cedric Yamanaka

GUERNICA
World
EDITIONS

TORONTO—CHICAGO—BUFFALO—LANCASTER (U.K.)
2022

Guernica Founder: Antonio D'Alfonso

Michael Mirolla, editor
Interior design: Jill Ronsley, suneditwrite.com
Cover design: Allen Jomoc Jr.
Front cover: Jason Oshiro

Guernica Editions Inc.
287 Templemead Drive, Hamilton (ON), Canada L8W 2W4
2250 Military Road, Tonawanda, N.Y. 14150-6000 U.S.A.
www.guernicaeditions.com

Distributors:
Independent Publishers Group (IPG)
600 North Pulaski Road, Chicago IL 60624
University of Toronto Press Distribution (UTP)
5201 Dufferin Street, Toronto (ON), Canada M3H 5T8
Gazelle Book Services, White Cross Mills
High Town, Lancaster LA1 4XS U.K.

First edition.
Printed in Canada.

Legal Deposit—First Quarter
Library of Congress Catalog Card Number: 2021948158
Library and Archives Canada Cataloguing in Publication
Title: Made in Hawaii : stories / Cedric Yamanaka.
Names: Yamanaka, Cedric, author.
Series: Guernica world editions ; 46.
Description: First edition. | Series statement: Guernica world editions ; 46
Identifiers: Canadiana (print) 20210327529 | Canadiana (ebook)
20210327537 | ISBN 9781771837224 (softcover) | ISBN 9781771837231 (EPUB)
Classification: LCC PS3625.A53 M33 2022 | DDC 813/.6—dc23

CONTENTS

To Laurie, Caleb and Ginger

SOMETHING ABOUT THE REEF, THE TIDE, THE UNDERTOW

(HONOLULU)—Nine people died today during a reef walk off Diamond Head. Witnesses say the group of teachers and students were on a field trip when a series of large waves caught them by surprise. Some of the victims were knocked into the ocean and panicked. Others were pulled out into deeper water where they drowned. "It was a freak accident," said windsurfer Sonny Souza. "It must've been something about the tide, the reef, the undertow."

MOM ALWAYS TOLD ME. NEVER cut your fingernails at night.

"Why?" I asked, clutching the clipper as I sat cross-legged, next to the trash can.

"Because if you do," she said, "you won't be around when your parents die."

Her eyes—the color of strong curry powder—reflected the light of the living room lamp.

"I don't understand," I said. "What's the connection between cutting my fingernails and ...?"

"I don't have time to argue with you, Lowell," she said. "Can't you listen to me for once? Between you and your sister, why can't one of you listen to me?"

Mom kissed me on the cheek and went to bed. She had to wake up early the next morning to lead her class on a reef walk. She'd been teaching the fourth graders about sea animals, and figured it'd be a perfect opportunity for them to see starfish, fish and turtles first hand. I put the clipper away, choosing to wait until the light of day to cut my fingernails.

* * *

The next morning, I walked into the backyard with a butterfly net, hoping to catch a bee. I still had a half hour or so before school. Mom had already left for her reef walk. There were a lot of bees out that day. Honeybees, bumble bees, yellow jackets, wasps. I walked towards a large hibiscus bush. I had to be careful. Catching the bees could be pretty challenging.

A yellow jacket buzzed industriously around a pink flower. Quickly, I trapped the wasp in my net. Then I gently tapped it with my slipper, not hard enough to kill it, just to knock it out. Then I placed the dazed yellow jacket into a glass jar. After a while, it would recover.

My older sister Renee came out of the house and told me to leave the bees alone.

"If you keep on bothering the bees, they'll get mad at you," she said. And sure enough, as soon as Renee walked back into the house, a honeybee stung me right on the palm of my hand. My whole forearm turned real red and swollen and Renee had to squeeze the stinger out, still beating like a heart.

* * *

Dad had a rep as the best bus driver at the Kamehameha Schools. Everybody wanted to ride in Dad's bus. And that made me feel good. I always felt safe as Dad drove us from the Kapalama Terminal up Skyline Drive to campus. He always looked like he knew exactly what he was doing—like he was meant to drive us to school every day—left hand on the big steering wheel, right hand on the faded yellow tennis ball on the stick shift. He clipped pictures of Mom, Renee and me on the large visors that protected his eyes from the sun.

There were all kinds of reasons why everybody lined up for Dad's bus. He always played cool songs—rock or Hawaiian. Some drivers refused to turn on their radios or, worse yet, played classical music. Some drivers were grumpy. Dad always wore a smile. Some drivers didn't say jack to you. Dad always said "good morning" or "good afternoon." Some drivers hit their brakes way in front of the stop, on purpose, to make you walk to their next bus or class. Even when it was raining. Dad always stopped right in front of you.

All my classmates said I was lucky to have a cool dad. And that made me feel good.

* * *

Mom always told this story to Renee.

One rainy night, a boy and a girl are driving along the dark, winding road near the Pali. When they get to Morgan's Corner, the boy says he's run out of gas, so he'll walk into town and look for the nearest service station. He tells the girl to roll up the windows, lock the doors, and wait in the car. The boy leaves and the girl waits. After awhile, she falls asleep listening to the tap-tap sound of the rain on the car roof. When she opens her eyes again, it's morning. The boy still hasn't returned. She gets out of the car to stretch her legs and feel the sun. It is a beautiful morning. The birds are singing and the sweet smell of ginger fills the air. Then the girl screams. The body of the boy hangs from a monkeypod tree and the tap-tap sound she'd fallen asleep to had been his blood dripping onto the roof of the car.

"Why does Mom always tell you that creepy story?" I asked Renee one day, after school.

"Because," Dad said, walking into the living room, filling the house with the smell of English Leather, "Mom don't want her only daughter driving off to Morgan's Corner with some no-good loser." He still wore his work clothes—the blue shirt with the short sleeves and his name, Marc, stitched on his breast pocket.

"Oh, Dad," Renee said, blushing.

"Mom loves her stories, doesn't she?" Dad said.

* * *

I was at the library doing some research for a history project on Kamehameha the Great. I sat in a carrel in the back, staring at my bee sting. My forearm had swollen to the size of Dad's. I hoped I'd have strong, muscular arms like Dad one day.

"Lowell," Dad said, walking into the library.

"Dad?" I said. "What are you doing in here?"

"We gotta go home," he said, struggling to get the words out.

"What? Why?"

"Your Mom is dead," he said, taking the deepest of breaths.

II

(HONOLULU)—Thousands of dead squid have mysteriously washed ashore on Hawaii's beaches. Officials from the Big Island to Kauai spent much of the morning clearing away tons of the creatures. Scientists say the unusual phenomenon may have been caused by a sudden change in the current, tide or water temperature. "I've never seen anything like it," said Aaron Davis, a surfer at Waikiki Beach. "It's the strangest thing."

I clipped this article out of the newspaper on the one-year anniversary of Mom's death. She would've loved this. Just like Dad always said, she loved her stories.

* * *

On her last night with us, Mom prepared tiny *pipi* shells for dinner. Black sea snails. An aunty from Kauai had picked them off the rocks at Kealia Beach and brought them over for Mom.

"You boil them alive?" I asked Mom.

"Of course," she said, smiling. "Just throw them in some hot water. Add salt. Then you poke the inside of the shell with a toothpick or a sewing needle and eat them. You wanna try one?"

"Yuck."

"Don't talk like that. Aunty Esther's boy died picking pipi shells. Big Island. Your cousin was climbing on the rocks and a wave came and swept him away."

"Wow. No wonder Aunty Esther always looks sad."

"Yup. Imagine dying in the ocean like that. Must be so cold."

* * *

Three days after Mom's funeral, Renee and I rode our bicycles along Nimitz Highway—near the oil refineries and the paper factory—towards Sand Island. We passed warehouses, bus yards, and auto repair shops. There was the sharp smell of pineapple from the cannery nearby, and from somewhere I couldn't figure out, rotten eggs. After about a half hour or so, we came to a huge steel drawbridge.

"Look," said Renee, as we passed an empty tollbooth with cracked glass. "Bullet holes."

As we crossed the bridge, I looked down and noticed tiny openings in the steel where you could see the deep blue ocean far, far below. It felt kinda scary. The water looked very cold and very angry. I was relieved when we reached Sand Island.

The air felt dry and hot. We rode our bikes down a dusty road filled with potholes. We passed rusted iron shacks, concrete barricades left behind from World War II, and hundreds of abandoned cars piled one on top of the other like twisted, metal towers. Soon, we reached the beach and walked.

"Listen," Renee said, handing me a large shell. "You can hear the ocean."

"I can't hear anything," I said, placing the cold shell against my ear.

We passed a huge sunfish—looking like a decapitated fish head—lying dead in a tangle of seaweed, drying and rotting in the sun. Flies buzzed over the stinking carcass.

Eventually, Renee and I stopped at an area lined with huge, black boulders and looked out at the ocean.

"Dad's not doing well," Renee said as we sat down.

"How do you know?" I asked.

"A woman knows these things."

"You're not a woman," I said, as a wave crashed on the boulders.

"I wonder why they never found Mom's body," Renee said, staring at the horizon.

"Maybe the ocean really wanted her," I said.

I threw a stone into the ocean and immediately regretted it, sickened, like I'd launched an unprovoked offensive against my poor mother's belly.

* * *

Every other Saturday morning, Dad builds a tool shed in the backyard, only to tear it down. He collects the wooden walls, the metal roof, and nails it all together. The shed is about eight feet high, the size of a small bathroom. Then he tacks the bills of marlins, the tails of ahi, to the wooden front door. Trophies of great fish from the past. Next, he fills the shed with his prized possessions. First the fishing poles, tackle boxes, scoop nets. Then the old car parts: bumpers, rims, windshield wipers, mirrors, license plates, carburetor fluid, steering fluid, brake fluid, WD-40, Armor All. Then, finally, the tools: drills, hammers, circular saws, screwdrivers, wrenches, saws, boxes of nails and screws of differing sizes, picks, axes, hoes, rakes, brooms, knives, machetes, mops, buckets.

At the end of the day, after the tool shed is assembled, Dad grabs a hammer and takes it all apart again. Lizards and roaches scramble out into the sun, confused.

14

* * *

Dozens of people showed up for Renee's graduation party. Everybody seemed to be having a good time. Except Dad. He sat in the corner of the garage, in a bright colored aloha shirt, staring at the moon.

Renee's boyfriend—Manny Rivera—piled rice, noodles, ribs, kalua pig and opihi on a plate and offered it to Dad. Dad ignored him.

"Mr. Botelho?" Manny said. "You should eat something."

Suddenly, Dad slapped the plate out of Manny's hand. The food went flying. The party went dead.

"Have you tried to get into my daughter's pants?" Dad said. "Have you taken her to Morgan's Corner?"

"Uh, no sir," Manny said, shaking his head.

"You better not!" Dad said, yelling. "I'll kill you, you fucker! Renee, don't you ever forget your mother! Don't you ever forget what she used to tell you about Morgan's Corner. You remember?"

"Yes, Dad," Renee said, sweeping the food off the floor into a dustpan.

* * *

"Lowell," Renee said, walking into my bedroom later that night, "can I talk to you?"

"Of course," I said. "Is it about Dad?"

"No. Well, yes."

Renee sat on my bed. She wore a robe and still smelled like the sweet lei she'd been wearing earlier.

"Lowell," she said, clutching a wet ball of Kleenex in her hand. "What am I gonna do? I'm pregnant."

III

When Renee told Dad she was pregnant, he snapped.

"You fucking slut!" he screamed. "You dumb bitch! I thought you was a smart girl! You're nothing but a stupid whore!"

"Dad," I said.

"Shut your mouth, Lowell," he said, fists clenched. "Before I kick your ass!"

"I'm sorry, Dad," Renee said. "But ..."

"But what?" Dad said. "What's Mom gonna say when she comes home?"

"When she comes home?" Renee said. "Dad, Mom's not ..."

"That's the problem with you kids! You don't listen! You didn't listen to Mom! You went up to Morgan's Corner and spread your legs! And now look what happened."

"Dad," Renee said, crying. "Mom is not coming home ..."

Dad slapped Renee in the face. My sister fell to the floor and crumpled into the fetal position, afraid to get hit again.

* * *

I woke up the next morning and something in the pit of my naau told me things were not right. I looked out my bedroom window. Sure enough, everything Renee owned—her clothes, her books, her CDs—had been tossed in the yard.

"Dad did it last night," Renee said. "When I was gone."

Dad was nowhere to be seen. I called the school. His co-workers said he hadn't shown up again. They were pretty used to this by now. Ever since Mom's death, it was pretty routine. Renee and me looked everywhere. Then Renee came up with an idea. We drove to Diamond Head beach. I thought we were too late. Police cars and fire trucks were parked at the lookout, near the lighthouse. We prepared for the worst. But there was Dad, sitting on a rock wall looking out at the ocean.

"Dad?" Renee said, gently grabbing Dad's arm. "Let's go home."

"Don't touch me, bitch," he said. "I don't like whores touching me."

"C'mon, Dad," I said. "What are you doing?"

"I'm looking for Mom. She's still out there. Somewhere."

The firefighters climbed up the hill, carrying a stretcher. Hikers had discovered the body of a homeless man decomposing in a grove of thorny haole koa trees. They wore surgical masks to protect themselves from the sweet, rotten smell. Renee and I had no masks. That night, even though I took three showers, I could not get that smell out of my hair.

* * *

Renee tried, but couldn't take it anymore. The last straw was when Dad chased her out of the house with a machete. She was moving to Oregon. She had friends there who were talking about opening a restaurant. They needed waitresses. I drove her to the airport.

"So, what are you doing about the baby?" I said.

"I don't know," Renee said. "My friends say they know doctors who can, um, take care of things. I don't know, Lowell."

"What does Manny think?"

"Manny left me, the asshole."

When the public address announcer called Renee's flight, we walked to the gate and hugged.

"Take care of Dad," Renee said. "He's suffering."

"We're all suffering."

I tried hard and didn't cry until I heard myself say the word "goodbye."

* * *

Dad was not at home again. The first place I looked was Diamond Head. It was dark. All of the surfers were gone. I ran down to the beach. There was Dad, a tiny figure. The only person in the water. Walking out to sea. A silhouette backlit by the moon.

"I need to bring Mom home," he said, when I finally caught up to him. The cold water came up to our noses.

"No," I said, wondering about the undertow.

* * *

(HONOLULU)—A 64-year old Kalihi man drowned off Diamond Head this morning. Witnesses say Marc Botelho—a Kamehameha Schools bus driver—appeared to be wandering on the reef when he turned towards the horizon and continued walking towards deeper water until disappearing. Ocean Safety and Services spokesman Edson Thompson said attempts to perform cardiopulmonary resuscitation on Botelho were unsuccessful.

I heard the pounding coming from the backyard and I knew Dad was building his tool shed again. But something seemed different this time. His movements were more urgent, his breathing harder. And this time, after he was done, he left the tool shed up. Then he got in his truck and drove off. Of course, I knew exactly where he was going. Call it stupidity, laziness—or murder even—I let him go. I can't explain why. I just let Dad go.

* * *

I've tried to avoid the ocean since losing Mom and Dad. I'd almost forgotten the feel of the sand and pebbles on my feet, the heat of the sun on my back and shoulders, how cold that first contact with ocean water can feel. As a kid, I used to love the beach the way young Travis loves the beach now. We walk towards the water cautiously. The first small wave covers our feet—a greeting from an affectionate but wary animal tentatively sniffing at our feet, trying to determine if we mean well or harm.

Renee—Travis' mom—sits on the shore watching us, a distant red spot. As Travis giggles, water swirls around the crater in the sand created by our feet, then just as quickly disappears. We walk towards the reef. The rocks are slippery and full of holes. We see reef fish, a sea urchin. Travis points. In a crack, I catch a glimpse of the spotted moray eel. Its sharp teeth and cold eyes remind me how dangerous the ocean can be. Eels, barracudas, sharks, undertows, drownings.

I look up at Diamond Head and lead Travis back towards shore. The wet sand on the ocean bottom collects around our ankles, hands refusing to let go.

WHAT I HAVE TO TELL YOU

ORION WONG LOOKS OUT AT the ocean off the Waianae Boat Harbor, wonders which is bluer—the sea or the sky—and asks himself how the hell he's going to tell his son what he has to tell him.

"Looks like a nice day, huh, Kona?" Orion says to the five-year-old boy.

Kona, of course, doesn't answer.

"Yeah," Orion says, starting the boat engine and steering past the breakwater towards the horizon. "Maybe we'll get lucky today. Maybe we'll hook up a nice ahi. Make ahi poke. With the *limu kohu* and the *inamono*. I can taste 'em already. My friend at the garage, Bobby, he and his boy caught a hundred-twenty pounder at the Ahi Fever Tournament. We'll catch one bigger than that, huh?"

Kona gazes out to sea, eyes the color of maple syrup. Since the day of his birth, the boy has never spoken a word. He does not laugh or cry. He rarely smiles. Therapists say Kona is of above average intelligence. At home, the boy plays with toy trucks and Kikaida miniatures, reads voraciously, draws pictures, watches TV. The experts scratch their heads and call it a rare and baffling case. They do studies, write reports, consult mainland professionals. Orion and his wife Nani simply have learned to consider Kona's silence a part of life.

Orion adjusts the lines and hooks on four fishing poles and casts them out to sea. Waves slam against the side of Orion's boat, a tiny 14-foot double hull with a 40-horsepower engine he bought second hand through the classified ads. The boat resembles a sports convertible car. There are two seats in the front and a steering wheel on the left side. Sea spray is everywhere.

"This sure beats being stuck in the garage," says Orion, breathing in the salty smell of the sea. "I've worked fifteen days straight, fixing car after car. It's nice to finally have a day off. There's gotta be a better way to make a living. I tell your Mom the place is driving me crazy. She don't listen. She don't understand."

Orion met Nani at the Kaneohe Body and Fender. She had a nail in her tire. Orion patched the leak. He wanted to tell her she had eyes as green as the ti leaves in his back yard. Instead, he told her the tire would run good as new.

"Cash or charge?" Orion asked.

"Uh, charge," Nani said, opening her wallet and handing him a credit card. Just like that, Orion had Nani's name, address, phone number. He returned the credit card and thanked her. Nani smiled, tilted her head to one side, and walked out of the garage.

It took Orion three days to work up the nerve to call her. It was the first time he'd ever called a customer, right out of the blue. She answered the telephone on the second ring. Right off the bat, Orion knew it was Nani.

"May I speak to Nani?" he said, nervous.

"This is Nani."

"Hi, Nani. Jeez, you're going to think this is weird but I'm the guy at Kaneohe Body and Fender. Orion. I fixed your tire, remember?"

"Yes, I do. Of course. Hi."

Orion felt relieved. She actually sounded happy to hear from him. Somehow, they wound up talking for an hour. Then Orion worked up the courage to ask Nani if maybe they could get together sometime.

"This is weird," Nani said. But she was laughing, so Orion guessed things were all right.

"Yeah, I know it is. But how about it?"

"Well, yeah, I'd like that, I guess. Why not? Boy, this is weird."

Orion picked Nani up the next Friday. She lived on a hill over-looking Chinaman's Hat. She worked as a nurse in the maternity ward at Queen's. They went out for Chinese food. She said she liked the sweet-sour shrimps but couldn't even look at the steamed fish with ginger and shoyu.

One year later, they went to court and got married before a judge. Orion wore his best aloha shirt, white pants, and white shoes to the ceremony. Nani said he looked like a member of the Royal Hawaiian Band. She wore a blue muumuu and a haku lei. After the fifteen-minute ceremony, Orion and Nani walked out of the judge's chambers. A bunch of news reporters and cameramen sprinted out of an elevator and rushed past them.

"What's going on here?" Orion asked a cameraman.

"A verdict in a murder trial," the cameraman said, breathing hard.

"Murder trial?" Orion said. "What kind?"

"You probably don't want to hear this but a guy just got convicted of slashing his wife's throat. He caught her in bed with another man."

Orion guessed the cameraman could tell Nani and he'd just gotten married.

"That will never happen to us," Orion said, winking at Nani. They were holding hands.

But the cameraman wasn't listening.

Orion steers his boat out towards the three-mile buoy. "Bull, the water is nice today, hah?" he says. Orion often calls his son "Bull." Just like his old man used to call him. "Clear. Glassy. I should drop the boat anchor and take a dive. I bet there's choke lobster holes down below."

Although his son never speaks, Orion often feels like he knows exactly what his son is thinking. It's a natural talent that has developed—perhaps through instinct, perhaps through necessity—over the years. On good days, Orion believes he is on the right track with his son's thoughts. On bad days, understanding Kona is as difficult as trying to predict the future by slicing open a goat and reading its entrails.

The wind blows through Orion's dark hair, which is slowly but surely revealing signs of gray. Kona looks out to sea. Orion remembers the day Nani told him she was pregnant. He'd never seen her so happy. They were at Ala Moana Beach Park early one Saturday morning, before it got crowded, casting for *oio*. Orion brought bottles of Coca Cola that had been covered with ice and placed in a small cooler. Even though the bottles had a fishy smell from the bait, the sodas were the best Orion ever had. They were so cold, they hurt Orion's teeth when he drank.

"It's going to be a boy," said Nani, blushing, hands on her belly. Her stomach was still rock hard from crunches done at 24-Hour Fitness. "I can tell."

"Do you have a name for him?" Orion said.

"Yes. Kona."

"Kona? That's the name of a town. Not a boy."

Nani explained. She came up with the name Kona because that's where the boy had been conceived. In the middle of a barren lava field, under the stars one summer night, while fishing lines probed deep into the dark, belly of the sea.

"The ocean is so big," Orion says, circling the three-mile buoy. The water is a very deep blue. "It looks like it goes on forever. I know what you're thinking, Bull. Nothing lasts forever. What about love? You think love lasts forever? I used to think so. In fact, I was positive. Now, I ain't so sure. Your mom says love lasts forever. I don't know."

Orion and Nani have been married for eight years. But over the years Orion started wondering if something had been lost somewhere. He wasn't sure what, but something that once felt so full of life had, over the years, died. Last night, after much debate, Orion told Nani how he felt.

"Life has grown stagnant between us," he said. "Don't you feel it, too?"

Nani asked Orion what he wanted. Orion said he wasn't sure. Maybe it wouldn't be a bad idea if they lived separate lives. Just for a while. Nani asked Orion if he'd found another girl. The young receptionist at work? A girl in a hostess bar? Orion said no, which was the truth. Nani started crying and said if that's what Orion wanted, go ahead. Go ahead and tell Kona.

"Son," Orion says, steering his boat towards Kaena Point,

sometimes following the flight of a sea bird. "I have something to tell you."

Orion has been thinking about it for a while now. When did things get so bad between him and Nani? The answer scares Orion. Things changed the day Kona was born, with the blue umbilical cord wrapped around his neck and shoulder like the silk banner of a beauty pageant contestant. Orion knows how horrible it sounds, but it's the truth. Everything was fine before Kona. He and Nani went to the movies, just like normal couples. They ate at restaurants, danced at clubs, wore matching green t-shirts and attended UH football games. The minute Kona was born, though, the child became the focus of their lives. That hasn't changed in five years. And somewhere, somehow, Orion and Nani focused so much on Kona, they forgot to focus on each other.

At first, they waited for Kona to babble, to talk, like other toddlers. He did not. Of course, this made things even more difficult. Still, they were both so thankful. Kona was growing up big and strong. He seemed bright—aware and intelligent. And he had a good heart. But why didn't he talk? Orion wondered if he had failed his son somehow. Where did I go wrong, he asked himself.

As a mechanic, Orion prided himself on his ability to solve problems. If a car engine fails to turn over, he'll check under the hood. A fluid leak means something else. A clutch that refuses to budge poses another dilemma. All of these situations can be fixed with the right tools and the proper techniques. It is hard for Orion to accept the truth that some things cannot—will not—be repaired.

One morning, several years ago, Orion looked out the kitchen window and saw Kona sitting on a stone wall outside the house, next to the tool shed. Orion read the morning paper, finished three cups of black coffee, and repaired a clogged drain in the bathroom. When he checked on Kona again, his son remained sitting on the same stone wall, seemingly staring into space. Curious, Orion went outside.

"What's so interesting out here, Bull?" he asked his son.

Orion followed the boy's gaze. Kona watched as a tiny spider built an intricate web, about the size of a basketball, across the wooden pillars of the tool shed. The sun sparkled against the fine web, like fire reflecting off the blade of a sharp sword. The web appeared as sturdy as the strongest monofilament.

"Too good, ah?" Orion said, quietly.

He sat next to his son, on the stone wall. For several hours, father and son watched the spider work. Suddenly, Kona picked up a rock and threw it at the center of the web. The project collapsed and tumbled into a field of high grass.

"What I have to tell you," Orion says. The sky over the ocean is blue, but clouds cover the sun so it's not blazing hot. "It's about me and your mom."

But Kona is not listening. His maple-syrup eyes are wide, his mouth open as if he is about to speak. Orion anxiously follows Kona's gaze to a point several hundred yards in front of the boat. Orion is not sure if he is seeing things. Something explodes in the water. He steers the boat towards the area. Suddenly, there are dozens of explosions all over the boat. Orion and Kona are in the middle of a school of hundreds of dolphins.

"Bull," Orion says, breathless. "This is amazing."

Kona watches the dolphins. Some leap into the air, the sun glistening off their wet and smooth bodies. Others swim right up to the boat, curious. Kona, for just a second, places his hand on Orion's shoulder. Orion is elated. It is a sign, an acknowledgement, an agreement. But then he wonders. Maybe his son had simply brushed him accidentally, heading back to the front of the rocking boat?

Suddenly, a fishing line begins to scream. Orion tends to the pole. He feels Kona's gaze shift from the dolphins to him. And this makes Orion feel even better.

Orion attempts to reel in a little bit of fishing line. He can tell by the resistance that something very large, something very strong, is hooked on the other end. Kona moves closer to him. Orion can smell his son's hair—apples, sugar, salt.

"Bull," Orion says. "Take the pole."

Kona's tiny fingers wrap around the pole. Orion covers his son's hands with his own.

The fish boldly takes some line out. Kona lets him run and then reels in more line. The fish takes more line out. Ten minutes later, the brave but exhausted fish is just off the side of the boat. An ahi, maybe twelve pounds. Orion admires the beautiful blue, green color of the fish just before it is pulled out of the water. He knows within only a few heartbeats, the brilliant color will disappear for good.

FOR SALE

I'M DRIVING TO ANOTHER OPEN house, thinking about interest rates and closing dates, when the body crashes through the windshield of my boyfriend's brand-new Infiniti Q45. For a split second, I wonder if I'm the victim of some cruel prank, the kind of thing my Princeton sorority sisters used to pull. But then I see the bloody face staring at me through the shattered glass—a young Asian woman, eyes and mouth wide open—and I somehow manage to pull my car to the side of the road.

Oh my God!

The woman fell from an overpass near the School Street off ramp, the police officer explains. Or maybe she was pushed.

Can I get your name, ma'am, he says.

Mary, I say. Mary Iwata.

I thought you looked familiar. You sold a house to me and my wife.

My body can't stop shaking. I've always been a careful driver. When my father taught me to drive many, many years ago, he told me three things. Plan my route in advance. Minimize left turns. And leave early to avoid rushing.

He never told me to watch out for falling bodies.

* * *

Thanks to the police officer, who is kind enough to offer me a ride, I get to my open house on time, early in fact. A spacious three-bedroom, two bath in Kaimuki. I sit at the koa kitchen table with the Sunday newspaper and a thermos of coffee, studying other listings. It always helps to keep up with the other Realtors. Somehow, this helps calm me. Maybe it's the routine. Work takes my mind off real life.

Even on a day like this.

The first people to come in are a nice, young couple. College educated, probably advanced degrees, a combined good six-figure income. Looking for a larger home. Preparing, perhaps, for a first child.

We love it, they say, opening windows, kitchen cabinets, bedroom closets.

It is beautiful, I say, in my best Realtor-slash-friend voice. The walls have been repainted. The carpet is new …

Why is the asking price so low?

It is low. 400-thousand. A quick scan of the MLS listings will reveal other comparable homes in the area selling for at least half a million.

The seller is motivated, I say.

A week later, the seller—Mr. Warren—offers his disclosure. His home had been a rental property. The first tenants, an Indian family, left behind the smell of curry. The second tenants, a Korean family, left behind the smell of kim chee. Mr. Warren's last tenant, a college student, left behind his splattered brains.

I should have told you earlier, Mr. Warren says.

Yes, I say.

* * *

I'm not a real estate attorney, he says, from behind his Raybans. But I don't think you had to disclose a thing.

But …

But nothing. You didn't even know.

My boyfriend, Darrin Simon, has just returned from a week-long conference in Hong Kong.

Honey, I say, clearing my throat. You're not going to believe what happened to me on Sunday. I was driving the car. Your car …

I try and stop the trembling again, remembering.

How'd you like the Infiniti? Pretty smooth, huh?

Yes, it's great. But listen. I was driving on the freeway, on my way to an open house, when ...

Hey, how about dinner? I've been invited to the Japanese Consulate for sushi. I'll pick you up at seven. Do you have my car keys?

Suddenly, I don't want to tell Darrin about Sunday. I don't want to tell him that his precious brand-new Infiniti is in the shop. I don't want to tell him anything.

The last thing I need now is another lecture from Darrin. I know that look in his eyes. Like I'm some stupid chick who can't do anything without him. Like it's my fault that some poor woman tumbled from the sky into my life.

Uh, I say, let's walk to the Consulate.

Walk?

Sure, it's not very far from town. It'll be good for us. Fitness and all, right?

Mary, are you okay?

* * *

I swim with the smooth strokes I've paid my personal trainer fifteen hundred dollars to learn. Oscar is great—a former Olympic bronze medalist. The waters off Ala Moana Beach Park are orange, almost like lava, late in the afternoon. The salt water calms me. I think of the evening to come—dinner at the Japanese Consulate with Darrin, martinis at Indigo later.

Suddenly, a giant manta ray leaps out of the ocean, flapping its great wings next to me. The fish possesses the wingspan of Darrin's damaged Infiniti's hood. Then it dives back into the water with an awesome splash. I freak out. Water shoots up my nose and down my throat. My calf cramps up. I try to tread water, but start to sink.

Help! I scream. But there is no one around. The pain is almost unbearable.

As I cough water, a hand wraps around my waist and takes me to shore.

You saved my life, I say. I lie on the sand, out of breath.

My name's Phil.

Phil is a large man, about my age. His head is shaved bald. He wears tattoos of snakes on his forearms and chest. I can see he works out. I thank Phil again and hand him my business card, Realtor-instinct. The one with my color portrait. Mary Iwata, R.A.

So, you're a Realtor, he says.

Yes, I say. And you? Are you a lifeguard?

No. I'm an ultimate fighting champion.

You're kidding.

No. Do you want to see my scars?

* * *

The party at the Japanese Consulate reminds me why I only go out with white guys. Every Japanese man in the room reminds me of my father. I bet they all go home and drink light beer with ice and watch sumo. I bet they have boring sons who drive souped-up Toyotas to Zippy's and wear t-shirts with ulua on the backs. The younger guys standing around, trying so hard to look cool, are probably no different. I bet they dream of posing in muscle magazines and hooking up with haole exotic dancers from Femme Nu.

That's another thing Darrin and I sorta have in common. I'm an Asian girl who only goes out with white guys. Darrin is a white guy who only goes out with Asian girls.

Is everything all right? he asks, over doses of maguro and ikura. You seem, I don't know, tense recently …

I guess I have a lot of things on my mind.

Like what?

Like life. Like death. Like freeways …

Death? Freeways? What are you talking about, Mary?

Nothing. I almost drowned this afternoon. I was pulled out of the water by an ultimate fighting champion named Phil.

Phil DeWayne? Darrin says. The guy's a nut. His fists are like sledgehammers. And he's deadly on the mat.

You go to ultimate fighting matches?

* * *

A quick search on Google displays 321,489 hits for Phil DeWayne, the Ultimate Fighting Champion. Born in Philadelphia, he now calls Hawaii home. He is a Gulf War veteran and holds black belts in kung fu, karate and tae kwon do. His hobbies include spear fishing and riding horses. He sports an impressive 15-4 record. In three months, he faces Neon Nicholas Ramirez, the number two-ranked contender.

One Sunday afternoon, Phil shows up at an open house I'm holding on Hawaii Loa Ridge.

I didn't know you were in the market for a home, I say.

Yeah, he says. We all need to live somewhere.

Yes. Well, as you can see, this is not a bad place to pick. Six bedrooms, three baths. Indoor waterfall and Jacuzzi. 1.6 million dollars.

I can't believe I saved your life, Mary. Can I call you Mary?

Yes.

I usually try and kill people. That's my line of work. Well, not actually killing them. Just hurting them very badly. I never thought I was any good at saving people. You're a first. Can I buy you a burger or something, Mary?

Um.

Okay. I get it. Maybe some other time.

* * *

It was creepy. That's what I tell Darrin.

We are in Darrin's Infiniti, driving to the Honolulu Club for our daily workout. The auto body guys have done an amazing job. The damaged hood, the windshield, all as good as new. I wish the poor woman could somehow, magically, have enjoyed a similar fate. Why did she jump? Or why would someone push her onto the freeway?

You're imagining things, he says. Darrin always accuses me of imagining things. He thinks I think every man in the world is in love with me, wants to get into my pants. He thinks I'm a narcissist.

I'm serious, Darrin. He looked at me funny.

Stop it, honey, he says at a light. Give me a kiss.

I do.

Did you clean the car or something while I was gone? It just feels, I don't know, different …

The bloody face stares at me, only me, through the newly repaired windshield.

* * *

Mary, when doing bicep curls, keep your elbows to your side.

Who is this? It's three in the morning.

It's me. Phil.

Phil?

The guy who saved your life.

The air in my bedroom goes ice cold. Phil continues.

I saw you at the Honolulu Club tonight. Last night. With that guy. Is that your boyfriend?

Yes. He's a sheriff. Police officer. FBI Agent …

Excuse me for asking, but does he make you happy, Mary? Or are you thinking of leaving him? That's the vibe I got, watching the two of you together. Maybe that'd be the best thing. Leaving him. I'm not sure if he's the best person in the world for you. You deserve better. He looks like a guy I once fought in a match. I broke his ribs and sent the poor bastard to his retirement.

How did you get my home number?

It's on your business card. I used to work out. With my wife. But …

Yeah?

The telephone is dead.

* * *

The property is gorgeous, the penthouse of a Makiki luxury condominium. I'm already debating whether to place my commission in the stock market, a Money Market or a shopping spree. I'm leaning towards the latter. Or maybe I should invest in a handgun.

When Phil walks into the open house, I nearly die.

Please forgive me, he says. I just can't get over it. I pulled you out of the water. Saved you from the clutches of death. It's like you've given me something. Hope or ...

You can't follow me around like this. Please. What do you want? Money? Sex? Drugs?

No, Mary. Please. It's nothing like that. I just want to be your friend.

* * *

At first I thought it was my imagination. But now I'm sure of it. My boss wants me to specialize in selling homes where death has occurred.

A twelve-year-old boy? I say.

Yes, says my boss. They don't know if it was an accidental death or suicide.

And now the parents want to move out of the house. Understandably.

And you want me to sell it.

Yes. It's not like he blew his brains out in his bedroom.

Yes.

I wouldn't ask you if I didn't think you could do it.

A twelve-year-old boy. Dear God.

* * *

The four-bedroom home is in Kaneohe, with a stunning view of the Koolaus and the bay.

Have you seen the garage? I say.

May we see the swimming pool in back? the couple responds. I should've known. They both look like athletes. Long, toned arms and legs. Swimmers, probably. Just my luck.

Of course, I say.

The pool is filled with salt water, says the man. I love salt-water pools. You come out of the water and you don't have that sticky, chlorinated feel. You actually have a glow. And the upkeep is a breeze. All it takes is a bag of salt every now and then.

And it's good for your skin, says the woman.

Why is the property so cheap? says the man.

I have to tell you something, I say, taking a deep breath. Here we go.

Yes?

A twelve-year-old boy drowned in this pool.

Oh. Thank you.

The professional swimmers are gone.

* * *

Something, I don't know what, compels me to visit the overpass near the off ramp where the poor lady leapt to her death. Why did she do it? Was she sick? Did she have problems with her family? Financial troubles? Suddenly, I see Phil walking towards me. The evil prick is stalking me. He's carrying a pot of flowers. Yellow marigolds, straight from Safeway.

I try to turn away. But Phil doesn't notice me. He leans on the concrete railing, staring down at the speeding cars on the freeway below. He is crying. *What's going on?* I surprise myself by walking up to him, gently placing my hand on his tattooed arm.

Phil? Are you okay? Why ...

Mary? My wife died here. She fell and was hit by a car on the freeway.

Your wife? Here? I-I'm sorry ...

I killed her.

You pushed her off the overpass?

She jumped. I guess she was just sick of it all. Sick of watching me get pummeled night after night. She always said she felt the pain of every blow she watched me take. Once, I came home blind. While an opponent choked me, the blood vessels in my eyes exploded. I got my sight back, eventually, but lost my wife. She asked me to choose. Fighting or love. I chose fighting.

I'm so sorry.

Phil hugs the flowers to his chest the way I, as a schoolgirl, once clutched my Hello Kitty notebooks.

* * *

I don't go home. Can't. Instead, I return to that first house. The one I sold the day Phil's wife crashed into the windshield of Darrin's car. The Kaimuki home that once smelled of Indian curries, then kim chee, then gunpowder and blood. I knock on the door. The young couple answers. They recognize me instantly and welcome me into their new home. I notice the bulge just beginning to show on the woman's belly.

I-I'm sorry to bother you, I say. I just wanted to check and see if you're pleased with your new home.

Pleased? they say. Very pleased. The house is wonderful.

I don't quite know what I want to ask them. *Did you know that someone blew his brains out in the middle bedroom, the one overlooking the avocado tree outside? Does it get cold in here at night? Do you see ghosts? Do you want to back out of the sale?*

Are you okay? the husband asks me. You look pale, Mary. Can I get you some water or something?

I thank them and leave. As I stumble towards Darrin's Infiniti, my insides feel twisted. I feel like I'm falling.

Tending Bar at the Happy Parrot Chinese Restaurant

TELL ME THE TRUTH, PLEASE.

Look at my face closely, dear friend. Do I truly resemble the great kung fu action star, Typhoon Chew? Yes, thank you. That's what everyone says. I could pass for his brother, no? Then how did our lives take such different paths? Mr. Chew learned the martial arts from none other than Bruce Lee, dates the fabulous Hong Kong film actress Shelly Chun, and rides motorcycles with Jackie Chan.

Me, my name is Timothy Louie and I'm a bartender here at the Happy Parrot Chinese Restaurant. In Chinatown—on the ground floor of the historic Y. Wing Lee Building—between R. Hong's Acupuncture and a theater that shows dirty, peep show movies. Sometimes, prostitutes with faces tough as rhinoceros hides smoke crack pipes in front of the sculpted lions guarding the doorway. Maybe you've eaten here, enjoyed our famous dim sum or cake noodle? At a birthday celebration, perhaps, or a wedding reception or Ching Ming?

Next time you come inside the Happy Parrot Chinese Restaurant, walk past the cashier and the tanks filled with doomed moonfish, prawns and lobsters. I'm the guy behind the bar in the red tuxedo. I think that's one of the worst things about this job. Wearing this cheap, red tuxedo that itches like a mother.

I'm surrounded by mirrors, glasses, bottles of Seagram's, Jose Cuervo, Johnnie Walker, Midori and Gallo. I know this sorry-ass bar station the way a prisoner knows every inch of his cell. To my left, the cash register and the certificate saying we've passed the Department of Health inspections and the room holds a maximum of 256 people. To my right, the drink pricelist the Honolulu Liquor commission makes us post.

Tsing Tao 3.00
Kirin 3.00
Asahi 3.00
Heineken 3.00
Budweiser 2.00
Miller 2.00
Coors 2.00

Directly in front of me is the empty jar with the hopeless sign that reads:

TIPS GREATLY APPRECIATED
MAHALO!

Ohhhhh, how I hate my job! Today was supposed to be my first day off in three weeks. I was at home, all set to go see Typhoon Chew's new movie—*The Mystery of the Crescent Moon Roundhouse Kick.* Just as I was headed out the door, the telephone rang. I could tell by the sound of the ring that it was Boss Wang, the owner of the Happy Parrot Chinese Restaurant. My brain said no answer, no answer, but, like an idiot, I answer.

"Hello?" I say, knowing full well what's coming.

"Timmy, come work tonight! Very busy!"

That's Boss Wang for you. No 'hello,' no 'please,' no 'goodbye,' no nothing.

Come to find out the other bartender, Anson Chock, called in sick. Again. Anson Chock is always pulling this crap. Originally from Guangzhou, in Southern China, he's now a University of Hawaii sophomore majoring in Accounting. With long hair tied in a ponytail, black leather jacket, Marlboro in mouth, and obnoxious Harley-Davidson. The chicks love Anson Chock. To make matters worse, he plays guitar in a rock-and-roll band called Angry Korean Heartthrobs. These young kids, they're not like us old timers. This younger generation, they're weak, spoiled, selfish, soft, able to think only about themselves. And—on top of everything—punks like Anson, they're know-it-alls.

"What's so hard about being a bartender?" he had the nerve to ask me once. "Especially in Chinese restaurant? Everybody order beer. What's the big deal? You get bottle opener. You open bottle. You take money."

Kids nowadays. Cocky bastards.

I wish I could be Anson's age again. If I had paid more attention in school, things may have turned out differently. Maybe I wouldn't be the black sheep of the Louie family. Instead, I cut classes to attend martial arts movies. I'd skip out of math and catch the bus to the rat-infested American Theater in Chinatown—next to the Prince Hanalei All-Male review at the Glades Nightclub—and watch the immortal Wang Yu in those One-Armed Swordsman movies. Or I spent countless Sunday afternoons in the old Liberty and Empress Theaters—admiring the exploits of David Chang, Ti Lung, Yueh Hua and Alexander Fu Sheng in Run Run Shaw films about flying guillotines and heads for sale. Other times, I sat in the New Kokusai—surrounded by glossy portraits of famous Japanese film stars hanging neatly on the wall—and watched Zatoichi the Blind Swordsman flicks. Then, of course, came Bruce Lee. And then everything changed. Bruce Lee was so big, they showed his movies in haole theaters.

No one could compare to Bruce Lee. Until Typhoon Chew. I've seen all of Typhoon Chew's movies. Two of my favorites are *Cobra Style Incident* and *Kung Fu Heartache, Part IV*. Sometimes, as I sit in the theater sucking on my li hing mui and watching Typhoon Chew digging out the livers of evil ninja guys, I wonder if me and

Typhoon, we'd get along. I think we would. In fact, I believe we could make some very good movies together. See, that's always been my dream—to be in the movies.

Anyway, just after high school, I started tending bar at the Happy Parrot Chinese Restaurant. I thought it'd be a temporary thing. A cool part-time job to make some side money and meet some hot babes until I was discovered by some big-time movie producer from Hollywood or Hong Kong. *HA!* Before I knew it, I was working fifty, sixty hours a week, for minimum wage, no holidays, no vacation, no nothing. It's been ten miserable years now! But let me tell you something. I've never called in sick. Not once. Not like Anson Chock, the panty. Not the day I had a 106-degree fever after eating some bad monks' food that had been left out too long. Not the Chinese New Year when the stray Roman candle exploded in my face. Not even the day my poor Popo passed away. Where has my life gone?

Oh, how I hate this job! It is very busy tonight. I should've been a computer genius like Byron Ah Choo. Look at him, sitting pretty at Table Number Nine, wearing his fancy suit and alligator shoes. We grew up together. He was always top in physics class, bottom in P.E. class. But he graduated from MIT and now works at NASA. Makes six-figure salary. Or look at Dr. Waldorf Ho, cardiologist, on Table Fourteen. Luxury condo. MidPac Country Club Member. Drive nice Jaguar.

"Look alive, for crying out loud! You sleeping, or what? I no pay you good money to sleep in my restaurant! Good-for-nothing!"

Boss Wang. He spits out insults the way a dragon issues fire.

I know what you're thinking. "Boy, Timothy Louie, you sure complain a lot. If you hate your job so much, quit!" That's a typical American attitude. Take this job and shove it kind of thing. I wish I could, but it's impossible. See, I have rent to pay. I'm not like Don Chung. His dad is a plastic surgeon. There's a guy, if he's not happy at work, he can take the job and shove it. He hasn't worked in years. Monday through Friday, he's golfing, fishing, living with parents, driving a BMW, using papa's Platinum Visa card. Some people have all the luck.

"One Special Martini. And make it quick!"

Boss's son. Roger Wang, Head Waiter. His face is as white as fresh lichee meat. He is prematurely bald, has a thin moustache, and is always running around his father like a puppy dog and a fire hydrant.

With the seriousness of a chemist, I prepare my Special Martini. You see, the Special Martini is my invention. Gin, vermouth, a splash of maotai, and, yes, a sliver of cold marinated jellyfish! Ha! As far as I know, the Happy Parrot Chinese Restaurant is the only place in the world where you can savor this delicious concoction!

"Hurry up!" Boss's Son says, shooting me a look that calls me a stupid bartender with no future. "Customers waiting!"

Relax, asshole.

Boss's Son—from now on let's call him B.S.—he's always telling me what to do. Wipe up the bar. My soda water is flat. I pour too much Bacardi in my rum and Coke. My bowtie is crooked. How many times have I dreamed me and B.S. are in a duel, like in the climax of a Typhoon Chew movie? We'd meet on a deserted sandy beach or the top of a windy mountain. I'd use the crane technique I learned in my youth at the Shen Shen Choy Physical and Cultural Academy. He'd use the dreaded parrotfish stance. In the end, the side of good would prevail over the side of evil and I'd knock him senseless with a lethal blow to the scrotum. One day, B.S. will take over the Happy Parrot Chinese Restaurant. That's the day I'm out of here.

At this point, there is a commotion in the Happy Parrot Chinese Restaurant like I've never seen. As if someone has released a thousand bees in the place. It is a buzz of excitement, of awe. Men cheer. Women scream. Children clap their hands.

Miracle of miracles, do my eyes deceive me? No, it is true! Here comes Typhoon Chew himself, world famous kung fu movie star! In a white suit, white shoes, sunglasses even though it's nighttime, gold chain around his neck. Typhoon Chew! My idol! Damn! Star of *No-Nonsense Kung Fu, Mighty Acrobat from China, Shaolin Boxing Giant* and, my all-time personal favorite, *Wicked Nunchaku Trick*. As Typhoon Chew's entourage glides past our scrolls of tigers, empresses and the limestone mountains of Guilin, The Great Man works the crowd, shaking hands with every customer like a politician in a tough race. He explains he is in town for the Hawaii International Film Festival, and wanted a nice Chinese dinner.

A beautiful girl escorts him. Imagine me, Timothy Louie, at the Chinese Jaycees Banquet with this Narcissus Queen. Boy that would freak people out. I wonder what that arrogant international lawyer Hector Po would say. I can hear him now. Ho, Timothy Louie get nice chick! Actually, the girl is as breathtaking as the stunning Honk Kong actress Shelly Chun. Ah, wait! It is, indeed, Miss Chun herself! Star of the classic movie *Kung Fu Sorority Girls*. Arguably her finest role. A lot of people say *Empress Pang, Queen of the Monkey Fist* is Shelly Chun's finest work but I say it's *Kung Fu Sorority Girls*.

Boss Wang is all excited. So is B.S. They're both jumping around Typhoon Chew like two ping pong balls bouncing on a linoleum table.

"Timmy!" Boss Wang screams, frantically waving me over. "Come here! Quick!"

I can't believe it! Boss Wang wants to introduce me to Typhoon Chew! This is my chance! My big break! I fix my hair, look in the mirror, and walk up to Boss Wang, B.S. and Typhoon Chew. I wonder if Typhoon Chew will see the resemblance between us.

"Timmy!" Boss Wang says, handing me a camera. "Take picture of me, my son, and Mr. Chew!"

"Okay," I say, sighing. "Smile."

Typhoon Chew flashes a peace sign. *Click!*

"Another one!" B.S. says. "This time, everybody make kung fu stance!"

Boss Wang assumes the position of the Eagle, ready to pluck out an eye. B.S. is the dreaded snake, ready to rip out an Adam's apple from your throat. Typhoon Chew, somewhat embarrassed, takes a boxer's stance.

"I'll hang these pictures on my wall so everybody can see!" Boss Wang gushes. "Of all the Chinese restaurants in town, Typhoon Chew picks Happy Parrot to eat!"

Click!

Before I can shake Typhoon Chew's hand, Boss Wang leads the entourage towards the V.I.P. room, reserved for special occasions. Whoo, the food we serve! Bowls of Shark Fin and Bird's Nest Soup. Heaping platefuls of Lobster in Black Bean Sauce, Peking Duck, Beggars Chicken, steamed mullet, Ma Po Tofu, Chinese Style Tenderloin Steak, Steamed Pork Hash with Salted Duck Egg. I must hand it to the chef, Orville Lo. He's so ugly, children cry when they see his face and dogs bark in alarm. But, ho, you should see him in the kitchen! Armed with a flaming wok, he becomes an artist on the scale of the great Gao Zheng, famous Ming Dynasty painter of masterpieces like *Sunset at Xian* and *Shanghai Nightingale*.

Me, I am crushed. My dream of sharing hot tubs with Hong Kong starlets is sinking faster than a mortar thrown into the Yellow River. But then, the winds of fortune finally blow Timothy Louie's way. At one point in the auspicious evening, Typhoon Chew himself walks out of the crowded V.I.P. room and—incredible!—sits at my bar.

"Nice tux," The Great Man says. "Red is your color."

"Uh, thank you, sir," I manage.

In a few minutes, I'm actually having a conversation with my idol. He speaks the majority of the time in English, but turns to Chinese when he hits a difficult phrase.

"I have everything," Typhoon Chew says, waving his hands in the air the way he wards off deadly spears and nunchaku sticks. "Money, women, looks. But there's one thing I don't have ..."

"I know what it is," I say. "Love."

"No," Typhoon Chew says. "Oscar. I don't have Oscar. I don't even have MTV Movie Award."

So, I listen politely as Typhoon Chew describes his lifelong quest to win the gold statue. How he thought the film *The Dragon Never Asks Twice* should have been nominated. His disappointment—even thoughts of suicide—when *Hands of Clay, Feet of Stone* was bashed by the critics. He even had his acceptance speech memorized. "Thank you, members of the Academy. This victory is a complete surprise to me. I did not expect to win so I do not have anything prepared. But I'd like to thank my agent and my fans."

"Sometimes life can be cruel," I say.

"How long have you been a bartender here?" Typhoon Chew asks.

"Over ten years," I say.

"Ten years?" Typhoon Chew says, marveling. "You poor bastard."

"Yes," I say. "It's been difficult. You know, Boss Wang believes in working overtime. But not paying overtime. Today was supposed to be my first day off in …"

"I once played a bartender in a movie," Typhoon Chew says. "Maybe you saw it? *Lightning Fist of the Bartender*. I played a bartender searching for righteousness in a world of corruption."

"I saw that movie. Twice. It was very good."

I cannot believe my good luck. This is a once in a lifetime opportunity. Typhoon Chew sits right in front of me. Here is my chance to finally shed this dreadful red tuxedo and escape this merciless hellhole known as the Happy Parrot Chinese Restaurant and live my dream. To celebrate, I offer my benefactor my specialty—a Cold Marinated Jellyfish Martini—on the house.

"Thank you," Typhoon Chew says, raising his glass and taking a sip. "Very nice."

"It is my invention," I say. "In fact, the Happy Parrot is the only place in the world where you can enjoy such a beverage. By the way, may I ask you something?"

"What is it?"

"Uh," I say, seizing the glorious moment. "Tell me the truth, please. Look at my face closely. Do I remind you of someone?"

"Excuse me?"

"Do I remind you of someone? Surely you must see the striking resemblance with someone you know. Someone very close to you?"

"Hmmmm," Typhoon Chew says, examining my face. The glare from one of his gold rings temporarily blinds me. "No. I'm sorry. Ah, wait! Of course!"

"Yes!" I say, elated. "You and I could pass for bro …"

"You are a dead ringer for my makeup artist, Mr. Look!"

"No."

"No? Ah! I see! My physician! Dr. Gao! No? My accountant? Hong? My mechanic? Mr. Long?"

"No," I say, grabbing my hero by a muscular forearm and leading him to the large mirror behind the bar. "Look at us! We could be brothers!"

"Uh …"

"Please take me to Hong Kong with you. I could help you with your next film 'The Revenge of the Kung Fu Brothers.' I've read about it in the magazines. I know Sebastian Song is supposed to play your brother. No question, a fine actor. But I hear the poor man is having terrible problems. I'm sure you are aware of the intense media scrutiny surrounding his affair, and the sad fact his wife is divorcing him. The situation is ugly and he can't focus right now. So perhaps you're looking for someone else to play his brother. Someone who can keep his mind on the job. I, Timothy Louie, am that man."

"You?" Typhoon Chew says, laughing so hard he doubles over. Soon the Great Man is gagging frantically, like the time he was blasted with a Hurricane Chop to the larynx in the classic *My Master's Kung Fu Technique is Superior to Your Master's*. Too much gin? Too much maotai? No. This is serious! Typhoon Chew's face is as red as firecracker paper. The man is choking to death!

Before I can do anything, Boss' Son—B.S.—rushes over, wraps his arms around the international film star's mighty chest, and performs the life saving Heimlich maneuver. Soon, a piece of jellyfish tentacle—roughly the length of one of those horrible curly hairs I always find when cleaning the men's bathroom—dribbles out of Typhoon Chew's photogenic mouth.

"Thank you," Typhoon Chew says, gasping for breath like the time he defused the underwater bomb in *Shaolin Scuba King*.

"You're welcome, sir," B.S. says. "Truly, it has been a pleasure to serve you."

Suddenly, someone in Typhoon Chew's entourage—his manager or agent or somebody who looks important—announces it's time to go. The crew is flying to Europe early tomorrow morning. Typhoon Chew folds a crisp hundred-dollar bill lengthwise, drops it into my empty tip jar, stands up and walks away.

"Wait, Typhoon!" I say. "What about me?"

"My friend," Typhoon Chew says, leaning towards me and speaking confidentially. "I am sorry. But I cannot take you with me. Not after what just happened. My fans think I'm invincible. If they found out I almost choked to death on a jellyfish tentacle, I'd be the laughing stock of Hong Kong."

"I won't tell," I say. "Your secret will accompany me to my grave."

"I'm sorry," the international film star says. "I cannot take that chance."

Typhoon Chew smiles for a few more photographs—he poses with Boss Wang again, smiling and aiming a fist at the tightwad's chin—signs more autographs, kisses a few more babies, and is out the door. As I stand on the street corner in my cheap red tuxedo, waving goodbye, Typhoon Chew and the breathtaking Shelly Chun climb into a pearl white limousine and disappear into the night.

I realize there goes a man who is living my dream. Driving away from the Happy Parrot Chinese Restaurant. Never looking back. Oh, what is to become of me? What does the future hold in store for poor Timothy Louie? Other people have pensions, retirement plans, 401ks. Me? I have nothing. Was I going to end up like poor Mrs. Choo? She worked here for thirty years. Waitress. The day she retired, Boss Wang gave her a lousy plate and a twenty-dollar gift certificate to, yes, the Happy Parrot Chinese Restaurant.

After awhile, everyone walks back into the Happy Parrot Chinese Restaurant to finish their meals and talk about the marvels they have witnessed this evening. Only me and Boss's Son remain outside. He is staring at my face, mesmerized, like he is seeing it for the first time. Is this finally the moment of our ultimate duel? I'm ready. What's your weapon of choice? Fists? Wooden staffs? Nunchaku sticks? Let's rock!

"You know something?" B.S. says. "Has anybody ever said you look like …"

Me, I look at the moon and say the only two words that wander into my troubled mind.

"Shut up."

THREE PHOTOGRAPHS
AND A LOOK BACK

THIS IS A PHOTOGRAPH OF me and my brother Everett. It was taken at a birthday party years ago. That's why the picture's all crumpled up and faded. There are some pictures, like wedding pictures, that people frame and put on their TVs or pianos or bookshelves. Then there are some pictures, like baby pictures, that people put in albums. This set of pictures here is the kind you get back from the drug store and maybe they don't look as good as you expected them to so you throw them in a closet or desk drawer and forget about them. I'm the guy on the right. Everett's the one holding the beer bottle up. Good looking bastard, isn't he? People are always comparing us. The Moniz brothers. Everett's two years older than me. He's the one always selling benefit tickets to some club he belongs to. Portuguese sausage for the swimming team. M&M's for the Key Club. Everett's the one that the neighbors call my mom about when they read his name in the newspapers. Me, I'm the other boy. The other Moniz boy. Everett's brother.

This is a pretty rare photograph because there aren't too many pictures of me and Everett together. I know that Mom has one of us taken on the Big Island when we were kids. We're standing in front of Halemaumau Crater, wearing shorts that came down to our knees. Then there's one of us in bow ties sitting in the front seat of Dad's Impala. And there's the one of us on the glass bottom boat in Kaneohe Bay, but that one doesn't really count because Everett has his hand in front of my face. Anyway, this picture here was taken at Sondra Hayashi's house. Sondra was Everett's fiancée. Very good-looking. It was a birthday party for her *grandfather. He was turning eighty. I'm wearing one of Everett's shirts. The picture is kinda blurry and dark looking because Sondra had one of those old cameras where the flash seemed to go off a half second after you snapped the picture. Sondra, I remember, took this photograph.*

* * *

Everett promised to let me drive his new Pontiac if I went with him to Sondra Hayashi's party. He'd saved up the money he made working at the gas station and came home one day with a black Trans Am he bought from a friend. I begged him to give me a chance to drive it, at least once around the block, but he wouldn't let me anywhere near the car. I wanted so bad to look the way Everett did when he wore his shades, adjusted his collar just right, and sat behind the wheel of his Trans Am. I didn't want to go to Sondra's party, but when he threw me the car keys and told me he'd let me drive, you better believe I changed my mind.

The Trans Am was jet black and I wished all my friends could see me as I sat in the bucket seat of the car. The steering wheel was covered with leather and when I tapped the accelerator, the engine rumbled and I could feel the vibrations pass through my leg and up to my brain. I turned up the radio and rolled down the windows.

"Sounds good, ah, the radio?" Everett said. "My friend Larry stole 'em."

The wind blew hard and I could smell Everett's cologne.

"Pick it up, Wade," Everett said. "You drive like a wahine. I didn't spend three months juicing up this engine block to go fifteen miles an hour."

"I ain't going fifteen miles an—"

"Don't grind the gears."

"Why do you want me to go to this party?" I said. "I don't even know Sondra. What the hell am I supposed to do at a birthday party for her grandfather?"

"She told me to ask you to come."

"How come you're letting me drive your car?"

"I'm in a good mood."

This was going to be the first time I ever met Sondra, face to face that is. See, every time Everett brought her over to the house, I left them alone and walked outside or went into the bedroom or something. It's funny in a way. I recognized Sondra's voice, knew how her perfume smelled, how her footsteps sounded on our floor. But I really had no idea what she looked like.

"I still don't understand why you want me to go to this party," I said. "Must have a catch someplace ..."

"Just be cool. Don't make me shame."

The birthday party was held at Sondra's house in Moanalua Valley. Most of the people were outside in the garage. Me and Everett walked into the house. A few folks played cribbage and watched television. A couple of ladies sat on the couch knitting. Sondra cut carrots in the kitchen. When she saw Everett, she waved and came over and gave him a kiss.

"This is my kid brother, Wade," Everett said to Sondra.

Sondra turned to me, tilted her head to one side, and smiled.

"Nice to meet you, Wade," she said. "I'm glad you could come."

I was speechless. Sondra had short, dark hair and deep brown eyes. She wore an ilima lei and a white dress. She was, by far, the most beautiful girl I'd ever seen. I should've known. Everett always hooked up with the awesome girls. You should have seen the wallet he used to carry around. It was full of these pictures girls gave to him. There were hundreds of pictures in his wallet. Every girl was a knockout.

"Where's your grandpa?" Everett said. "The birthday boy?"

"Outside grilling some fish," Sondra said. "I better go check on him."

Sondra left. Everett opened an ice chest and took out two beers. Then he looked at his wristwatch.

"Did I ever tell you how Sondra and I met?" Everett said. "It was the weirdest thing. We met at a bookstore."

"You're right," I said. "That is weird. You never go to the bookstore."

"Yeah, I do. I always check out the body building magazines. Or the drag racing stuffs. Anyway, I was at the bookstore when Sondra walked in. Ho, I thought she was a hot looking chick. So, I followed her around. Guess what section she wound up at?"

"I have no idea. The fashion magazines? Computers? Romance novels?"

"No, brah. The fricking occult section."

"Hah?"

"That's right. She was reading all these weird books about spirits and witches and fortune telling and stuffs. I walked up to her anyway. The rest, as they say, is history. But Sondra's really into that stuff. Heck, she collects tarot cards. Can you believe that? Must have something to do with the grandfather. Wait till you meet him. The buggah is one amazing dude."

"Why?"

"He sees ghosts."

"Hah?"

"Yeah. He's some kind of Japanee priest or something."

"I've never met anyone who sees ghosts," I said.

Sondra walked over to us carrying a rice cooker full of rice. "I told Grandpa to come inside," she said. "But he insists on sitting out in the garage."

"The fresh air is good for him," Everett said.

"I guess you're right."

"You need help with that rice cooker?"

"No. I'm fine. Thanks."

Sondra put the rice cooker down and picked up a camera lying on the kitchen table. It was one of those old Kodak Instamatics. "Here, Everett," she said. "Stand next to your brother and let me get a picture of you two. The Moniz boys."

Everett walked over to me and put one arm around my shoulder. He smiled and held up his beer bottle.

"What handsome brothers," Sondra said, looking through the camera viewfinder. "Okay. Smile."

She snapped the picture and the flash hurt my eyes. Everett patted me on the back and gave Sondra a kiss on the lips.

* * *

This second photograph here is my brother and Sondra. It was taken at the same party. All three of these pictures were. It smells a little funny, doesn't it? Yeah, these pictures were in a cardboard box in the back of my closet for the longest time. What is that smell? I'd like to say it's mothballs but Mom doesn't use mothballs any more. Not since the time our cat ate a bunch and got sick all over the carpet. It smells more like chewing gum that's been left sitting in a desk drawer too long. Or the ointments in a medicine cabinet. Bactine, Vicks, what is that stuff you use for rashes, Calamine Lotion? You should see my closet. I got bathrobes in there I wore when I was five, boxes of checkers and chess, Monopoly and Scrabble, footballs that can't be inflated any more. Yeah, I'm not the neatest guy in the world. Neither is Everett, though. But I'm drifting away from my story. What was I saying?

Oh yeah. I think Sondra is one of those girls who takes nice pictures, but she looks even better if you see her in person. In this photo she looks a little shorter than she actually is. She's about five-seven, with heels. My brother, yeah, he looks good here, doesn't he? Everett always looks good in his pictures. Mom says it's his dimples and long eyelashes. The neighbors are always trying to get Everett to meet one of their daughters. They voted him most photogenic in high school. Everyone complimented him on his graduation picture in the high school yearbook, sitting on a stool in some professional photographer's studio downtown, wearing a boutonniere and a rented tuxedo. And everyone loved his prom picture. Him and Jamie at the Sheraton. Her in a pink dress and long white gloves, Everett in a white suit and cummerbund. Everett must've been invited to more proms than anyone I know. He went to at least nine. I think it was because he was a great athlete. Just about everyone in Hawaii seemed to know who Everett Moniz was. When he was on the basketball team, the coach said he had one of the cleanest jump shots he had ever seen.

It's funny because I keep on thinking if it wasn't for me, Everett wouldn't be the basketball player he is. See, one winter, Everett and I walked over to Damien High School and played hoops every day, rain or shine. I caught pneumonia and didn't realize it until I started coughing up hard pieces of blood

Everett was also on the swim team and came within a tenth of a second of beating the state record for the one-hundred-meter free style. His coach, Coach Choo, said Everett was the greatest student he had ever coached. Everett was most famous for his diving. He was a helluva diver. He did things off the board I didn't have the guts to try. He'd wait till the girls came around after cheerleading practice or volleyball and then he'd dive off the high board and do twists and somersaults in the air. Once or twice he belly-flopped and a couple of guys had to pull him out of the pool, but that never stopped him. He'd catch his breath and be up there again the next day. Everett often pulled off dives I couldn't believe, awesome dives, spinning like a top and landing straight as a knife into the water without a splash. The girls who came to the pool just to watch him dive would clap. They thought he was a helluva diver.

Jeez, where was I? Oh yeah. That Sondra is quite a looker, huh? Everett and Sondra. I have to admit. They made a great looking couple. I mean, look at them here. It's like a picture out of a fashion magazine or a Sears catalogue or something. I know, I know. It looks like the bottom of Everett's pants is on fire. That's just my thumb. I always seem to manage to stick my thumb in front of the camera lens when I take other people's pictures.

* * *

Everett and I walked outside carrying huge plates filled with food. Lumpia, sushi, kalua pig, noodles, the works. We'd drunk maybe four beers apiece. That's the problem with me. If I drink too much, I can't eat. And I almost always drink too much at parties.

"Try the pancit," Everett said. "The buggah is winners. Squeeze the lemon on top."

"Lemon?"

"That's what the lemon is for. Whatchoo thought was? Decoration?"

"No. I knew."

"You knew," Everett said. "Sure, kid."

"You're always telling me what to do, Everett."

"Just make sure you don't spill food on my shirt."

I stuck my hand in the cooler to get another beer. Someone had put the sodas on top of the beers so I had to reach way down in the freezing ice water to grab the beers.

"Don't get the sleeves wet," Everett said. "You're wearing one of my slickest shirts."

"No worry."

Sondra was running around like crazy. She served coffee and rocked crying babies to sleep. She listened patiently as the old ladies outside complained about it being too cold and the old ladies inside complained about it being too hot.

"Wade," Everett said. "I need to ask you for a favor."

"A favor?" I said. "I knew it. Here it comes. What?"

"I need you to, um, take care of Sondra tonight."

"Whatchoo talking about?"

"I'm going to leave pretty soon. So, uh, can you keep her company?"

"What? Why? Where are you going?"

"I'm meeting Lynelle for drinks."

I couldn't believe it. Lynelle was a good-looking girl but she had this reputation for being sorta, how do you say, loose. We used to stand under the bleachers at pep rallies and try to look under her skirt. I couldn't believe Everett would do something like this to Sondra.

"What?" Everett said. "Why are you looking at me like that? Oh, I get it. You think I'm a bastard." I didn't answer. "See, the fact of the matter is I'll be married soon. Married! Then it's one girl for the rest of my life. You see what I'm saying? *One girl!*"

"Sondra seems very nice," I said.

"What am I supposed to do? Lynelle calls and asks me to have a couple of drinks. What's the big deal? Hell, this marriage thing, it's so iffy. What if Sondra and I get married and a year later, I meet someone I like better? What if Sondra does? Things like that happen all the time. Everything depends on, like, circumstance."

"Circumstance?"

"Wade," Everett said. "Do you know what a marriage is? A marriage is a promise. A promise to be faithful, to love your husband or wife for the rest of your life. What the hell is a promise? Nobody keeps a promise. To think that a person keeps a promise is like, it's like, arrogance. It's circumstance that keeps a promise. Think about it. The only thing a person can do with a promise is break one."

"You brothers look like you're having an intense conversation," Sondra said, walking up to us. Several old ladies had asked her to search the house for a deck of *hanafuda* cards.

"We were just talking about, uh, how nice you look tonight," Everett said.

"Sure," Sondra said.

"I'm serious. You really do look nice. Hey, tell Wade here about your tarot card collection."

"I don't have a tarot card collection," Sondra said, looking at me and rolling her eyes towards the sky. "I have *one* deck of tarot cards. That's not a collection …"

"I don't know anybody who has tarot cards," Everett said. "Do you, Wade?"

"No," I said.

"This girl has it all," Everett said. "Tarot cards, I Ching sticks, crystal ball …"

"A girl can never be too sure about things," Sondra said.

"I've got a Ouija board," I said.

"You do?" Sondra said. "So do I."

"Yeah? That Ouija board is pretty scary. I want to throw it out but a friend of mine says that you can't just throw it out. The only way to get rid of a Ouija board without being cursed is to give it away. But I can't find anyone who wants to take it …"

"Jeez," Everett said to me. "Your face is all red. How much you drank? Two beers? What? Cannot handle?"

"I can," I said.

"You know what, Sondra?" Everett said. "I have to hit the road pretty soon."

"How come?" Sondra looked disappointed.

"I need to run some errands."

"Errands?" an old man sitting in a corner of the garage in front of a hibachi said. "Where you going?"

"Oh, Grandpa," Sondra said.

"No, no," Sondra's grandfather said. "Where you going?"

Sondra's grandfather had a long face, gold, wire-rimmed glasses, and his hair was slicked back with pomade. He wore shorts, an aloha shirt, and a maile lei around his neck. Something about Sondra's grandfather shook me up. Right from the start. I don't know why. I guess I was one of those people who can't get too comfortable around folks who see ghosts. Maybe it's like the Ouija board in my closet. I try to avoid it at night. My philosophy is to stay as far away as possible from things I can't understand.

"Uh," Everett said. "I'm going to, uh ..."

Sondra smiled and placed her hand upon Everett's.

"Uh," I said, trying to cheer Sondra up. I reached for her camera. "Let's take a picture of you two." Sondra smiled and moved over next to Everett.

"Come and take a picture with us, Grandpa," Sondra said.

"No."

"C'mon, sir," Everett said, looking at his wristwatch and running his hands through his hair.

"No."

"Move closer," I said.

Sondra's grandfather picked at the spaces between his teeth with his little finger.

"Okay, good," I said, looking through the viewfinder of the camera. "One, two, three." I pressed the shutter and the camera made a clicking noise.

"I hope you kept your finger off the lens," Everett said.

"Don't worry," I said.

Everett gave Sondra a kiss on the cheek.

"Thanks," Sondra said.

I didn't know if she was talking to me or Everett.

* * *

This third shot is a picture of me and Sondra. Yeah, my eyes are closed. I always blink just before my picture is taken. Even the picture on my driver's license. My eyes are half closed, like I'm about to fall asleep. I'm holding Sondra's grandfather's guitar. Yeah, I play a little bit of guitar. So does Everett. We used to take lessons together on the second floor of an old music store in Moiliili. From a Japanese guy who always left his glasses on top of his head. Mr. Ifuku. It's strange. Everett was the best. He had an old Ovation and I swear he was so good he could play just by using his left hand. But one day, he just quit. I don't know why. I kept on going to the lessons and I started getting pretty good, but then I quit too.

I get the strangest feelings when I look at old photographs like these. One time I was walking through Aala Park for some reason and an old man with a bent back stopped me and took out a crumpled picture from his wallet. It was a black and white shot of a young man with well-oiled hair and a tie standing in front of a polished Ford and the old man looked me in the eye and said, "This was me." Or when we're all sitting around the kitchen table at my Aunty's house and all the grownups are sipping instant coffee and it's late at night and Aunty takes out the old family album and all the photographs are yellow and faded and every-one—even the people who have long since died of old age—looks young. Can you imagine the thoughts running through the mind of someone who is looking at a picture of you after you've died?

Look at Sondra. Her cheeks seem a little red, don't they? That might have been from the champagne they were passing around but I can't remember seeing her drink any. She seemed like one of those girls who if they just take a sip from your drink, their cheeks turn all red. Look at her smile. She had the straightest, whitest teeth in the world. I always wanted to ask her if her father was a dentist but I never got the chance.

* * *

Sondra's grandfather threw several pieces of butterfish onto the grill of the hibachi. He sipped from a tiny cup of hot sake. The juices seeped out of the fish and made angry, hissing noises on the hot coals.

"Sir," Everett said. "This is my kid brother, Wade."

I smiled and Sondra's grandfather extended his hand and I shook it. His hands were warm and he held my hand tightly. The orange coals of the hibachi reflected off his glasses.

"Next weekend I'm teaching Sondra how to swim," Everett said.

"That's good," Sondra's grandfather said. His skin was dark and covered with liver spots.

"I'm on the swimming team. I came this close to …"

Next to Sondra's grandfather was an old guitar. It was so old I couldn't read the make because the ink had been rubbed off. The metal strings were thick and black. Sondra's grandfather began to play. It was a very slow song. I had never heard it before. It sounded a little like those songs they play on the classical radio stations. I took the tongs and began turning over the cooking butterfish.

"When I was young like you fellas," he said, "I could really play this buggah."

"You're very good," I said. "What song are you playing?"

"I forget the name. I always used to play this song when I was young. On the sugar plantations in Waipahu. I'd sit on the porch at night after cutting sugar cane for twelve hours and play this song. I wish I could remember the name. You play?"

"I used to," I said.

"I bet you're a good player," he said, offering me the guitar. "You get long fingers."

The guitar felt very heavy and the wood was scratched and chipped. I hadn't touched a guitar in a while and the calluses on my fingers had long since disappeared and it stung like hell when I slid my fingers along the metal strings to make a fast change from one chord to another. I began playing a song I used to hear on the radio all the time when I was a kid, *Classical Gas*. Everyone seems to be able to play one song well, one song that they'll play when someone asks them to pick up a guitar. That was mine. *Classical Gas*.

"Eh," Sondra's grandfather said. "You sharp, boy."

Sondra smiled and walked over to us and sat down. I liked the way she ran her hands on the back of her thighs to smooth her dress before she sat down. She looked pretty classy when she did that. Sondra was a very classy girl.

"I taught him this song," Everett said. "Long time ago."

Every time I did a bar chord, I couldn't press the strings down hard enough and they made a buzzing sound. But little by little it was coming back to me, and the more I played, the smoother things got.

"A minor," Everett said. "Back to A minor."

"I know," I said. "I know."

"Well," Everett said, standing up and looking at his watch. "Sorry to interrupt your show, Wade. But I've got to go …"

I stopped playing.

"No stop," Sondra's grandfather said. I continued, only more softly.

"Don't spill anything on my shirt," Everett said. He looked at Sondra's grandfather. "He's wearing my shirt."

Sondra's grandfather broke off a piece of grilled butterfish with a pair of wooden chopsticks and offered it to me. I took the fish with my fingers.

"Careful," he said. "Hot."

I blew at the fish and placed it in my mouth. The sweet fish melted on my tongue. Sondra's grandfather poured me a tiny cup of sake.

"Misoyaki butterfish and sake," he said, winking at me. "Cannot beat."

I watched as Everett and Sondra stood on the other side of the garage, holding hands. Everett kissed Sondra on the cheek and then walked down the driveway. Lynelle was going to pick him up. I was supposed to drive his car home. The glare from the street lamps reflected off the jet-black body of his Trans Am.

"Your brother is a busy man," Sondra's grandfather said.

"Yes," I said.

"He needs to take better care of himself. Maybe you should watch out for him, Wade. How about you? You have a girlfriend?"

"No," I said.

"Me, I met one girl. One girl in my life, understand? Some folks run around, run around. Me, one girl. And I married that lady. And we was in love until the day she died."

Sondra walked back into the house. She caught me watching her and she smiled and looked at the ground.

"Sondra sweet girl," her grandfather said to me. "You think she pretty?"

"Uh, yeah."

"She looks all over the mother when the mother was her age. Around the eyes and the hair."

"She must've been beautiful."

"Oh, yeah," he said, smiling and looking into the fire. "Oh, yeah."

"I think Sondra is the prettiest girl I ever met."

"Go talk to her."

"Nah. Wouldn't be right."

"Wouldn't be right?" he said, placing the grilled butterfish onto a paper plate. "Why wouldn't be right?"

Right about here, Sondra's grandfather and me started talking about ghosts. He said he was what the Japanese call an *odaisan*—a person who can heal illnesses without medicines, see into the future, talk to the dead. In some cases, he told me, he was called upon to chase away evil spirits, to exorcise demons that had possessed the soul of living people. I don't know how we got on the subject. But I can tell you the conversation gave me the creeps.

"What kind of ghosts have you seen? I asked him.

"All kinds," he said. "Ghosts—*obake*—they're like a part of my family. Some are good. Some are bad. They're like people. Some are good. Some are not so good. But, eh, I tell you, friendly ghosts are the nicest things in the world to have around. And most of the ghosts in Hawaii, they're friendly buggahs. How about you? You believe in ghosts?"

"Yeah," I said, after awhile. "I've never seen one. But I think I believe in them."

Sondra's grandfather said over the years, he'd seen hundreds of ghosts—good and bad. He told me about the faceless lady who haunted the restroom of the old Waialae Drive In. He also told me about the woman who walks in knee-deep ocean water, forever looking for her drowned baby. And he also told me about the Green Lady of Wahiawa, who hid in forests and tried to kidnap children on their way to school.

I asked Sondra's grandfather what was the scariest thing he'd ever seen. He sipped his sake for a while, like he was debating whether he should tell me what was going through his mind. Then he took a deep breath and looked me straight in the eye.

"There's a family who lives in Hawaii nobody speaks to," he said. "These people have the power to bring bad luck, illness—even death—to their enemies. For some reason, they set a curse upon another family. Their only daughter, a pretty 16-year-old honor student and cheerleader, became weak, refused to eat, and couldn't sleep. One night, she lay in her bed crying.

"'What's wrong?' her mother asked.

"The girl didn't answer.

"'She's just tired,' her father said. 'Let her rest.'

"He bent down to kiss his daughter on the cheek. Just then, the father noticed that something was horribly wrong. The girl's bed sheet was completely soaked with blood. The girl had been cutting up her body with a razor. They rushed her to the doctor. The doctor could clean the three dozen wounds, but he couldn't do much else. Finally, the parents asked me to see the girl. When they brought her here, she screamed and swore at me like a stevedore after a twelve-hour shift. I told the girl to kneel down in front of me. 'Who are you?' I asked her.

"'Go to hell,' she told me.

"But the voice wasn't the voice of no 16-year-old girl. No, sir. I had heard that voice before. It was the voice of the dead."

Right about here, I was seriously considering excusing myself and going into the house and asking Sondra if she needed any help washing the dishes.

"For nineteen hours, I prayed in front of the poor girl," Sondra's grandfather said, eyes shut tight, like he was in pain. "I was tired, but something inside me told me, 'no stop, no stop.' Something told me I was doing good. Sure enough, slowly but surely, I could feel the evil leaving the room. All of a sudden, the girl started screaming. She ran into the kitchen and grabbed a steak knife and started cutting up her body. I rushed over to her and used every ounce of my old aikido training to take the knife away. But not before she stabbed me in the stomach." Sondra's grandfather unbuttoned his shirt and showed me a three-inch long scar, just to the left of his belly button.

"'Where am I?' the girl said, looking up at me.

"I could tell by her voice and the look in her eye that she was cured. Whatever had possessed her had left."

"W-were you scared?" I said, looking over my shoulder. Just in case.

"I was," Sondra's grandfather said. "I had never seen anything like that in my life. And thank goodness, I haven't seen anything like that since. Damn, I never was more scared in my life than I was with that poor girl."

"What happened to the girl?" I said.

"She's doing okay."

"Yeah? That's good. Did you ever see her again? I mean, after …"

"Oh yeah. In fact, she's about to serve her grandfather some cake."

Happy birthday to you! Happy birthday to you!

Sondra walked up to her grandfather carrying a huge birthday cake. Everyone was singing. There must've been about fifty candles on that cake.

Happy birthday, dear Grandpa …

Sondra placed the cake in front of her grandfather.

Happy birthday to you!

"Make a wish and blow out the candles, Grandpa," Sondra said.

"Help me out, Wade," he said.

He held onto his wire-rimmed glasses and blew out all of the candles. Then Sondra gave him a kiss and everyone clapped their hands. It was strange seeing Sondra and her grandfather together like that. They almost looked the same. It wasn't in the eyes or the chin necessarily. It was in something I couldn't place.

After Sondra cut the cake and served it, her grandfather called her over.

"Here," he said, offering her a folding chair. "You sit down here. You running around so much. Relax with Wade here …"

Sondra smiled at me and sat down.

"You two get to know each other," her grandfather said. "You young ones. So shy. You have enough to eat, Wade?"

"Yes, sir."

"Sondra cooked lots of the food. She's a good cook." He sipped his sake.

"Can I get you more sake, sir?" I said.

"Don't worry about me," he said. "If I want some more, I'll go get some more. I get two legs. You two talk to each other." He looked at me and smiled. Then he walked away.

"Thanks for all your help tonight, Wade," Sondra said.

"Don't mention it," I said, thrilled to hear Sondra say my name. "Anything you need, you let me know. Okay?"

"And thanks for keeping Grandpa company. I can tell he likes you. I hope he wasn't boring you, or …"

"Your grandfather is great. I could sit and listen to his stories for hours."

"Stories?"

"Yeah, I've never talked to anyone who met ghosts before."

"He told you about the ghosts?"

"Yeah."

"Um, do you think I should make a plate for Everett? I mean, gosh, there's so much food. I bet your brother will be hungry when he gets home tonight. What do you think? Maybe I'll just give him some noodles. He loves noodles."

"Sondra," I said. "Can I ask you something?"

"Yes?"

"It's kinda a weird question. But here goes. What is it about Everett that you like so much?"

"I don't know," she said. "The usual things, I guess. He's a sharp guy. Funny. And he can be sweet when he wants to be. And he doesn't look too shabby, either. What more could a girl ask for?"

The wind blew and Sondra brushed her hair out of her face.

"Are you excited about getting married?" I asked.

"I am. But sometimes, a lot of times, I don't know if your brother is …"

"Why?"

"It's just a feeling. And some of the things he says …"

"Like what?"

"I don't know," Sondra said, turning towards me. "Where does Everett go every night?"

"I don't know," I said, after a while.

"Would you tell me if you knew?"

"Probably not."

Sondra smiled and nodded her head slowly.

"You're a good brother," Sondra said, gently placing her hand on mine. Was the light playing tricks on me or did I see scars thin as white hairs crisscross her fingers, knuckles and wrist?

"No," I said. "I'm not a good brother. I might just be a stupid one."

Sondra's grandfather returned with the camera and said, "Lemme take a picture of you two young ones."

Sondra looked at me and I looked at her and we sorta smiled at each other.

"Get closer together, for crying out loud!" he said.

Sondra and I moved closer together. I could tell Sondra was embarrassed.

"Wade," her grandfather said. "Put your arm around her waist! She not going bite!"

I put my arm around Sondra's waist and Sondra, she leaned her head on my shoulder. It was very nice. I could smell the perfume in her hair.

"I hope you'll excuse my grandpa," she said. "He always gets like this when he's had too much to drink."

"I think he's great."

"I'm glad."

"Okay," Sondra's grandfather said. "On the count of three. Ready? One ..."

"This is so much fun," Sondra said. "I'm glad you could come tonight, Wade."

"Two."

"Sondra?" I said. "I have to tell you something. About Everett ..."

"Yes?"

I wanted so bad to tell her that Everett was a bastard and that right now, he and Lynelle were probably in the back seat of some car at a drive-in movie or something. I wanted so bad to tell her how pretty I thought she looked and how she was too good for Everett and yeah, I didn't have the Trans Am or the nice clothes and maybe I couldn't jump off the high board the way Everett did but if I had the chance—if she gave me the chance—I'd treat Sondra better than any girl has ever been treated.

"I'm sorry," I said. "Never mind."

"Three."

Sondra's grandfather pressed the camera and the flash went off and for a while I saw nothing but blue and red stars in front of my eyes. Sondra gave me a tiny kiss on my right cheek and her grandfather smiled and ran his hands through his gray hair.

MORTUARY STORY

THE CHILDREN STOOD ON TIPTOE, peering over each other's shoulders.

"Holy cow!" one said, staring at the street.

"Damn!" another one said.

That was the first thing I noticed. The kids. The second thing I noticed was the cops. Dozens of them, talking on radios, taking notes, shaking their heads, blue lights spinning on the roofs of their cars. The third thing I noticed was the blood.

"Jeez," a third boy said.

* * *

I worked as a graphic designer on the second floor of a Nuuanu Avenue office building. Kay's Design. I'd been gifted with a Mac G5 and a corner cubicle with a lovely panoramic view of not one but three mortuaries. I tried to convince myself that the view outside the window was in no way symbolic of my current status at my dead-end job but always inevitably wound up failing miserably.

I'd been wrestling with one of the issues my profession often encounters. Specifically, the weight of the paper for a demanding non-profit customer's newsletter—70# Matte or 80# Gloss? It was a draw, a deadlock, a standstill. Who gave a rat's ass? So, I did what any graphic designer stuck in my position would do.

Lunch.

I walked past Fort Street Mall, the Hawaii Theatre and Chinatown, weighing my options. Homeless men and women lay curled in alleys and stairwells. Art gallery employees wiped their plate glass windows with rags. I wandered into a Vietnamese restaurant and ordered pho with tendon and beef balls.

"What's beef balls?" I asked the waiter.

"You will like," he said. "Try."

He brought my pho and a plate full of fresh basil, bean sprouts and green chilies. As I sipped the rich broth, the clutter of paper sizes and corporate logos began to leave me. Instead, I thought about the girl I'd met the night before. I'd gone to a wedding reception at the Moana Surfrider Hotel for a buddy of mine named Trent, an investment banker. If you wanted to learn how to master your Xbox, load your iPod, know which J-Horror flick to download, Trent was your man. If you wanted to know which stock or mutual fund to consider for your portfolio, you'd best look elsewhere.

Oh, the girl. Pauline Chang stood by herself listening to the band play—the only person in the room doing so. I worked up the courage and tapped her on the shoulder and she turned around real quick, like I'd startled her or something. Somehow, we sorta struck up a conversation and I asked Pauline if she wanted to go out to dinner sometime. She said fine, after awhile, but added pretty quickly that she could only make it on weekdays. I wondered about that for a while.

"How about tomorrow?" I said. "Tomorrow is Monday. Monday is a weekday."

"Tomorrow?" she said. I hoped I wasn't sounding too anxious. "Sure. Tomorrow is okay."

Pauline left the wedding reception early but I stuck around the open bar and listened to the band play but I didn't think they were very good and, before I knew it, it was last call so I had one more beer and left.

* * *

After lunch, I walked back to the office. A blue hearse was parked in the lot of one of the mortuaries surrounding my building.

Two transvestites stood on the sidewalk, thin and frail with sandy brown hair and bad teeth. They smoked cigarettes and talked about how much prison sucked.

That's when I saw the kids, the cops, and the blood.

The blood belonged to a poor man who had apparently been the victim of a hit-and-run. He lay in the middle of Nuuanu Avenue, broken, lying in a pool of blood and glass. A woman kneeled next to the man, crying. She looked Filipino, pretty, wearing a red blouse and white skirt. The hem of her skirt was stained with blood.

"I saw the whole thing," one of the boys said. "The car hit the man. The guy flew ten feet in the air. The car raced towards the freeway. He didn't even stop."

* * *

Pauline lived all the way in Pacific Palisades, past Pearlridge. When I picked her up, she said she wasn't hungry or anything so we drove around and wound up at a bar in Waikiki. Paula—she asked me to call her Paula after awhile—looked real nice. The only thing that bothered me a bit was that she wore pants and I was kinda hoping she'd wear a dress because she's one of those girls who could knock you out when they wear a dress.

Paula ordered a white wine. Me, I had a beer. She said she enjoyed teaching kids how to play the ukulele. She laughed when she told me she must've heard the song "My Favorite Things" from *The Sound of Music* about five million times. But she said she didn't mind because every time the children played it, it sounded totally different. It never once sounded the same. I said that "My Favorite Things" was one of my all-time favorite songs. I even sang the parts I remembered to her, but she wouldn't believe me.

Then the strange thing happened.

"Do you ever think about the end of the world?" she said.

"Excuse me?" I said, surprised.

"I wonder if it'll occur in our lifetime. Things are so crazy now. Can you imagine? Living through the end of everything?"

Wait a minute. This was the kind of dark, cynical stuff people were used to hearing from me. Folks at the office accused me of being a skeptic because I doubted everything I was told. Some great philosopher we studied in history class way back when is supposed to have been like that, Hume or Humis. I forget his name.

"No, I can't imagine," I said.

"I can," Paula said. "I just hope I'm not here when it happens."

Paula explained. After nine years, today was her last day as an Intensive Care Unit nurse at Queen's. She worked as a music teacher on the weekends. I thought about mentioning the man lying in the middle of Nuuanu Avenue, but decided against it. Paula said she'd been thinking about quitting for a while. She worked sixty-hour weeks, treating patients who needed medical attention most. The sickest of the sick. It was tough work. The line between life and death was such a thin one.

What really pushed her over the edge, though, was participating in a bio-terrorism training exercise several weeks earlier. In the scenario, Bubonic plague hits all of the islands. Brought over by a terrorist on an airline flight from Southeast Asia. Thousands are dying. There's panic outside of the hospital. Folks don't know how to dispose of the bodies of their loved ones.

"It's chaos," Paula said. "Horrible. And my job was to report to work and tend to the sick and dying. Can you imagine? I guess I'm weak. A coward. But I realized that, if doomsday ever hit, I couldn't drive to the hospital and work. I'd want to be with the people I loved."

Paula said she was thinking about moving to New York City and living with her sister in Brooklyn. Then she started peeling at the wet label of my beer bottle. I took this as either a sign of affection or boredom. I noticed she got the label off without tearing it.

After awhile, I drove Paula home. We reached her stairway and the lights were all off in her house and she thanked me and looked up at me as if maybe she wanted a kiss. Her nose sorta shined in the glow of the street lamps and the moon, with the foundation and all. I told her what a nice time I had and how we should do this again sometime. She smiled and thanked me again.

Then she went into the house and turned on all the lights. I stuck around for a while and looked at the *bonsai* plants in her yard. The air in Pearl City is very cold and clean smelling late at night. I looked at all the lights leading back to town, and the moon reflecting off the deep, black waters of Pearl Harbor. I felt like kicking myself for not kissing Paula. Then I drove home, whistling "My Favorite Things."

* * *

I came up with the idea somewhere on the freeway, near Fort Shafter and the Moanalua Gardens.

The man lying on Nuuanu Avenue. I had to visit him. See if he was all right.

I didn't know how I'd find him. I'd just follow my instincts, like an *oopu* traveling from its birthplace in a mountain stream to the ocean and back again. Instincts.

My first stop was Queen's, the busiest trauma center in Hawaii, Paula's old stomping grounds. Sure enough, the Filipino woman who'd been on her knees in the middle of Nuuanu Avenue sat on a couch in a waiting room, alone, in the darkness. The hemline around her white skirt was still stained with blood.

A doctor walked up to her. She stood.

"He's still unconscious, Mrs. Campos," the doctor said, sighing. "But there's no more internal bleeding. I think we stopped it all. He does have broken bones. Ribs, both legs, his hip."

"Carnegie," the woman said, shaking her head.

* * *

I grew up in a two-story apartment complex on School Street, above a Korean grocery store, across the street from the Mee Lin Chinese Restaurant. The restaurant was famous for its four-dollar dinner plate, which featured generous portions of jasmine rice, chop suey noodles, oily *kau yuk*, sweet sour spareribs, and fried shrimp. On Friday and Saturday nights, however, a live band took over the Mee Lin Chinese Restaurant and played disco music in a large room on the second-floor. The band was solid, tight. They played so loud, it felt like they were right there in my living room. My folks hated the band. I loved them. These were the first songs on their playlist:

> K.C. and the Sunshine Band's "That's the Way I Like It," and "Boogie Shoes"
> "Shame," Evelyn "Champagne" King
> Village People's "YMCA"

Although I was only eight years old, I snuck across the street one night and watched the band play. There were nine young Filipino men on stage, wearing matching white polyester jackets over long sleeved silky dress shirts and Angels Flights pants. The thing that impressed me most was the brass section, playing the charts just like on the records.

The trumpet player seemed to be having the best time. He danced and sang and snapped his fingers. When he blew accents on his trumpet, he made faces like he was surprised by the brilliant sounds escaping from his instrument. When he spun his trumpet around his index finger, he reminded me of a gunslinger in a cowboy movie twirling a six-shooter.

"Boy," he said to me, during a break, "ain't you a little young to be here?"

"Y-you're great!" I gushed. "All of you! You guys can jam!"

"Ah," he said, with a very slight Filipino accent. "We're okay."

His name was Carnegie Campos.

Over the next several weeks, I saw him buying Campbell's Soup at Ambassador Market, long johns from Kamehameha Bakery, baby Lowenbraus from Bruddah's Liquors. I figured he must live nearby. Sure enough, one day, he was cutting the grass in front of a tiny wooden house on Bernice Street.

"Do you live here, Mr. Campos?" I said.

"No, sir," he said. "I'm a yardman."

Carnegie explained that he was saving up money for a one-way ticket to New York City. A friend of a friend of a friend knew someone who could hook him up with Donna Summer's band, maybe.

"Will you look at that?" Carnegie said, smiling.

The plumeria trees in the yard were filled with dozens of chrysalises of Monarch butterflies dangling from the branches.

* * *

"I'm sorry," I said.

The woman in the hospital lobby looked up at me.

"For everything. I saw you today. I knew Mr. Campos. I hope he'll be all right."

The woman nodded.

I told her about the Chinese restaurant and the music and the trees with the Monarch butterflies. The woman smiled and said her name was Virginia. She asked me to call her Virgie. She'd been married to Carnegie for twenty-one years.

"You knew Carnegie when he was happiest," Virgie said. "Playing the trumpet. Singing. He loved music. Why couldn't things stay that way? I guess everything turns out for a reason."

"Does he still play?"

"No. Not for years. Not since he started working at the mortuary."

Mortuary? Damn. A musical genius like Carnegie Campos? I wondered if he worked at one of the three mortuaries closing in on me at Kay's Design. Maybe we'd been working across the street from each other all this time.

"Carnegie is an embalmer," Virgie said. "At first, he said it was scary. He always worried about having one of the bodies jump out of their coffin. Or their eyes popping open. One thing he never got used to is the smell."

Virgie asked me if I wanted to see him. I followed her into the Intensive Care Unit.

Carnegie lay in bed, surrounded by machines. He looked much older, tired, but there was no mistake that this was the same man who once danced to "Boogie Nights" and sang lead on "Maneater" at the old Mee Lin Chinese Restaurant. There were cuts on his forehead, cheeks, and nose from the shattered windshield. The skin around his temples appeared damp, as if tears were slipping out of his closed eyes.

Virgie placed her hand on Carnegie's frail arm, careful not to upset the tubes.

"Don't you dare leave me, Old Man," she said, gently, into his ear. "Please. Stay."

* * *

I excused myself, allowing Virgie to spend time alone with her husband. I needed to talk to Paula, tell her she was right. The world was messed up. I dug some coins out of my pocket and walked to a pay phone. I dialed Paula's number—hoping beyond hope that she hadn't gone to bed yet—and after a couple of rings, she answered the phone. It sounded like I woke her up.

"Paula?" I said. "Hi, it's me. I ..."

"Hi," she said. "What time is it?"

"Uh, half past eleven. I'm sorry to wake you. I just wanted to thank you for coming out with me tonight. I had a nice time. I've been thinking about what you said. About the world and all. You're right. Things are crazy. The world is ..."

"Where are you calling me from? Is everything all right? Is that music? Where's the music coming from?"

"Music?" I said, puzzled. "There's no music here."

"I need to get some sleep. Call me again."

"Sorry to wake you."

"That's all right. Goodbye."

When I got back to Carnegie's room, Virgie was gone. I didn't want to leave Carnegie alone. So, I sat in a chair in the corner and stared out a window. Outside, the night was so black I couldn't tell if I was facing the mountains or the ocean.

* * *

"Whether you're a brother or whether you're a mother,
you're stayin' alive,
stayin' alive!"

Over the next few days, I visited Carnegie every day before work, during my lunch break, after work. He lay in bed, eyes closed, silent. Virgie visited every day, also. She wanted to be with him 24-7. But she worked three jobs to pay the mortgage on a house they'd just built in Waikele. Truck dispatcher during the day, dishwasher at Waikiki restaurant at night, nursing home custodian on weekends. Virgie was too afraid to tell her bosses what had happened to her husband so she just continued going to work.

As nurses took Carnegie's temperature and blood pressure every fifteen minutes, I tried to imagine Paula once performing the same tasks.

One day, Virgie and I sat at Carnegie's bedside. She talked about the day Carnegie waited at the airport, ready to leave for New York and chase his musical dreams, when he got word that his father had suffered a massive stroke. Carnegie rushed home, never to leave the island.

Then she spoke about divorce. "He's been unfaithful," she said, sighing. "I saw him. With another woman. A young girl. Pretty. Half his age. She was carrying a ukulele."

"A ukulele?" I said, stunned. "No."

"The day this accident happened, I was going to leave him. Accident. Is that the right word?"

"Ahhhhh, freak out! Le freak, c'est chic!"

Virgie and I looked at each other, puzzled. Then we turned to Carnegie who lay in bed, asleep, with a smile on his face. Virgie laughed and hugged me. Then she fell on her knees.

Once an hour, Carnegie began delivering lines—hoarse, but always in perfect pitch—to disco songs he used to perform on stage at the Mee Lin Chinese Restaurant. *"Do a little dance, make a little love, get down tonight!" "Get down, boogie oogie oogie!" "Macho macho man! I wanna be a macho man!"*

The doctors were encouraged by Carnegie's progress. That made me—skeptic and all—feel encouraged, as well. All the while, Virgie never let go of her husband's hand. She held on, tapping the soft skin between his knuckles and wrists with her fingers like a musician working the valves of a favorite trumpet, gently, tenderly.

JUST LIKE MAGIC

THE PORCH LIGHT AT BILLY Kalihi's beachfront Kahala Avenue home is always left on, day or night. Ever since the afternoon his eleven-year-old daughter Faith—his only child—disappeared from the face off the earth. Faith was in the sixth-grade. Billy dropped her off at the Palama Dance Academy for her hula lessons, as he'd done for several years. That Thursday, however, turned out different. When Billy returned to take his daughter home, Faith was nowhere to be found. He parked the car and walked into the classroom.

"Good evening, Mr. Kalihi," Mrs. Ahuna, the hula teacher, an old lady in her seventies, said. "How are you?"

"Mrs. Ahuna," Billy said, confused. "Have you seen Faith?"

"Faith? She was waiting outside by the curb."

Billy and Mrs. Ahuna looked everywhere. Billy wondered if his wife, Tracy, had picked the girl up. He called home, standing in a pay phone booth that reeked of urine. His wife said Faith was not at home. Billy searched the area. Then he called the police. They searched the area again. Nothing. At eleven that evening, numb and defeated, he drove home.

"Where could she be?" Billy said to his wife. "What the hell happened to her?"

"I don't know," Tracy said, helpless.

"If anyone's hurt her, I'll kill the bastard," he said, pacing the room. "Who the hell would harm an innocent eleven-year-old girl?"

"The world's a messed-up place."

"I used to think that," Billy said, looking out the window. "Now I know it." The full moon hovered like a balloon in the night sky, the color of an ambulance siren. "Why did Faith have to take those hula lessons? Why the hell did you want her to take them, Tracy?"

"Billy," his wife said, hugging a sofa pillow to her breast. "Please."

"Damn it!" Billy said, slamming his fist into the wall.

The couple spent the night waiting for a knock on the door, a phone call, anything. At one point, as Tracy lay asleep on the couch—rolling over and mumbling restlessly—Billy thought he heard a noise coming from Faith's bedroom. He slowly walked down the dark hallway, heart pounding, and opened the door.

Faith lay in bed, awake.

"Faith?" Billy said, rushing to his daughter and holding her. "I was so worried about you, Honey. Where were you?"

"I'm sorry, Daddy," the little girl said. "I'm sorry for the trouble I've caused."

"Are you okay, Sweetheart? I love you."

Billy, elated, ran into the living room and woke his wife.

"She's here!" Billy said. "Faith! She's okay! She's safe!"

Tracy placed her hands on her mouth—daring to believe—and followed her husband. Faith's bed was empty, untouched. But the room was filled with a thousand butterflies of all shapes and sizes, clinging like multi-colored refrigerator magnets to the pink walls, the dresser, the closet doors. Others fluttered around the ceiling light. Still others escaped out of an open window.

* * *

The name Billy Kalihi still sounds familiar to many. He is, quite simply, the greatest magician in Hawaii history. You may recall the night he made Aloha Stadium and fifty thousand screaming fans disappear during a University of Hawaii football game. Or the afternoon he sauntered across the muddy surface of the Ala Wai Canal. Or the New Year's Eve he shot the Aloha Tower into the skies above Waikiki like a rocket.

What very few people know is that, before achieving these successes, Billy had lived a difficult life—a life, many would opine, that often seemed the farthest thing from magic.

Back in the old days, he was simply known as Billy Carvalho from Kalihi Valley Homes. His mother had died in a house fire. Three months later, his father drowned after being washed off the rocks near the Makapuu lighthouse while fishing for ulua. That night, Billy cried so hard he felt his eyes had turned into spigots. The next morning, Billy awoke to the frantic screaming of the landlord, complaining about faulty plumbing. The entire apartment was ankle-deep in water. Billy, eyes bloody and raw, secretly touched a ruined rug with his index finger and recognized a flavor he knew he'd discover.

Salt.

It was at that moment Young Billy discovered his connection with magic. Perhaps one day a biographer will examine the great magician's life and recognize the fact that Billy simply used magic to compensate for the dreary history and world he'd inherited. Billy eventually found work at the Kalihi Fish Market. During breaks, the novice magician entertained his co-workers by playing card tricks on friends, making coins disappear, repairing torn dollar bills.

"You're good," Tracy Kau, a long-legged cashier with dimples the size of marbles, said. "You ever thought about becoming a magician?"

"My dream is to get out of Kalihi Valley," Billy said. "Maybe I'll be the best damn fish cutter Kalihi has ever seen."

"Is that why you always keep your knives so clean? And line them up all nice and neat?"

"You bet. I've lived a tough life, Tracy. I've learned that you've got to be careful. You've got to be ready. For anything. Always. Because if you ain't, life will bite you on the ass."

* * *

It was there—amidst the kajiki, the menpachi, the onaga—that Billy Carvalho and Tracy Kau fell in love. On their first date, they sat in a car on a moonlit night at Sandy Beach and Billy articulated the similarities between cutting fish and magic and why he loved both skills equally.

"Both require tremendous hand and eye coordination," Billy said. "And in both, you've got to prepare. Preparation is everything."

"That's what my dad always says," Tracy said, studying the stars.

Tracy took Billy to her Kahaluu home and introduced the star-struck fish cutter to her father, the legendary magician Kealia the Unreal. Outside the house, near the washing machine, three tiny puppies slept in a cardboard box.

Kealia the Unreal was getting old, and had been searching for someone to pass his knowledge on to. He found the perfect disciple in Billy, someone sharp, curious, eager to learn. Kealia the Unreal quickly took a liking to the young fish cutter and, over time, generously disclosed every secret he possessed. He even came up with the name Billy Kalihi.

Eventually, Kealia the Unreal announced his retirement and a grateful Billy Kalihi inherited his mentor's six-night-a-week contract with the Outrigger Waikiki Beach Resort.

"Ladies and gentlemen," the announcer always said to the breathless, sold-out audience. "Preeeeeesenting, Hawaii's greatest magician … BILLY KALIHI!"

A drum roll and a cymbal crash. The house lights flash and there he is—entering from stage left—Billy Kalihi.

"Aloha!" he says to the crowd, dapper in a top hat and black tuxedo.

Billy starts off his two-hour show with the easy stuff. Handing out red roses that appear out of midair to pretty tourists. Setting fire to hundred-dollar bills. Pulling doves out of handkerchiefs. At one point, Billy asks the audience to give a warm round of applause as his lovely assistant—Tracy Kau, dressed in black sequined tights—walks on stage. Through the remainder of the evening, Billy throws flaming daggers at his faithful girlfriend, saws her in half while she lies in mysterious mirrored boxes, handcuffs and submerges her in deep glass pools.

"I always wonder how people like you and my dad do magic," Tracy said backstage after a show one night.

"There's no such thing as magic," Billy said. "You know that. It's all preparation, illusion."

"Don't say that. You can't tell me the look I see on those people's faces doesn't come from seeing magic."

* * *

The years went by. Billy Kalihi's reputation blossomed like the *pua kenikeni* in spring. There were Vegas gigs, appearances on Carson, Letterman, Leno. Sadly, amidst the numerous business deals, contracts and negotiations, Billy's love for magic—and Tracy—slowly but surely began to wane.

"Maybe it's time we get married?" Tracy asked one night before a show. "Have children? Don't you think that would be wonderful?"

"One of the arts a magician—and his assistant—must master is the art of patience," Billy said.

"But I want to get married. Go to some place with snow for our honeymoon. I've lived in Hawaii all my life so I've never seen snow."

"Look. Your dad has given me a wonderful gift. It's going to lift me—us—to a higher level."

Billy rushed out on stage, bowing to his adoring audience. The Governor and the First Lady sat in the audience alongside popular jazz singer Joe Lum.

"The Lovely Tracy will now step foot into this booth," Billy said, midway through the show. "And I'll make her disappear."

"Listen here," Tracy said, whispering into Billy's ear. "I'm the best thing you'll ever find. If you want to see me again, you'd better learn to perform some real magic."

Tracy moved aside the velvet curtain, waved to the crowd, and walked into the booth. Billy made mysterious motions with his hands and pulled the curtain open. A gasp from the audience. Tracy, of course, was gone.

"Now," Billy said, closing the curtain and winking confidentially at the audience. "I'll bring her back."

There were more mysterious hand motions and then, voila, the curtain was pulled open again. A hush fell over the crowd. Billy scratched his head. The booth remained empty.

After the show, Billy rushed over to Tracy's Kahaluu home. She was not there. He visited the places they frequented. Restaurants, cafes, magic shops. Nothing. "Ho boy," Kealia the Unreal said when Billy told him his plight. "Tracy, she's a special girl. It's going to take some big time magic to bring her back."

Billy pored through every magic book he owned. "How do I perform real magic?" he wondered. "She's gone. I'll never see her again. What a fool I am. I love her. Why didn't I tell her that?"

That night, for the second time in his life, Billy cried himself to sleep. The next morning—lo and behold!—Tracy appeared in Billy's living room and hugged him.

"You did it!" Tracy said, face flushed red with excitement. "You performed real magic! I love you!"

Tracy opened the curtains to the living room window. Outside, white flakes fell from the sky. Was Old Man Bolosan plucking chicken feathers again? No, this white stuff was different. It was snowing in Honolulu!

"I-I love you, too," Billy said, mystified, eyes searching the heavens.

And they ran outside hand-in-hand, like thousands of incredulous Honolulu residents. People caught snowflakes on their tongue at Ala Moana Park, skied down the slopes of Diamond Head, built snowmen on the shores of Waikiki Beach.

"How'd you do it?" Tracy said, eyes sparkling.

"Maybe it was you who did the magic?"

"Silly, I'm just the magician's assistant. Gosh, this is so beautiful."

"Tracy," Billy said, falling to his knees in the fresh snow. "I'm so sorry. I've been such an asshole. But everything I've ever loved, I've lost. I don't want to lose you."

"You'll never lose me," Tracy said, tears sliding down her cheek and freezing into icy pellets in the cold.

* * *

The wedding was beautiful. The hundreds of guests all commented on how perfect Billy and Tracy looked together. "Here's to a long, healthy life," Kealia the Unreal said, holding up a champagne glass. "And tons of keiki!"

Hours later, after the band had stopped playing and the liquor had all been drunk, Billy walked up to Kealia the Unreal. There they stood, ties loosened, sleeves rolled up to the elbows, faces flushed with beer and champagne.

"That was a great speech," Billy said. "Except the part about the kids. Ain't gonna be no kids. I don't care what Tracy says about wanting a bunch of kids. Not me. I've never carried a baby in my life. Ain't that amazing? Here I am, thirty-something years old, and I've never held a baby. Can you believe that?"

"Kids can be okay," Kealia the Unreal said.

"I know people so busy raising children, they have no time for themselves. I don't want to be like that. I've still got a lot to accomplish. Besides, who'd want to bring a poor kid into this crazy world?"

Tracy, on the other hand, loved children. She volunteered at pre-schools, was the favorite aunty of a dozen nieces and nephews. One day, Billy came home and found his wife sitting on the sofa, crying.

"What's wrong, honey?" Billy said, startled. He had never seen that look in Tracy's eyes before, a look of defeat, of loss.

"It's the doctor," Tracy said, sniffling into a moist Kleenex. "He says I can't have any children."

* * *

Two months later, puzzled obstetricians scratched their heads as Tracy wrestled with bouts of morning sickness, fatigue, an increased appetite, mood swings, and the changing contours of her body.

Faith Gina Carvalho was born on the tenth floor of the Queen's Medical Center.

"Ain't she the prettiest thing?" Billy said to Kealia the Unreal, as they stood in the hospital lobby, the child in his arms. "This kid will have it all. I'll make sure of it. She'll be the happiest girl in the world." He turned to the child. "You hear that, little girl? That's a promise." The child wrapped its tiny hand around Billy's finger. "How about that? Maybe I can perform magic, after all."

"How'd you come up with the name Faith?" Kealia the Unreal asked, smiling.

"All my life," Billy said, not taking his eyes off the child, "things have been tough for me. I've lost so much. But deep inside, I always tried to believe, to have faith. You gotta believe."

* * *

Faith grew to be a very pretty girl. Billy got her involved in a myriad of activities. Baton twirling, piano lessons, flower arranging, painting, charm school, ice skating. The one she loved most, though, was hula.

One afternoon, she participated in a hula competition at the Kamehameha Schools. Billy, Tracy and Kealia the Unreal sat in the gymnasium stands watching. Suddenly, about halfway through the dance, Faith made a mistake. She raised her hands to the heavens when she should have been gesturing towards the earth. Faith performed the rest of the hula perfectly. She placed fourth. As they drove home, Billy knew Faith was disappointed. But she never said anything. In fact, when they got home, she kissed her father on the cheek and spent the rest of the day practicing the same hula. Over and over again.

"Faith is the best thing that ever happened to me," Billy said. "I don't deserve her."

"Don't talk crazy," Kealia the Unreal said.

One day, Faith offered Billy a painting she'd done in school. A very deep, blue ocean filled with fish.

"This is for you, Daddy," she said.

Billy, speechless, smiled and ran his fingers through his daughter's soft hair.

"You sure you don't want to keep that?" he finally managed. "It's very pretty."

"I want you to have it, Daddy," she said.

"Thank you, Sweetheart," he said. "You know what this painting reminds me of? Did Daddy ever tell you he once worked in a fish market? I met your Mom there. Daddy used to be the best fish cutter in Kalihi. It was a long time ago."

Billy framed the painting and hung it on the living room wall, where it remains to this day. The next night, while washing the dishes together after dinner, Tracy gave her husband some disturbing news.

"A boy called for Faith," Tracy said. "Can you believe that? Some kid in her reading class. And she's talking about earrings and makeup and nail polish. Pretty soon, before we know it, it'll be high school and the prom and asking for the car keys and college entrance exams. It's happening too fast."

"Gosh, they grow up quick," Billy said.

* * *

The next day, as he'd done for several years now, Billy dropped Faith off at the Palama Hula Academy.

"Take care, Princess," Billy said, watching his daughter climb out of the car.

"I will, Daddy."

And Billy never saw his daughter again. Perhaps, the disturbing case may bring back memories for you. The television and newspaper reports. The rumors. The leaflets with Faith's picture displayed on every telephone pole, cash register, shop window. "MISSING," it read, in big capital letters. "Faith Carvalho. Age 11. 4 feet, 2 inches.

65 pounds. Black hair. Brown eyes. Last seen at the Palama Hula Academy. Wearing a white blouse with pink balloons on the pockets and blue shorts. Reward. Call the Honolulu Police Department."

A week later, Billy and Tracy and about fifty other people conducted an island-wide search for Faith. Many of the people, Billy had never met before. The group divided Oahu into four sections. East, west, north and south. Searches were held on four consecutive Saturdays. Beaches, mountains, streams. One group at Kaena Point discovered a pile of bones. Police carefully placed the remains into a plastic bag and took them to the Office of the Honolulu Medical Examiner. Two days later, the bones were determined to be those of a cat.

"She's gone," Mrs. Ahuna said, during a search near the Pali Lookout.

"Shut the hell up!" Billy said, turning towards the hula teacher.

"I'm sorry," Mrs. Ahuna said, looking down.

"I'm sorry, too."

Another day, Billy consulted a psychic who worked out of a house in Maunawili Valley.

"Her body is near the water," the psychic said, eyes closed.

"You're wrong!" Billy screamed. Tracy restrained her husband. "Faith ain't dead!"

One night, the lead detective in the case called Billy and reported that police had received an anonymous tip. A girl fitting Faith's description had been seen in the passenger's seat of a brown Chevy Camaro, on Farrington Highway near Makaha. Three days later, the fire department responded to a fire in an Ewa canefield. What they found was, in fact, a burning Camaro. Cops and news crews converged at the scene in minutes. To this day, however, no connection has been made between the burning car and the car seen carrying the girl that may or may not have been Faith.

Sometimes, on good days, Billy believed that Faith was still alive. That she was just lost somewhere. That one morning, just like magic, he'd get a call from Tracy saying Faith had come home. All too often, though, Billy lay awake at night while the rest of the world slept and wondered if he was right that first day in the hospital when he held the tiny, fragile Faith in his arms.

"You gotta believe," he said back then, so many years ago.

* * *

Billy Kalihi does not practice magic anymore. He and Tracy are separated. Once in a while, they'll meet for lunch or talk on the telephone about the weather, the UH football team, their favorite television shows. But no, they never talk about Faith.

Except one time.

On what would've been Faith's sixteenth birthday, Billy invited Tracy to the house for dinner. Over roast chicken and Kahuku corn, Billy told his wife he honestly doesn't know if he can ever have another child. To take care of her so—to pour all of his love into her—only to have her taken away like that.

"I consider myself pretty tough," Billy said that evening. "But if something like this happened to me again, it wouldn't just break my heart. It'd kill me."

"You make hula dancers levitate," Tracy said, whispering, tears in her eyes. "You made Diamond Head erupt. You even made snow fall over Honolulu. I saw all of these things. With my own eyes. You can perform magic, Billy. Maybe you can bring Faith back?"

"Tracy, what you saw was not magic. It may have been just like magic. But it was not magic. There is too big a difference."

"Billy?"

"I'm sorry. No."

At that point, something caught Billy's eye. On the painting Faith had created—the very deep ocean filled with fish—Billy saw an image of his lost daughter. She sat on a tiny boat floating upon the surface of the water, smiling and peaceful.

"D-do you see that?" Billy said, quietly leading his wife to the framed painting.

"See what? I see a brown smudge or ..."

"It's not a smudge. L-look closely."

"Oh my God," Tracy said, suddenly, hands covering her mouth. "Faith?"

"She looks like she's studying something. Far off in the distance."

"Butterflies?" Tracy said, whispering, a tear slipping down her cheek.

Billy wrapped his arms around Tracy for the first time in years, wondering.

DANCES WITH KRISTY

HER REAL NAME WAS KRISTAL, but that night, she introduced herself as Kristy. Jeff Kane met her at a Nuuanu YMCA dance. Junior year in high school. The boys sat on one side of the gymnasium. The girls sat on the other. Jeff leaned against the wall with his best friend, Ignacio Perez.

"Nicky," said Jeff. "Who's that girl in the blue dress? I've been watching her the whole night. It's the damndest thing. She's the best-looking girl here, but no one's asked her to dance. No one's even talked to her. I wonder why?"

"Maybe nobody has the guts," Nicky said.

"Yeah, that's probably it. You think she'd dance with me, Nicky?"

"Hmmmm. Hard to say. She's pretty cute. But, then, you're okay, too. I guess. Give it a shot. I'll give you two-to-one odds."

A five-piece band began playing Earth, Wind and Fire's "Reasons." Jeff held his breath and walked across the gym to the girls' side, where Kristy sat on a metal folding chair. It felt like the longest walk of his life. Jeff asked Kristy to dance. She smiled and stood up. Jeff looked up at the ceiling and exhaled, relieved.

"Thanks for asking me to dance," Kristy said, placing her hands on Jeff's shoulders. "This is my favorite song."

"Really?" Jeff said, hands around Kristy's slender waist. "This is my favorite song, too."

"But this is a love song," Kristy said, smiling. For some reason, her hands were cold. Her hair smelled sweet, minty. Like a flower garden. Maybe fresh orchids. "Guys aren't supposed to like love songs."

As the lead singer of the band sang in an impressive falsetto, Kristy hummed along.

"Do you want to be a singer?" Jeff asked. "I bet you'd be great."

"Oh, no," Kristy said. "I think I want to be around plants. Something simple like that. I want to grow things. Surrounded by photosynthesis going on all around me. Simple is best. That's what my dad always tells me. How about you?"

"My dad's a cop. His dad was a cop. I guess I'll end up being a cop, too. It's a family tradition."

After the dance, Jeff looked all over the gym for Kristy. He did not find her. He went home but couldn't sleep. Outside, the wind blew hard and he swore as he lay there in bed that he could still smell Kristy's hair.

* * *

Years passed. Jeff eventually went to police recruit school for three months in Waipahu. He learned how to handcuff people, how to administer pepper spray, how to utilize pressure points that would force the most uncooperative criminal into submission. One day, though, Jeff realized he was not cut out for police work. He dropped out of the academy.

Instead of wearing a gun and a badge, Jeff wound up waiting tables at the Hinalea Bistro in Waikiki. Every now and then, he wondered about Kristy. Sometimes he thought he saw her. There she sat, on table four, sipping a Zinfandel. Or selecting breakfast cereals at Costco. Or maybe standing in line at the bank across the street on payday. But Jeff would have to wait ten years to see Kristy again.

It happened like this.

Nicky Perez—now a cook at the Hinalea Bistro—admired a poster a customer had recently brought into the restaurant. *Miss Honolulu Pageant. Neal Blaisdell Center.* There were photographs of fifteen young ladies arranged neatly on the poster. One of them was a girl named Kristal Hookano. Jeff had to look twice. Her hair was longer now, past her shoulders. The cheekbones seemed higher, the nose sharper. The eyes, though, were the same. Big and brown. Yes, it was her. Kristy.

"I know that girl," Jeff said. "Kristy Hookano."

"Cutie," Nicky said, nodding his approval.

"I met her at a YMCA dance ten years ago. You were with me."

"I was? That's the amazing thing about you, Jeff. You can remember people you met at some dance ten years ago. Me, I can't remember people I met ten minutes ago. By the way, can you loan me twenty bucks?"

"Again? Don't tell me you're still gambling."

"It ain't gambling."

"Black jack? Poker? Payote? Roulette? Craps? That ain't gambling?"

"No. Those are games of skill and chance."

All of a sudden, three refrigerator-sized hoods in aloha shirts and dark glasses walked into the kitchen of the Hinalea Bistro.

"Gentlemen," one of the men said. "We are associates of Mr. Ace Tonga. We're looking for a man named Ignacio Perez."

"Y-yes?" Nicky said, shaking.

"We believe you have some money owed to Mr. Tonga."

"Yes. No. I mean …" the quivering Nicky said. "Look, gimme another week. I'll have the money then. Five thousand dollars plus interest. I promise! Pretty please?"

One of the men grabbed Nicky and shoved him against a wall. A second guy picked up a bowl of shrimp tempura batter Nicky had been mixing and dumped it on Nicky's head. The third guy stuck a gun down Nicky's throat.

"If we don't have the money by Saturday," the guy with the gun said. "Mr. Tonga will be very, very disappointed."

"Five grand?" Jeff said when the three men had left. "Nicky, you need to lay off that gambling stuff. How're you supposed to come up with five grand by Saturday?"

"Easy," Nicky said, wiping tempura batter out of his eyes. "Some sucker is giving me ten points on the UH game."

* * *

The Miss Honolulu Pageant was held on a cool spring evening. Jeff sat in the back of the auditorium—a dozen long stemmed roses on his lap—fingering through the program. There she was, on page 17. Kristal Hookano. Age 24. Born in Honolulu. Graduated from St. Andrew's Priory School for Girls. B.F.A.—University of Santa Clara. Majored in Music. Interests: Playing the violin, going to the beach, traveling, animals, meeting new people. Does volunteer work with the elderly at the Hale Aloha Care Home in Makiki. Ambitions: To one day play the violin with the Honolulu Symphony.

Kristy was contestant number seven. As soon as she walked on stage, Jeff was blown away. It was the pageant's opening number—a tribute to Disney. With all the girls singing "It's a Small World" in different languages. Next came the swimsuit competition, and Kristy wore a white, one-piece bathing suit and twirled a bamboo umbrella. The audience cheered, applauded and whistled. The night progressed. Jeff watched as Kristy played Mozart on the violin in the talent competition, walked down the ramp in a long silk dress during the evening gown competition, and told the panel of seven judges during the interview portion of the program how the world would be a better place if everyone just took more time to talk to each other.

Jeff wasn't surprised when Kristal Hookano was named the new Miss Honolulu. They gave her a crown and she stood next to a six-foot high trophy. Local celebrities, politicians, sports heroes, and leaders in the business community waited in line patiently to congratulate her. They handed her roses, pikake, maile and if you had been there, you would have smelled the flowers all the way in the back of the auditorium, where Jeff sat and watched.

When the pageant was over and the stage had been cleared, Kristy stood in the parking lot, surrounded by friends. Hundreds of them, it seemed. She talked to each one, exchanging hugs and kisses. Jeff waited nervously for his turn, recalling his younger days as a North Shore surfer, watching the ocean for the right swell.

When he felt the perfect wave—as if the ocean was taking the deepest breath of her life—Jeff walked over to Kristy.

"Congratulations, Kristy," he said, handing her the dozen roses.

She accepted the flowers with a meek smile.

"Thanks," she said, holding the roses up to her nose. "They're lovely."

"You're probably wondering who I am," Jeff said, smiling. "You won't remember me. We haven't seen each other for a while. I'm Jeff Kane. We met at a YMCA dance years ago."

Kristy continued to smile at Jeff, looking a bit puzzled.

"Oh, gosh!" she said, a second later, laughing and then covering her mouth with her hand. "Oh, gosh!"

She opened her arms and Jeff and Kristy hugged. The smell of flowers was everywhere.

"How are you, Jeff?" she said, as they separated. Kristy's eyes were red and her mascara was smeared. Jeff could tell she had been crying for some time. "Gosh, how long has it been?"

"Ten years. I've been good."

Kristy grabbed Jeff's hand and introduced him to several people in the crowd. She explained to them how they had met at a YMCA dance many years ago, how she couldn't believe he had come out to see her after five, no ten, years.

"Daddy," she said. "Come here. You're not going to believe this." A large man in his sixties walked over to Kristy. Thin moustache, dark skin, black hair combed neatly with pomade. He held a little girl in his arms. "This is Jeff Kane. Jeff, this is my dad, Samuel Hookano."

Samuel Hookano looked familiar and Jeff had heard the name before but he couldn't place where he had seen the man. Kristy's father shook Jeff's hand, a hard and firm grip.

"Whoo, you're heavy," Samuel Hookano said, looking at the little girl he was carrying. "Sweetheart, you're getting too big for Uncle."

Another girl, about six or seven, walked up to Kristy with an ilima lei.

"Here, Aunty Kristy," she said.

Kristy bent down and the girl placed the lei around Kristy's neck. They kissed on the lips and then the girl walked away. Kristy adjusted the lei and turned to Jeff, her cheeks flushed.

"She's so cute," Kristy said. Jeff smiled and nodded. "So, are you a policeman now? I remember you saying you were going to become a policeman one day."

"You've got a good memory. No, I'm a waiter."

"You know what? The pageant people are having a reception later tonight at the Kahala. Can you come?"

"Yeah, I'd love to."

Kristy smiled and thanked Jeff for everything and then she turned to several other people who'd come by to congratulate her. Jeff looked at Kristy's father, who bounced the little girl up and down in his arms and, suddenly, he remembered where he had heard the name Samuel Hookano.

In the 1960s, it was said that just about every restaurant and bar, every nightclub, every gambling game, and every pimp paid a tax—a protection fee, it was called—to a man named Lloyd "Waikiki Boy" Naha. That, however, changed suddenly on New Year's Eve, 1966. That night, two police officers discovered the Waikiki Boy's body in the trunk of his Cadillac. The car was parked in the middle of a Kunia canefield. The Waikiki Boy lay in an inch-deep pool of blood. It actually took the coroner several weeks to make a positive identification on the body because the Waikiki Boy had been shot fourteen times in the face and his fingertips were cut off his hands. There was no identification on the body—no driver's license, no credit cards, no wallet. The fact of the matter is when the two police officers opened the car trunk and found Lloyd "Waikiki Boy" Naha, they found only what was left of the top half of him. To this day, everything from the belt down remains missing.

The crime caused a stir. The police brought in one man for questioning, but he was released pending further investigation. That man was Samuel Hookano, Kristy's father. The theory goes that Samuel Hookano was a lieutenant in the Waikiki Boy's hui. No one would have more to gain from the Waikiki Boy's death than

Samuel Hookano. And sure enough, when the Waikiki Boy was no longer able to perform his obligations, it is said that none other than Samuel Hookano assumed his mentor's responsibilities.

* * *

The hotel room at the Kahala was packed. People stood shoulder to shoulder. In the middle of the room, on a glass table, lay a spread including yakitori sticks, chicken wings, sushi, shrimp wrapped around tiny pieces of apple, tiny won ton the size of marbles.

When Kristy saw Jeff, she waved and walked over to him.

"I'm so glad you came," she said, holding a plastic cup full of crushed ice and Coke. "I can't believe you remembered me. After all these years. I mean, it was one dance …"

"I'll always remember asking you to dance," Jeff said. "It was the first time I'd ever asked a girl to dance. I was so nervous. The amazing thing is that you remembered me. How did …?"

"It's simple," Kristy said. "You were my first dance, too. Isn't it amazing how, sometimes, a five-minute song can change your entire life?"

As the crowd in the hotel room thinned, Jeff and Kristy walked outside to get some fresh air.

"Isn't it weird, having to go to parties where half the people are strangers?" Kristy said.

"Yeah," Jeff said, smiling. "By the way, should I call you Kristy or Kristal?"

"Kristal's my real name. The one on my birth certificate. My friends call me Kristy."

"Then I'll call you Kristy."

The cool night air smelled of salt water. The only sounds were the waves lapping against the shore and the hiss of the gasoline powered torches that lined the walkway. Kristy took off her white sandals, wrapped the straps around her fingers, and walked on the sandy beach barefoot.

"Thanks for coming tonight, Jeff," she said.

"I wouldn't have missed it for anything," he said. "So how does it feel to be Miss Honolulu?"

"I don't know. I'm a little numb. That's a question you'll have to ask me maybe fifty years from now. It's too early to say."

"Did you always want to be in a pageant like this?"

"Oh, no!" Kristy said, smiling to herself. "Actually, all of my friends were pretty surprised when I told them I was going to do it. No, I was never one of those girls who went to modeling school and walked around with books balancing on my head and stuff. In fact, I was always kind of a tomboy. You want to know why I decided to run? Okay. I work at Hale Aloha. That's a care home for the elderly in Makiki. There's this adorable lady there named Mrs. Aiona. She's 92 years old. She told me one day that I should run for Miss Honolulu. Just like that. I thought about it for a while, and I decided, yeah, why not? I mean, before it's too late."

Jeff and Kristy walked past a waterfall and then crossed a concrete bridge that stretched across a lagoon. Two dolphins swam under the bridge—sleek and mysterious gray shadows gliding just below the water's surface.

"You play the violin well," Jeff said.

"My dad insisted on it. I was six years old when I started. I used to hate those lessons. But now, I'm glad he made me take them."

"By the way, where is your dad? I didn't see him in there."

"He went home. He said he was tired. So, was your dad disappointed? About you not becoming a police officer?"

"I remember the day I told my Dad I was dropping out of recruit school. I was so scared. I told Dad I wasn't cut out to be a cop. He placed his hands on my shoulders and looked me in the eye and said, 'I want you to be happy. That's the main thing. That's what it's all about.' Those were his exact words. It was the first time he'd ever said anything like that to me. And he never said anything like that to me again."

"He sounds like a good man."

"He was. Dad passed away a couple of years back."

"I'm sorry, Jeff."

"It's funny. I always used to worry about Dad getting hurt as a police officer. I thought about high-speed chases, hostage stand-offs, shoot outs with crazed gunmen. Instead, Dad died from a massive stroke."

Kristy placed her hand on Jeff's and they both looked out at the dark water.

* * *

"You're going out with Samuel Hookano's daughter?" Nicky said the next day at work. "Are you crazy, my friend?"

While he stuffed a Cornish game hen—one of the night's chef's specials—Nicky told Jeff dozens of stories about Samuel Hookano. There was the one about the time Samuel Hookano lost sixty-five thousand dollars at a Chinatown crap game to a man named Leyton Choy. Choy, who stood 6-8 and weighed 325 pounds, was a bouncer at the Club Top Cat. After the game, Choy turned the ignition to his Lincoln Continental and the car exploded into a million pieces. Fragments of the windshield were found three blocks down the road. Choy survived, but walks with a severe limp because his legs are mangled beyond repair.

Still, Nicky said, Choy was a lucky man compared to, say, Caesar Castro—a heroin dealer who refused to pay the collection fee to Samuel Hookano. No one has seen Castro in the last twenty years. Officially, the police call it an unsolved missing person's case. But, off the record, they'll tell you that Castro will never be found because he was taken in a boat several miles off Sand Island and fed piece by piece to a school of tiger sharks. The police won't comment on persistent rumors that three kids discovered Castro's head washed up on the beach the day he was reported missing.

Samuel Hookano, however, has never been convicted of this crime. Or any other crime, for that matter. He has never spent a minute in prison.

"Oh, my goodness!" Nicky said, all of a sudden.

"What?" said Jeff, thinking Nicky had left one of his hens in the oven too long.

At that point, Ace Tonga's boys—the three thugs that earlier dumped tempura batter on Nicky's head—stormed into the kitchen again. Nicky, Jeff feared, was a dead man. But Nicky was nowhere to be found. All that remained of him was the garlicky smell of Cornish game hen stuffing.

* * *

Jeff and Kristy saw each other just about every day the next couple of months. These were busy times for Kristy. Appearances at shopping malls, television interviews, visits to elementary schools where she played the violin, and a banquet where she danced to "E Ku'u Morning Dew" with the Governor.

One day, after a Hawaii Visitors Bureau Luncheon, Kristy asked Jeff over to her house for dinner.

"It'll be nice," Kristy said. "You've never been over to the house before. You can keep my dad company. What do you say? It'll be fun. Is something the matter?"

"No, no," Jeff said. "What time?"

Nicky came into work that afternoon with two black eyes, a bandage wrapped around his forehead, and five missing teeth.

"Jeff," he said. Jeff could tell by the tone of Nicky's voice that his nose had been broken. "You've been going out with Samuel Hookano's daughter for a while now, ah? You must be getting, uh, tight with the old man."

"I'm going to the house tonight."

"Perfect," Nicky said. "Do me a favor, buddy. Ask 'em to tell Ace Tonga's boys to leave me alone."

"I can't do that."

"Why not?" Nicky said, checking the consistency of a lobster bisque.

"For one thing, we don't even know if Samuel Hookano is, uh, involved in any illegal activity …"

"C'mon, Jeff!" Nicky said, rolling his black eyes.

"And, even if he was involved, what would Samuel Hookano have to do with Ace Tonga's people?"

"Samuel Hookano owns this town. He could buy uku million Ace Tongas. If Samuel Hookano tells Ace Tonga to lay off the poor cook at the Hinalea Bistro, I'll bet everything I own Ace Tonga would lay off."

"Why don't you just give up the gambling?"

"Games of skill and chance."

"Whatever. I'll, uh, see what I can do."

That night, Jeff thought that Samuel Hookano—sitting in front of a hibachi on the porch of his house preparing steaks, lobsters, crab legs, oysters and Kahuku prawns—looked a lot different in person than he did in the pictures they ran in the newspaper and television.

"Kristy tells me you work at the Hinalea Bistro?" Samuel Hookano said, looking at Jeff. He had a deep, gravelly voice. The kind that made you pay attention.

"Yes, sir," Jeff said.

"Nice restaurant," Samuel Hookano said, turning over a steak. "I ate there one time. Years ago. I love those little shrimps they give you, with the lemon and the cocktail sauce."

"My friend, Nicky—Nicky Perez—is our cook. A good guy. Great guy. Hard working. Family man. Wife. Three kids …"

"Eh, eat up. Get planny. My old man, he always used to make me finish off everything I had on my plate. Everything. Until this day, I always wipe my plate clean. Ask Kristy. The only time I couldn't clean my plate was at this party for some Chinese friends. They put this thing on my plate and told me to grind. I did. Not bad. I asked them what it was and they told me. Monkey brains. That was it for me."

Jeff, Kristy and Samuel Hookano laughed.

"Mr. Hookano?" Jeff said, taking a breath. "About my buddy Nicky? The cook?"

"Yeah? What about him?"

"Uh, sorry. Never mind."

"Well," Samuel Hookano said after a while. "If you'll excuse me, I'd better go take care of the yard." He stood up and shook Jeff's hand. Then he turned to Kristy. "Miss Honolulu, make sure Jeff here gets enough to eat."

Kristy smiled. Samuel Hookano walked away and uncoiled a long, green garden hose. Jeff and Kristy walked into the house.

"So, what do you think of my dad?" Kristy said, turning on the radio. "I think he likes you. Great guy, huh?"

"Yeah," Jeff said. "Where's your mom? She must be happy. I mean, married to a guy who actually cooks. My mom, she'd think she walked into the wrong house if she saw my dad fixing dinner. When he was alive ..."

"My mom passed away when I was a little girl," Kristy said, trying to smile.

"I'm sorry. Was she sick, or ...?"

"No."

Outside, Samuel Hookano began watering the lawn.

"I guess that's why Dad and I get along so well," Kristy said. "It's just us. It's been that way for a while, now."

"Can I ask you a question?"

"Sure."

"What does your dad do for a living?"

Kristy smiled. Then she looked Jeff straight in the eye.

"I don't know," she said. "Sometimes he leaves for work early in the morning, like anybody else. And sometimes he'll come home in the evening, like anybody else. But other times, the phone will ring in the middle of the night and he'll go out. Or, he won't leave the house for days or he won't come home for days." Kristy shook her head and smiled. "I remember one day in the first grade. I was playing jacks with a couple of other little girls at school. These boys came over to us and said, 'Eh, you better let Kristy win. Bumbye her dad going kill you.' Gosh, that was so mean. I remember chasing those boys down the hall, throwing my slippers at them, tears in my eyes, screaming, 'Not! Not!'"

"That sounds pretty rough."

"Sometimes, it hurts me, what people say about Dad. I mean, he's the sweetest, most loving person …"

"Do you and your dad ever talk about these things?"

"What things?"

"The things people say?"

"No, we never have." Kristy paused for a moment. "You know what scares me, though? Sometimes, I start thinking that maybe everybody's right. Everybody's right and I'm the one who's wrong. That Daddy owns half of the judiciary and he was the one who locked that legislator guy in the tiger cage at the zoo and gosh—who knows?—maybe I'm Miss Honolulu because I'm Samuel Hookano's daughter. It scares me that after everything Dad's done for me, I could still wonder about that, that something like that could even enter my mind."

"Hey," Jeff said, pointing to the radio, changing the subject. "They're playing our song! Will you dance with me?"

Sure enough, it was the very same song Kristy and Jeff had danced to at the YMCA ten years ago. Earth, Wind and Fire's "Reasons." Kristy placed her hands on Jeff's shoulders. Jeff put his arms around Kristy's slim waist. She still smelled like fresh flowers.

Then Jeff noticed it. Kristy was crying.

"What's wrong?" Jeff said, quietly. "Did I say something wrong? Or …?"

"Dad could never do any of those terrible things people say he did," Kristy said, just as quietly. "Could he? You've heard the stories. Do you believe them?" She looked into Jeff's eyes. "Do you?"

Behind Kristy, Jeff saw Samuel Hookano water some ti leaves, stop for a moment, and look up at the rising moon.

"No," Jeff said, finally. "No, I don't believe them."

AN AMERICAN TREASURE

B E VERY CAREFUL.
You are holding an American treasure in your hands. Action Comics, No.1. The first appearance of Superman. There are believed to be less than a hundred copies of this rare work of art in the world. Published in June 1938, the comic book originally sold for a dime. A recent Internet search revealed that a mint condition specimen, like this one, is worth one million dollars.

The American treasure lies in the back of my closet, in a cardboard box next to a vacuum cleaner, deflated footballs and an ab machine I bought after watching a TV infomercial but never used.

I am an orthopedic surgeon. I used to be a comic book collector.

Ever since I was a young boy. I purchased mint condition, multiple copies of—among others—Superman, Batman, Spiderman, Hulk, Captain America, Silver Surfer, Daredevil, X Men. I never read the comic books. I never even opened them. Instead, I carefully placed these specimens in plastic bags that protected the fragile pages from oils and dusts that would mercilessly destroy them. The covers still remain attached to the first page. Unmolested, virginal.

How did I come upon this rarity of comic book artifacts, Action Comics No. 1? Where do I begin?

* * *

I grew up in Kalihi, living in a cramped one-bedroom apartment over a sheet metal factory. The place was infested with cockroaches. At breakfast, the insects crawled out of the toaster the minute I turned the appliance on. When I took a shower, the bugs rushed out of the faucet when the water turned hot. Once, I opened a potato chip bag left on the kitchen counter and dozens of roaches leaped out. At dinner, they made appearances in my chili, my beef stew, my Portuguese bean soup, my rice. The roaches sprinted across my desk as I tried to do homework. When I went to sleep at night, they crawled into my mouth and hair.

My childhood smelled like bug spray.

Raid, Spectracide, Black Flag, Combat, Ortho. There was so much bug spray in the house, the walls and cupboards were covered with the glossy sheen of the toxins, and the dishes and cups had the flavor of poison. Often the sprays didn't seem to work. I doused an army of roaches foraging for crumbs near the kitchen sink. The bugs scampered away—wet, but seemingly unharmed.

I wound up killing hundreds of cockroaches the old-fashioned way, slapping them with shoes, slippers, dish clothes, bare hands. After awhile, I felt like I was in a war.

I started taking things personal.

* * *

Laureen always brought the best stuff to Kapalama Elementary School for show and tell. Every Wednesday, she stood in front of the classroom and displayed cool possessions that made the rest of us third-graders sick with jealousy. Sometimes—as a member of the Book of the Month Club—she brought in a new book. Other days, she exhibited ovens that actually baked cakes. Or chemistry sets. Or cool K-Tel record albums with all the songs we heard on Casey Kasem's American Top-40. Me, I didn't have shit to bring for show and tell. Marbles, baseball cards, maybe some stupid hot rod magazine.

One day, Laureen brought in a box of comic books. She said the old comics were lying around in her Grandpa's house and she took them home. She held up a bunch of junk—Richie Rich, Archies. Then, I couldn't believe my eyes, she displayed a copy of Action

Comics No. 1. I gasped, but no one noticed. No one seemed to know, seemed to give a shit, that Laureen held the most valuable comic book in the world in her unsuspecting hands.

Laureen passed the comic books around. When Action Comics No. 1 came my way, I quietly and quickly slipped it into my folder. Then I took it home. No one saw me. It was so easy. I carefully placed the comic book into a plastic bag and added it to the rest of my collection.

The next day, Laureen came to school with a black eye. The teachers asked her what happened. I eavesdropped, expecting to hear the worst. She cried and said she fell down some stairs.

Within a week, Laureen had withdrawn from school.

* * *

Sick to death of the roaches, I vowed to get out of Kalihi. I studied my ass off and applied to colleges on the mainland. I wanted to get as far away as possible from Hawaii—both geographically and sociologically. I did everything I could to raise the tuition money—part-time jobs, financial aid forms, student loans. I even sold my entire comic book collection. Except for my prize—Action Comics No 1. That one, I kept.

Eventually, I wound up going to medical school in Boston. Boy, there were a lot of haoles on the mainland. That's the first thought that came into my mind as I tried to make my way around a bustling Logan International Airport. After all, I'd come from Kalihi—a place where I could count all the haoles I knew on one hand. Let's see. There was Christian Moore, who ran on the track team. And Victoria Brown, who smoked weed with her buddies in the Drama Club. And Duke Hubert, who walked around wearing Black Sabbath t-shirts, telling anyone who'd listen he worshipped the devil.

They lost my luggage. Great. We were off to a wonderful start. I caught a brown taxi to the huge Boston University campus on Commonwealth Avenue. My first stop was the registration office where I signed up for my classes. Then I wound up renting an over-priced studio on Park Drive, near a Belgium restaurant and a taxi cab business. That's when I learned a hard lesson. I hadn't gotten away from the roaches. Boston, like Hawaii, had more than its share.

One day—jaywalking across Commonwealth Avenue as an ancient looking Green Line T train raced past me—I realized I was homesick as hell. Hawaii seemed so far away. *Was* so far away. I wondered if I should dip into my slim savings account and splurge on a couple of slices of pizza at Kenmore Square. I couldn't cook anything. The airlines had lost all my pots and pans. An icy wind blew off the Charles River and made the hairs on the back of my neck stand up, like I was listening to the scariest ghost story in the world.

I doubted I could ever call this new, strange place home.

Several weeks later, I walked down Newbury Street to kill time and try to forget how homesick I felt. I wandered into used bookshops and tiny art galleries displaying autographed John Lennon lithographs. Then I turned into a sidewalk cafe called Cammie's Coffees. I'm not sure why. Something about the place just made me want to walk in.

A girl with blue eyes and hair that smelled like honeydew melon introduced herself as Robin and took my order. I selected the coffee of the day, whatever that was. The place was pretty empty—I was the only customer—so we started talking.

"I don't want to sound ignorant or offensive or anything," Robin said. "But what are you? Mexican? Eskimo? Indian?"

"No," I said, smiling. "I'm from Honolulu, Hawaii."

Robin was from Upstate New York and studying to be an architect at MIT. She kept on thinking Honolulu was an island and even when I told her it was the name of a city, the state capital—not an island—she still wouldn't believe me.

"Do you all live in grass huts?" she said. "Walk around in, like, hula skirts?"

"No. Not quite."

"What language do you speak there?"

"Uh, English. Mostly. But we do have a lot of immigrant families from Asia and the Pacific and …"

"What about money? What kind of currency do you use?"

"Actually, Hawaii is a part of America. The fiftieth state and all? We, uh, use American money."

"Where is Hawaii anyway? Is it somewhere off Washington State? Isn't there a bridge connecting Seattle with Hawaii?"

Robin said the coffee was on the house, a welcome gift to Boston. I objected but she wouldn't hear any of it. And even though spending three bucks for a cup of coffee went against everything I learned growing up in Kalihi, I became something of a regular at Robin's place on Newbury Street.

One day, I asked Robin out for lunch and she agreed.

"It must be so cool living in Hawaii," Robin said over clam chowder, lobster and bread pudding at the Union Oyster House. Robin knew a manager at the restaurant and got us a good price.

"Yeah," I said, digging into my scrod. Whatever the heck scrod was.

"I'd love to live there, actually. Seems like a wonderful place to have kids, raise a family. Hey, did you know we're sitting in the oldest restaurant in America?"

"We are?" I said, looking around the place. The restaurant did look pretty old. So did the busloads of tourists sitting around us. "No kidding?"

"Greg," she said, after our meal, as we walked out of the oldest restaurant in America. "Do you have protection?"

"Excuse me?" I said, not sure I heard correctly.

"Protection," she said.

"Uh, no," I said. "But I could get some. I mean, if you …"

"We better get some," she said.

"Okay. But …"

"It gets pretty cold here."

"Cold?"

"Greg, this is not Hawaii. You'll die in Boston wearing the clothes you have on. You need protection against the raging elements."

So, Robin and I walked to Filene's Basement, where I purchased a heavy coat, gloves and a scarf. After awhile, Robin and I saw each other pretty regularly. She took me to the Freedom Trail, and we walked past Paul Revere's home and Bunker Hill. Names and places from my history books. We ate linguine with clam sauce at a tiny Italian restaurant in the North End. We admired Renoirs and Monets at the Museum of Fine Arts. I put on the only suit and tie I owned—a clip on, alas—and we drank over-priced Scotch at the Ritz Carlton and the Plaza Hotel. One brisk day in October, Robin drove me to Lexington and Concord and we admired the colors of the leaves. Old men in flannel shirts raking fire-colored leaves in their yards and driveways looked at us funny. I was pretty used to it by now. It happened all the time. From the museum guards, to the vendors selling Italian Sausage sandwiches outside of Fenway Park. What the hell was this Eskimo guy doing holding hands with one of our girls?

Somehow, two years later, Robin and I got married in Boston. I wondered if Robin's parents were bummed out. The last guy Robin dated before me now wrote speeches for the Governor of Massachusetts. If they were disappointed—to their credit—they never showed it. As we drank Dom Perignon and Verve Cliquot and single malt scotches at the reception later that evening, I wondered if everyone at that reception was trying to figure out the same thing I was. How the hell did a guy like me from Kalihi wind up with this East Coast girl with the most amazing blue eyes?

* * *

After graduating from medical school, I convinced Robin to move to Hawaii. We lived high on Waialae Iki Ridge, in a splendid home without roaches. Our only son, a six-year-old named Kainoa, seemed to have a gift for spelling. My office was located in the Kalihi Medical Arts Building. I kept my staff small—two assistants and myself. My wife worked as a freelance photographer—taking pictures of foods, clothes, pets, models. I came to work about nine, treating patients for their knee, shoulder, back, hand and hip problems. Some days, I performed surgery. Life seemed fairly routine.

Until the day I realized my wife was having an affair. I don't know how I came to this conclusion, exactly. Robin just seemed to act different. She started going to the gym, something she never did before. She bought more clothes, giggled on the telephone, sang in the shower. Sometimes she worked late, saying she had a photo shoot, and came home smelling of alcohol unsuccessfully disguised by a heavy dose of Altoids. One afternoon, I discovered a note crumpled in her sweater pocket, written in someone else's handwriting. *The Wild Wahine, Friday, 11 p.m.*

That Friday night, I carefully made my way into the Wild Wahine, a strip bar off Keeaumoku Street. Was Robin having an affair with some thick-necked bouncer, or a tequila bottle juggling bartender, or a disc jockey spinning hits by rappers and head bangers? I had to find out. Dozens of strippers roamed the stages, slapping their butts and stuffing garter belts around their thighs with dollar bills. Maybe I had it all wrong. Maybe my wife wasn't having an affair. Maybe Robin had become an exotic dancer. Maybe my life had turned into a Movie of the Week. *I Married a Stripper. The Shocking Story of Dr. Greg Peralta.*

One could only hope.

Alas, this was no Movie of the Week and my dreams—my life—were smashed to bits in the span of a heartbeat. For there was Robin—sitting in a dark booth—cozy in the arms of another. I snuck over for a closer look and almost fell flat on my ass. My wife was French kissing another woman, a local girl with long brown hair. A stripper, it turned out. As I wobbled out of the club, unseen, I wondered what was worse—my wife having an affair with another man or another woman. For some strange reason, I almost felt a sense of relief that it wasn't another man. Don't get me wrong. It sucked. Of course, it sucked.

But not as much.

* * *

Three nights later—when I shook off some of the shock—I returned to the Wild Wahine. My wife wasn't there, thank goodness, but her stripper friend was. She sat at the bar, one long leg crossed over the other, sipping iced water.

"Hello," I said. "May I talk with you?"

"Would you like a lap dance?" she said.

"Can we talk during a lap dance?"

"We can do anything you want."

She grabbed my hand and led me towards the back of the Wild Wahine. We wound up in a tiny, dark room the size of a broom closet. There was nothing in there except a wooden bench and a box of Kleenex. I sat on the bench. She asked for twenty bucks and I gave it to her. The DJ played a Nine Inch Nails song. "Closer." The girl began to take off her clothes.

"So, what do you want to talk about?" she said.

"I've never had a lap dance before," I said, not knowing quite where to begin.

"Well, you just relax. What's your name?"

"Greg."

"What do you do, Greg?"

"I'm an, uh, doctor. Orthopedic medicine."

"Wow."

"What's your name?" I said.

"My stage name is Roxy. But since you're a doctor I'll tell you my real name. It's Laureen."

At first, the name meant nothing to me. But somewhere between the point where she slipped out of her bra and red leather skirt, it hit me. Laureen? Could this have been the girl from school who I stole the priceless Action Comics No. 1 from? I tried to look into Laureen's eyes, to see if I could see the tiny schoolgirl who had mastered the art of show and tell.

"Do you like me?" the gyrating Laureen asked, hands in hair.

"Yes," I said. I tried hard to bravely tackle the task at hand, but Laureen's breasts, thighs, and belly button ring were messing with my concentration.

"Do you want to touch me, Doc?" she asked. "Go ahead. You're a doctor."

I gently reached out my hand and placed my fingers on Laureen's hips. The skin felt soft, warm, inviting. This, I realized, was what my wife had elected to sacrifice our marriage vows for. This was skin Robin had touched, kissed, caressed. For just a second, I came up with the idea of forgiving my wife for everything and bringing Laureen home for the weekend. Just the three of us. Wouldn't that be something?

"Be careful with those, Doc," Laureen said. "Your hands are playing with a true to life American treasure."

"Did I go to school with you, Laureen?" I said, cheeks hot. "Kapalama Elementary School? You always brought the best stuff for show and tell?"

I thought about my theft of her Action Comics No. 1, the million-dollar specimen still in the back of my closet. It was perfect, wasn't it? I steal the priceless artifact from Laureen. In return, she steals my priceless wife. Life was exactly the way my mom described. What goes around comes around. Something about karma.

"Show and tell?" Laureen said, peeling off white panties and sitting on my lap. "How's this for show and tell?"

* * *

Of course, I'd see Laureen again.

One Thursday afternoon, she brought Paiea into the office. Paiea was her husband. The couple said Paiea had hurt his leg playing basketball. I asked him to lie on his stomach and raise his right leg. I immediately saw that his Achilles tendon had been ruptured.

"It's very common to rupture the tendon playing ball," I said.

"Yeah?" Paiea said. "What do I do now, Doc?"

"Basically, you have two choices. I could cast it. Let it heal on its own. Or you could have surgery and I'll repair it."

"What do you recommend?"

"There's always risk with surgery. But that's what I recommend."

We scheduled the surgery for Tuesday. Meantime, I wrapped an Ace bandage around Paiea's ankle and set him up with a pair of crutches.

"No basketball," I said, smiling.

"Yeah," he said, walking out of the office.

* * *

I slept with Laureen three days later. The surgery on Paiea went pretty much as planned. In the hospital, I explained to Paiea and Laureen that he'd be in a cast for six to eight weeks. After that—and some rehab—the repaired Achilles tendon would be as good as new. Heck, he could be back out on the basketball courts before he knew it.

I offered to drive Laureen home. She accepted. And as Paiea lay in his hospital bed—knocked unconscious by a shot of Demerol to the ass to ease the pain of his foot—Laureen invited me into her house and gave me another lap dance.

"I came to you because you're the only doctor I know," she said, afterwards.

Paiea hadn't ruptured his Achilles tendon playing ball, she admitted. Paiea was one of several Native Hawaiian sovereignty leaders involved in a three-day festival honoring the *kanaka maoli*—the men and women of the Hawaiian nation. He'd been leading a rally in front of the Bishop Museum when the cops came. Instead of facing arrest, he ran and jumped off a third-floor balcony of the T. Chin Building on North King Street. That's how he ruptured his Achilles tendon. That's how he became a fugitive.

"Paiea's always hated haoles," Laureen said, shaking her head. "I knew him when he was a kid. Back then, you could find him hanging out at Waikiki Beach, with his surfboard and the power cord tied to his ankles. Paiea always yelled at the tourists. I never felt too good about that. Sometimes he hassled them. Other times he asked them for money. Paiea had this thing about tourists. He was always talking about how he hated the missionaries and how they took the land from the Hawaiian people and in his words 'fucked the place up.'"

"I thought your, um, husband looked familiar," I said. "I think I've seen him on TV."

"Can I ask you a favor, Doc?"

"Yes."

"Please don't tell Paiea where I work. He doesn't know anything about the Wild Wahine. If he found out, he'd go crazy. Promise?"

"Yes. Of course."

"Thank you. Are you married, Doc?"

"Yes. My wife's name is Robin. I think you might know her."

* * *

Paiea was released from the hospital the next day. As I placed the hard cast around his leg, he complained about living in an apartment infested with cockroaches.

"I'd give anything to live in a house without roaches," he said. "I bet you live in a clean house, Doc. No roaches, right?"

"Not anymore."

"Lucky."

"So, you're a sovereignty activist?" I said.

"You've been talking to my wife?" he said.

"Um, yeah," I said, focusing on his leg, avoiding the eyes.

"I'm fighting for you and me, brah. I love Hawaii. And I love her people. I'm fighting to be a beacon of light for us. I've dedicated my life to correcting the wrongs and the injustices that have been done to us. I'm fighting to get our land back. I'm fighting to get our rights back. I'm fighting to get our pride—our *haaheo*—back. You're Hawaiian, right? You should come join us."

"I'll think about it."

"The haoles are like the cockroaches in my house. They're everywhere, taking over everything. They walk around like they own the place. I've got to stop it. We've got to stop it, Doc. Before it's too late."

"But ..."

"Me and Laureen, we live simply. Our house is filled with cock-roaches, but that's okay. We got each other. One day, we'll have our land back, too."

As Laureen helped her husband to his crutches, I tried to keep a tally of the secrets I had to keep. Number one, Paiea's wife worked as a stripper. Number two, I'd slept with her. Number three, she'd slept with my wife—a haole from Boston, no less.

Things were getting a little crazy.

* * *

"You slept with her," Robin said one night, over a dinner of stroganoff and arugula.

"What?" I said.

"Laureen. You slept with her."

"I don't know what you're ..."

"I smell her on you, asshole! I smell her in your hair, in your clothes, on your fingers! How could you do this to me?"

"How could I do this to you? How could you do this to me? You slept with her first. You started it."

Robin came clean. She said she met Laureen during a photo shoot. Negligees for a large department store. They started talking. Robin said Laureen was the first person in Hawaii who made her feel comfortable, welcome. She said she had never felt at home in these islands. Not for a second. The locals looked at her funny, treated her different. She always thought about going back to Boston, but never worked up the guts to tell me.

"What's going to happen to us, Greg?" Robin said, staring suddenly at the TV.

* * *

Paiea was the lead story on the six o'clock news. The police had arrested him and were escorting him into the cellblock. He had no shirt on. He wore handcuffs. He'd been hiding out in a Maili beach house.

"Laureen used to take me there," she said. "To that Maili home. It was so beautiful. Large turtles used to rest on the beach outside the house and lie in the sand."

"How'd the cops know where to find Paiea?" I said.

"Easy," Robin said. "I told them."

* * *

The protestors formed a circle around the courthouse. A hundred or so men, women and children joined hands and sang songs of Hawaiian pride and unity. Police watched. I walked into the courtroom, packing my mint condition copy of Action Comics No. 1 in a briefcase. I had made up my mind. I was going to give the American treasure back to Laureen. She could do with it what she would. She could use its million-dollar pedigree for her husband's legal defense, to escape from the nasty clutches of the Wild Wahine, to get rid of the roaches in her apartment, to advance the cause of the Hawaiian people. Action Comics No. 1 had become a symbol, for me, of Hawaii's land. It had been unfairly taken and should now be returned to its proper owner.

The large crowd of supporters did not stand when the judge entered the courtroom.

"These are not our laws!" one man screamed. "You are not our judge. This is wrong. Free Paiea!"

Paiea held up a hand. The man stopped talking.

Prosecutors argued that Paiea was a flight risk and a danger to the community and should be held on one hundred thousand dollars bail. The defense called that amount ridiculous, a sum reserved for murderers and rapists. The judge placed Paiea on supervised release and allowed him to walk out of the courtroom.

After the hearing, Laureen hugged her freed husband. As we walked out of the courthouse, I offered her my gift.

"What is this?" she said, staring at the plastic bag, puzzled. "A joke?"

"No," I said. "I took it from you years ago. Now I'm giving it back."

"What?"

"Be careful, you are holding an American treasure in your hands. Action Comics No. 1, the first appearance of Superman. There are believed to be less than a hundred copies of this rare work of art in the world. Published in June, 1938, the comic book originally sold for a dime. A recent internet search revealed that a mint condition specimen, like this one, is worth one million dollars …"

"How could you do this to me?" a woman screamed, suddenly. My wife. "Laureen, how could you do this to me? I thought you loved me. Didn't you say you loved me? Lying on the beach, with the gorgeous turtles?"

"Robin?" Laureen said.

"Paiea, did you know that your wife is a stripper?" Robin said.

"Please, Robin," I said, raising a hand.

"No, it's true," Laureen said, clutching Action Comics No. 1 tightly to her breasts. "I am a stripper. And I slept with Robin."

"What?" Paiea said.

"I slept with him, too," Laureen said, pointing at me. The crowd gasped. I heard at least three "auwes."

"Doc?" Paiea said, staring at me in disbelief.

Before I can say anything, Paiea rushes me. The cops intervene, wrapping their arms around the charging activist and a dozen or so of his partners. Paiea's head—either by accident or by wrestling technique—violently strikes the concrete sidewalk. Laureen rushes over to her fallen husband and wraps his head with, of all things, Action Comics No. 1. I am stunned. The famous cover of Superman effortlessly lifting a green car on a city street is now nothing but a crumpled bandage.

"I love you, Paiea," Laureen says. "Please forgive me for my mistakes."

The blood pools around Paiea's head like a thought bubble in a comic book cartoon.

THE SINCEREST
FORMS OF FLATTERY

One Night

Y OU KNOW THIS IS GONNA be a bad idea, Baby.

You should never have agreed to attend your ten-year high school reunion. The plan has bad news written all over it. But your agent, Natalie Boucher, insisted. It'll be a great public relations move, she said. It'll show the world that you—Ernie Pacheco—have not forgotten where you'd come from. Sure, you had to cancel a couple of choice gigs, hot parties, big money opportunities to squeeze this trip in your schedule. But Natalie said it'll be worth it. So here you are, flying in from Las Vegas. You haven't been back to Hawaii in years.

You won't have much time in the islands. You'll hit the reunion, shake a few hands, then hop back on the first plane home.

Heck, Baby, you have things to do.

(Now and Then There's)
A Fool Such as I

The reunion is held at the Royal Hawaiian Hotel in Waikiki. You dress low key—black shirt, pants. The emcee is none other than Tito Nakata—former quarterback—now some disc jockey at a Jawaiian radio station. He calls lucky numbers, tells lame jokes, tries to force us to sing the alma mater. The crowd eats it up. You have only one question.

Where's Asa Furtado, your old flame?

Knowing Asa, she has to be here somewhere. She wouldn't miss the class reunion for the world. You wonder what she looks like now. Is she married? Does she have kids? You wonder where she works. She always wanted to be an astronaut.

Slowly but surely, folks walk up to you.

"Eh, Ernie," they say. "Long time no see. So, what are you doing now?"

"I'm in the entertainment business," you say. "Vegas, Hollywood ..."

"Haolewood? No act, Bull! Whoah! What are you? A movie star? Singer? Porn star?"

"I'm an Elvis tribute artist."

"Say what?"

"I pay tribute to the King. On stage."

"You're an Elvis impersonator? You heard that, everybody! Ernie is a fricking Elvis impersonator!"

Some of the assholes actually have the nerve to laugh. Do they think it's easy being an Elvis Tribute Artist? Hell, no. It's hard work. You need to stay in shape if you want to honor the young Elvis, stay out of shape if you choose to memorialize the later Elvis. You have to remember words to a large catalogue of songs, feel comfortable with karate choreography. And last, but not least, you better know where to purchase the right accessories. The wrong jump suit will make or break a tribute.

One moron asks you to sing. Soon the whole mess of them are whooping and hollering. "Sing, Elvis!" they scream. You politely decline. But they won't take no for an answer. Finally, you decide to give the assholes a treat. You get up on stage and hit them with a dose of "Blue Suede Shoes." Do you resemble the King? Not really. But folks say during your performances—as you wiggle your hips, sneer and flash shaka signs—you slowly but surely morph into The Man.

On stage, you search the adoring masses for your missing Asa. You don't see her. But at one point during "Love Me Tender," someone throws a hotel room key at you. Paydirt! This could've only come from Asa.

After the concert, they show a slide show about your class. There is not one picture of Asa. You find this odd. Not one picture of the Senior Class President, National Honor Society President, track star. How can this be? It's like she never existed.

As you try to make an early exit from the festivities, Bruce Lim—wrestler turned comptroller—stops you.

"Eh, look averybody," he says. "Elvis is leaving the building!"

Are You Lonesome Tonight?

But Bruce is mistaken. You're not leaving the building. You're heading for room 1412, the number on the key thrown at your feet. That is one of the perks of your Elvis gig. Back when you were just Ernie Pacheco, living in a duplex near Kam Bowl, nobody threw keys at you. You lived in a dump. For some reason, the house next door always seemed to smell like fingernail polish. Your father said a beautiful girl lived there, a manicurist who modeled her fingers for fashion magazines. You never saw any beautiful girls in that house.

"Howzit, handsome."

You walk into the hotel room. A hot chick sits on the bed, removing her stockings. It isn't Asa.

"Sweetheart," she says. "You remember me?"

"No, ma'am," you say.

"Ma'am? Ooooh, you're so polite, honey. Just like The King. I love The King, you know. Come closer, darling. My name is Ramona."

Ramona grabs your hand. She has the softest hands. Hands, you imagine, that could've belonged to the manicurist, finger model next door. You kiss. Her lips are soft, inviting. She tastes like Doublemint gum.

116

"I don't remember a Ramona in school," you whisper.

"That's because back then, I was Raymond."

"Raymond Correa?" you say, pulling back. "Math League Champion?"

"That's the one, Studly," Ramona says. "I bet you're probably wondering where Asa is. You two were quite the couple. Then you dumped her for the bright lights of Las Vegas. Ain't that right, sweetie?"

"Yeah. Afraid so. So, what happened to her? Where is she?"

"You never heard?"

"No. Heard what?"

Ramona leans over and whispers in your ear, dramatically. Her highlighted hair smells like Vidal Sassoon and cigarette smoke.

Don't Be Cruel

You guess if you must blame somebody for this fiasco, you might as well start with Elvis. Elvis and your Dad.

As a kid, you tried everything to impress the Old Man. You got good grades in school, worked as the editor of the school newspaper, was named treasurer of the Key Club.

"Key Club?" you remember Dad saying. "What the hell is that? You guys pick locks, or something?"

Needless to say, he was not impressed. That was the problem. Nothing impressed him. Actually, you take that back, one thing did impress him. Big time. Your Dad worked as a security guard. You remember the night that forever changed his life. And yours, too. He worked the big Elvis concert at the Honolulu International Center and came home singing Elvis songs. He went to the old Kress at the Kamehameha Shopping Center and bought all his records, hung posters on the wall, sat hypnotized in front of the TV during reruns of *Blue Hawaii*.

You realized Dad liked Elvis better than you.

That's when you came up with your plan. If you became Elvis, Dad'd like you, too. Mom didn't want to become Elvis to win Dad's

117

approval. She just up and left, hooking up with a mailman who didn't give a rat's ass about Elvis.

"Son," Dad said one day. You were in Dad's car, the one with the KISA bumper sticker and the dice dangling from the rear-view mirror. You sang along with an Elvis song on the radio. "Heartbreak Hotel." "You're pretty good. You sound like the King."

And that's all it took.

Dad signed you up for singing lessons, taught you how to play the guitar, enrolled you in karate school. He combed your hair like The King, bought you your first pair of bell-bottom pants.

"You have a gift," he said, one night, as the fingernail polish smell from the house next door drifted into your living room. "A special talent."

"Is the manicurist lady working on her fingernails again, Dad?" you said.

"Never mind, son."

Memphis

Things to do in Memphis:

Graceland
Beale Street, birthplace of the blues
barbecue

One day, Dad came home with the biggest smile on his face. Bigger than the time he won four hundred bucks shooting craps with Reynold and the boys.

"This is your lucky day, Ernie," Dad said. "We're going on a trip."

"Where?" you said, excited. "Disneyland? Magic Mountain? Dodger Stadium?"

"Better. We're going to visit Elvis' home, Graceland, in Memphis."

"Oh. Uh, thanks a lot, Pops."

So, Dad and you flew to Memphis and took a bus to Graceland. You walked with other tourists through Elvis' living room, music room, kitchen room, trophy room. The place didn't do much for you. All shag rugs and mirrors and funky couches. After the tour of the house, Dad told you to follow him.

"I want you to meet somebody," he said.

"Who?" you said.

"The King."

You thought Dad was actually going to introduce you to Elvis. What would you say? Instead, you both wound up standing in front of Elvis' grave, in a place called the Meditation Garden.

"Elvis is dead, Dad?" you said.

No one else was around. It was just you, Dad and The King. You wondered why the other tourists in your group declined to pay their respects, opting instead for the souvenir stands searching for t-shirts and shot glasses.

"Sir," Dad said, with more reverence than you'd ever heard in his voice. "This is my son, Ernie. He is going to dedicate his life to you. Is that cool? Give us a sign."

The whole thing felt a little creepy. Suddenly, a wind blew and—from nowhere—a smell of sweet, musky cologne emerged.

"You smell that?" Dad said, sniffing the air like a dog around a T-bone steak. "The King is giving us his blessing."

"Oh."

"This whole trip is kinda mystical kine, Ernie," Dad said, wiping a tear from his eye. "I was thinking about it. You and Elvis have the same initials. E.P. You both have five letters in your first name. You both have seven letters in your last names."

"So?"

"So? You think that's coincidence?"

"Yeah. Planny people have the initials E.P. Choke people have five letters in …"

"You got a lot to learn, boy, about the ways of the world."

For the Good Times

"My Dad is weird," you told Asa.

"He's not weird," Asa said. "He's actually pretty cool."

You both sat at your favorite hangout, Makapuu Beach, watching the waves break and the hang gliders soar above the lighthouse.

You remember Asa back in those good old days. How the sea wind blew through her hair. How her eyes were as green as naupaka leaves. How she body surfed with one hand out, like she was reaching for treasures in the breaking wave. She had her entire life ahead of her, and you knew she was destined for good things.

Heck, Asa'd tackled unimaginable odds. She grew up in Kuhio Park Terrace. Her Dad was doing time for cracking safes. Her Mom worked two jobs and raised four kids. One brother was in a gang, running drugs. Another brother was dying of AIDS. Asa's sister worked as a prostitute, standing on street corners in front of the Nuuanu mortuaries.

"You know what I'm going to be, Ernie?" she said. "An astronaut. I want to fly in space. See stars and moons and planets. I'll be the first astronaut from KPT."

That's when you noticed the creepy looking old guy standing by the showers taking pictures. You figured it was some pervert after Asa. You were wrong. The guy was after you. He introduced himself as Flash Peterson, talent scout. Flash Peterson's cologne smelled like the musky winds swirling around the Meditation Garden at Graceland.

The rest, as they say, is history. You said goodbye to Asa and flew up to Vegas. Flash Peterson set you up. Your career paying tribute to Elvis was born. Soon you were playing gigs—church groups, fundraisers, conventions, wedding receptions, birthday parties, dinner shows.

"That's my boy," Dad wrote on a postcard with Diamond Head and Waikiki Beach.

It was your eighteenth birthday.

(You're The) Devil in Disguise

You have to ask three different people for directions before you find the place. In Ewa Beach, past the golf courses and the strip malls. Basically, in the middle of nowhere. A guard waves you onto the dusty property and you park the rental car. You walk past the kitchen, which smells of beef stew, and the gym where patients lift weights. You don't belong here, have no business here. But you've pulled strings with a social worker who'd caught your act while vacationing in Vegas.

You and Asa sit outside, at a table covered with a brown veneer. Birds sing in the trees. The years have not been kind to Asa. Her eyes—once green as Makapuu naupaka—are tired and dim. Her teeth are stained yellow. She wears a white sweat shirt, denim shorts, and tennis shoes.

"So, what brings you here?" Asa says, sipping Diet Coke out of a plastic cup.

"I came here to see you."

"You did? So, what do you do nowadays? For a living?"

"I'm an entertainer."

"Actor? Singer? Porn star?"

"Elvis Tribute Artist."

"I guess your Dad must be happy. Mind if I smoke?"

"No. Not at all."

Asa takes out some rolling papers and a pouch of tobacco and expertly rolls a cigarette.

"I never thought about it," she says, inhaling the cigarette smoke and holding it in her lungs. "But you kinda look like Elvis."

"Really?" Of course, you are flattered.

"Yeah. Your hair, forehead."

"Thank you. Thank you very much."

"So, what brings you back home? The reunion?"

"My agent thought it'd be a good idea."

"You have an agent?"

"Yes. Well, sort of. Natalie Boucher is her name. She also works at Caesar's Palace."

"Wow. Promotions and stuff?"

"No, seafood buffet. She's a waitress."

Asa flicks her cigarette ashes into a coffee can.

"So how was it?" she says. "The reunion?"

"You didn't miss anything," you say. "How long have you been here?"

"I've been clean fourteen months now. They let me out three, four times a week. I'll be out for good soon."

"How did this happen, Asa? How'd you wind up here?"

"I'm weak."

"You're not weak."

"You want the truth? The truth is power, right?"

"Yes."

"When you left me, everything fell apart," she says, rolling up the sleeves of her sweatshirt. A horrible scar runs down the inside of her arm, from the bicep to the wrist. You want to ask how she got it, but don't. "I'd built my life around you. It sounds fucking corny to say, but you were my world. When I didn't have you anymore, I drank, smoked weed, sniffed coke, did ice. Anything to forget about you. Pretty soon, all I could think about was the next hit, the next drink, you know? It was the only time I felt good."

"I'm sorry."

"It's funny. Do you know where I used to buy my shit from? Your neighbor."

"What?"

"You lived next door to the biggest crack house in Kalihi."

"The house that always smelled like fingernail polish?"

"Acetone. An ingredient used to make drugs."

"Oh."

"I'd better go," she says, standing up and clutching her blue AA book to her chest. "It was nice seeing you again, Ernie. You watch. I'll beat this."

Don't Cry Daddy

You drive to Kalihi, budgeting fifteen minutes to catch up with the Old Man before heading off to the airport. You even bring him a gift, a plate with Elvis' portrait painted on it. The early Elvis, looking at the heavens like a man searching for the answers.

When you get to the old duplex, you're shocked to see the place on fire.

"No!" someone screams, on his knees. You recognize him as your neighbor. Ponytail, tattoos, skinny. "The place just went up, man," he says, gulping breaths like a drowning man. You realize in twenty some odd years, you never got his name.

Flames poke through windows, doors, and what used to be your roof. Firemen in thick yellow jackets shoot water from their hoses at the blaze. Black smoke is everywhere.

"S-someone ran into the house," the guy on his knees says, shaking his head.

"Who?" you say. "Where's my Dad?"

"Maybe it was him, man. I don't know. Could be. Somebody ran in."

Paramedics carry your Dad out on a stretcher. Dad's face is black, almost unrecognizable. Portions of his peeling skin are bloody and pink and burned. You're not sure if it's your imagination, but a tear seems to slip out of the corner of his eye.

"Dad?" you say, clutching the Elvis plate.

The paramedics look at you, shake their heads, and drive your Dad away. That's when you see her. Asa. Standing in a corner, blanket wrapped around her shoulders, crying.

In the Ghetto

Later that evening, as you wander through the charred house with the smell of smoke in your hair and clothes, you figure it all out. Asa, the poor sick bitch, had visited the drug lab to buy her shit.

She'd told you she'd kicked the habit, but had been lying. While she was in there, the place caught fire. Dad ran in to save her. He managed to get her out. But could not save himself. You'd always thought of him as just some Elvis wannabe, a groupie. Now you realized he was a fucking hero. As you stare at horrible, desperate fingernail marks scratched on the black walls, you make two promises. From now on, you will dedicate every show you do to Dad's memory. And you'll dedicate the rest of your years to imitating his life.

I Want You, I Need You, I Love You

"Mama, I hope I look as good as you when I turn eighty," you say to the birthday girl, Willow, sitting in her wheelchair. "*If* I turn eighty."

The crowd eats it up. At least one set of false teeth hits the floor in an uncontrollable burst of laughter. You're playing to a feisty group of thirty senior citizens at Sisto Banditos, a small Mexican restaurant off the Strip. You wonder if the tacos, enchiladas and burritos will play dirty tricks with the sensitive digestive tracks of your audience.

As you break into "I Want You, I Need You, I Love You," you start thinking about Asa. She's tried to call you several times, but you never called back. The bitch killed your Dad. If she hadn't gone back to the drug house, Dad would never have had to run into that burning hellhole and pull her sorry ass out. No, you left for Vegas without returning her calls. Just like that first time, all those years ago.

After the show, you pose for pictures with Willow and sign a few autographs. That's when Asa walks up to you.

"Nice jumpsuit, dude," she says.

"What are you doing here?" you say.

"I've been released from the treatment center. I'm clean."

"I don't know why I'm talking to you," you say, as you both walk out of the Mexican restaurant. The lights from the Strip blink on and off in Asa's green eyes. "I feel like you killed my dad. You lied to me, you went back to the drug house to buy drugs, Dad pulled you out of the flames."

"Truth is power, right?" Asa says, stopping under a streetlight in the middle of the sidewalk. The night air feels very thin and cold. You place your hands in your pockets.

"Yes," you say, stopping also.

"You got it all wrong, Ernie. I went to your dad's place, hoping to see you again. The crack house next door was on fire. Someone said your Dad was still in his house. I ran in. Sure enough, your Dad's arms were full of his Elvis scrapbooks, posters, records. He wouldn't come out. I tried to pull him out. He wouldn't move."

"What?" The Strip begins to spin like a crazy roulette wheel. Las Vegas sinks beneath your feet. You do everything you can not to fall on your ass.

"I tried to get him out, Ernie. But I failed. That's the truth."

"I'm sorry," you say, wrapping your arms around Asa. "I'm so sorry for doubting you. For everything."

"That's all right."

"Have you been to Graceland before?" you say, after a long while, when you've saved up enough strength to start walking again.

"Graceland?" Asa says. "No."

"You have any interest in going?"

"No. But with you, I might make an exception."

"Good," you say, placing your hand in Asa's. "I have a buddy there I want you to meet."

BENNY'S BACHELOR
CUISINE

BENNY AKINA AND DENISE PARK met at a New Year's Eve cocktail party thrown at the luxurious Diamond Head beach house of Jules Reinnard. Monsieur Reinnard, of course, is the famous owner of Waikiki's Silver Oyster Pub and Cafe. Benny Akina was a restaurant critic for the *Honolulu Advertiser*. Denise Park, one of Hawaii's most respected chefs. Over spinach salads, crab cakes, fresh oysters and rigatoni, they talked about the weather, politics, sports and—the subject they shared the highest mutual interest—food. Great banquets, unforgettable dishes, secret recipes, and favorite restaurants.

A year later—after dozens of dinner dates and home-cooked meals—Benny Akina and Denise Park were married. Together, they were a happy couple. Gifted with looks, intelligence, grace, style, success, and youth. Life was as sweet and smooth as a perfect cabernet.

Three years later, they bought the Silver Oyster Pub and Cafe in Waikiki. Jules Reinnard—after fifty-nine years in the restaurant business—retired. Benny handled the administrative affairs. Denise created amazing dishes in the kitchen. Lines formed outside the restaurant. The guest list included kings and queens, presidents, Hollywood stars, champion athletes.

Two years later, Benny Akina and Denise Park finalized their divorce. Denise hired the finest attorney in town and got the houses, the cars, and the Silver Oyster Pub and Cafe. Benny got the shaft.

What had happened to this promising marriage? Benny asked himself the question hundreds of times.

Their union seemed to have been filled with love, respect, friendship. Denise always kept the house neat, made sure Benny's clothes were clean and pressed, prepared delicious meals. Benny brought home chocolates and dozens of long-stemmed roses, took Denise on long drives around the island on Sunday afternoons, politely endured the opera on public television with her—even though he wanted to watch Monday Night Football.

Perhaps, Benny thought, he was just not cut out for marriage. Had never been. He was a natural bachelor. And, basically, a slob. Leaving his bed unmade in the morning because, at night, the sheets just got mixed up again. Leaving clothes on the floor because a shirt on a carpet was easier to find than one hanging in, say, a dark closet. Leaving his hair brush uncleaned for years until it resembled a sea anemone because hair just needed to be combed again and brushes, well, they just got dirty again.

Denise, on the other hand, was the opposite. She was a woman who liked neatness, order, and organization. Everything had its place. She arranged pots in her cupboard by size. Placed spices in alphabetical order. Made sure the television remote control was exactly perpendicular to the television set.

Maybe, thought Benny, little by little, it was these tiny differences that had disintegrated the real love Benny and Denise had shared. Like waves breaking on rocks, turning them gradually into sand.

One day, destitute and unemployed, Benny Akina walked down Beretania Street and came upon an empty shop with a "For Lease" sign taped to the window. That's when the idea hit him. A voice in the wind told him to open up a restaurant. A restaurant solely for bachelors. There must be millions of them out there, thought Benny. A place to make them feel at home. Or a place for married men to go so they, too—even for just a meal—could feel like a bachelor once again.

"What used to be here?" Benny said to the realtor.

"A dress shop," the realtor said.

"It's perfect," Benny Akina said. "I'll take it."

Thus, Benny's Bachelor Cuisine was created. The menu was enough to bring a tear to any bachelor's eye. Spam and rice. Campbell's Soup. Instant Saimin. An assortment of TV dinners. Bologna sandwiches. Vienna Sausage. Pretzels. Pork and beans, with the option to eat them straight out of the can.

And the decor. Pure bachelor gems. Laundry baskets. A weight bench. Ashtrays with coins and car keys inside. Various athletic equipment. Magazines like *Sports Illustrated, Popular Mechanics, Esquire,* an occasional *Playboy.* Black, velvet glow-in-the-dark posters of panthers, dragsters, Elvis and Bruce Lee hanging on the walls.

On its first day of business, Benny's Bachelor Cuisine received no guests. Not a soul. The second day was no different. Alas, neither was the third day. Benny began wondering if he had made a terrible mistake. On the fourth day, a young man wearing a silk shirt, Angels Flight pants and Famolare shoes walked into the restaurant. He had perfect, blow dried hair. A gold teardrop around his neck. Benny thought he was seeing a ghost from the seventies.

"You look familiar," Benny said.

"You might have seen me in the movies," the ghost from the seventies said, sitting down at table five. "I was in *Saturday Night Fever.*"

"Of course. I should've known."

"Remember when John Travolta wins the disco dance contest? I'm in the background, watching him do his thing. Second guy from the left."

The ghost from the seventies became the first official customer of Benny's Bachelor Cuisine when he ordered the spaghetti with Ragu sauce. It was on the house.

Soon, word of mouth spread and Benny's Bachelor Cuisine flourished. Bachelors began gathering by the dozens. There were the young downtown professionals. Accountants, architects and attorneys. Eating dinner before attacking Restaurant Row or

Ward Centre. Thinking they ruled the world. Then there were the working-class guys. Construction workers, stevedores, bus drivers. Enjoying a beer before heading off to a night of Hawaiian music. And then there were the older customers. Like the balding, sixty-year-old doctor who wished more than anything he was a bachelor again. While his wife was at the symphony, he was driving his red BMW convertible up and down Keeaumoku Street, looking for the perfect Korean Bar.

"What's the secret to the success of Benny's Bachelor Cuisine?" a curious bachelor asked one day.

"I'm not quite sure," Benny said. "All I know is there's a lot of bachelors out there who are lonely. They need a place to go, a place to meet. And bachelors do get hungry."

"But let's face it," the curious bachelor said, looking at his plate of canned chili, "the food here is kinda terrible."

"That's part of the charm, I think. If folks want good food, they can go to thousands of other restaurants."

Benny did it all. He bought the ingredients, prepared the food, served it, cleared the tables, washed dishes. Sometimes, he even played the role of psychiatrist. Take, for example, the case of the gloomy account executive who thought he'd never find a girl.

"Girls don't like me," the account executive said, staring despondently at his plate of canned sardines. "I'm too dorky."

"You'll find a girl," Benny said. "In the meantime, enjoy the freedom of your bachelorhood. Think of it like, uh, like you're a caterpillar."

"Caterpillars are worms, aren't they?"

"Have patience," Benny said. "And before you know it, you'll find the girl of your dreams and your life will be transformed. Like a caterpillar turning into a beautiful butterfly."

"Bachelors are worms, huh?"

Sometimes, Benny performed the duty of social worker. Here is the dilemma of Ray, a fireman.

"I lost my girl," Ray said. "My life is over."

"Don't talk like that," Benny said. "There'll be others."

"Not like Suzanne," Ray said, a tear falling into his bowl of canned chunky stew.

"Sure there'll be," Benny said. "Trust me. I was married once."

Yes, bachelors gathered at Benny's Bachelor Cuisine and talked of fish that got away, waves that had been surfed, cars, deals, beers that had been drunk, and—of course—women.

"There's a girl with the best set of legs at work," one bachelor said. "When she uses the Xerox machine, I wait patiently behind her and tell her to take her time."

"There are too many wahines calling me up," another bachelor complained. "I can't get any sleep. As soon as I lie down, the phone rings."

"Listen to us," one brave bachelor finally said, standing up. "We sound like a bunch of kids in a high school locker room. Treating women like objects. Aren't you fellas ashamed of yourselves? Don't you all wanna get married? Have kids? Take on responsibility? Share your life with someone? Experience true love?"

The poor soul was booed louder than a BYU touchdown at Aloha Stadium.

As for Benny, he returned to the lifestyle he had once thrived upon before his unfortunate marriage. Sitting around the laundromat with other bachelors. Playing poker until the wee hours of the morning. Drinking a dozen different liquors in a dozen different places with a dozen different girls. Laughing, joking. While other less fortunate bachelors stood around dance floors like those statues on Easter Island, Benny Akina was the king of parties.

Secretly, though—very secretly—Benny often thought about Denise. Not only did he miss her venison, her rabbit, her soufflés. He missed her. Her smile, her warmth, the way she filled an otherwise empty house.

One day—one magical day—the unthinkable occurred. The afternoon began like any other, feeding hungry bachelors.

"I'll have the hot dogs," a customer in Levis jeans said. "Three of them."

"Hot or cold?" said Benny.

"Don't ask stupid questions," the somewhat belligerent bachelor said. "Cold, of course. Right out of the refrigerator. How else do real bachelors eat hot dogs?"

"What's your special today?" another bachelor asked.

"We have a potato chip and beer combo," Benny said, somewhat proudly. After all, he had come up with the dish himself.

"Potato chips?" the discriminating bachelor said, rather disappointed. "That seems so, I don't know, boring."

"Boring?" Benny said. "You call seventeen different kinds of potato chips boring?"

"Seventeen? No way. Get out of here."

"Sour cream and onion, barbecue, cool ranch, extra crispy, low salt ..."

All of a sudden—for the first time ever—a woman walked into Benny's Bachelor Cuisine. Jaws dropped. The insurance men turned off their calculators. Two crane operators stopped comparing tattoos. Dead silence. It was Denise Park.

"W-what are you doing here?" Benny said, not realizing he was walking backwards, moving away from Denise as if she was Frankenstein's monster.

"I'm hungry," Denise said, smiling meekly. "This is a restaurant. I'd like to order something to eat."

"C-can't you read the sign outside? It says Benny's Bachelor Cuisine. You know what a b-bachelor is?"

"So? Women can eat cold hot dogs and Spam and rice too." She studied the menu. "The eggs simmered in Tabasco sauce sounds interesting. But let me give you a little tip. People are becoming a bit more health conscious. You should turn towards lighter, healthier foods. That's what we're doing at the Silver Oyster Pub and Cafe. One of our most popular dishes is a linguine with asparagus and eggplant."

"I'll have you know, Miss Smarty Pants, that our Vegetarian special is one of our most popular selections. Kim chee and rice. Dill pickle on the side."

"May I sit down?" Denise asked.

"Jeez," Benny said, throwing his hands up to the ceiling in despair. "Yeah. Sure. Go ahead."

"Thank you," Denise said, selecting table four. A popular window seat with a view of the health club across the street. Bachelors fought like rabid dogs to sit there and watch the aerobic instructors going home from work. "I think ... I think I'll have the Benny's Bachelor Cuisine Blue Plate Special. Cold, two-day old frozen pizza."

"Excellent choice," stockbroker Hank said.

"What did you really come here for?" Benny asked.

"What do you mean?"

"You didn't come here to eat two-day old pizza."

"Doesn't the aging process bring out the flavor of the cheese?"

"Denise?"

"All right," Denise said, taking a deep breath. "I was worried about you. I missed you and I wanted to see you. Okay? Is there anything wrong with that?"

"I've missed you, too," Benny said.

"Oh, Benny," Denise said. "I miss rinsing your hair from the bathroom sink after you shave. I miss the way you squeeze toothpaste from the top of the tube, not the bottom. I miss the way you perspire after working out and still insist on lying on the couch without taking a shower."

"I miss the way you always complain about me leaving the toilet seat up. The way you arrange your CDs in alphabetical order. The way you insist on wiping your silverware before eating with it."

"Why did we fall apart?" Denise asked.

"Maybe it's true what they say," Benny said. "Everything that's created is destined to fall apart."

"You think there's a chance that we could, uh, we could try again?" Denise asked.

"Anything's possible."

"Do you want to?"

"Yes," Benny said. Then: "But what will happen to Benny's Bachelor Cuisine?"

"Leave it open," Denise said.

"Really?"

"Of course. There are a lot of bachelors out there who need a place to go to. A place to talk, share their triumphs, their sorrows."

"I love you Denise."

"I love you, Benny."

And to this day, Benny Akina and Denise Park are together. Living in a three-bedroom house in Aina Haina. Monday to Saturday, they work at their respective restaurants. Sundays, they spend together. Denise prepares a breakfast of waffles, eggs Benedict, and iced coffee. Like thousands of couples here in Hawaii, they may go to the movies, spend the day at the beach, or stay at home with their two children.

Of course, there are still arguments every now and then. About Benny leaving crumbs in the carpet or dripping water on the bathroom floor after a shower. About Denise having to make sure the clocks in the house match the time given by the recording on the telephone. But both Benny Akina and Denise Park have learned that the love they have rediscovered is a precious gift that cannot be taken lightly, that these differences in personalities are what makes the world go around.

Yes, even for bachelors.

OZ KALANI,
PERSONAL TRAINER

O z Kalani was the kind of person who believed a life could be created, transformed, defined by a single moment. This was his.

Hawaii Five-O. Episode Number 21. "Aloha Means Goodbye." A pyromaniac extortionist threatens to set the entire island on fire unless he is given a priceless feather cape once worn by ancient alii, now under lock-and-key at the Bishop Museum. Remember that episode? There's the scene where a Lincoln Continental explodes on a Chinatown street. The extortionist guy ducks down an alley. Steve McGarrett, immaculate in dark suit and tie, gives chase.

"Which way did he go, bruddah?" McGarrett asks a young taxi driver.

"That way," the young taxi driver says, pointing towards Diamond Head. He is wearing a blue aloha shirt and a straw hat.

McGarrett, without another word, runs after the extortionist.

That young taxi driver was none other than the hero of our story, Oz Kalani. And *Hawaii Five-O*, Episode 21, was Oz Kalani's television debut.

"This is it, boys!" I remember an excited Oz Kalani saying the night the episode aired. We watched the show in the living room of his Kuhio Park Terrace one-bedroom apartment. "This is Da One."

"Da what?" one of us asked, confused.

"Da One!" Oz Kalani said, wearing a puka shell necklace and Hang Ten t-shirt. "Da Big One!"

"Da Big What?" someone said, still confused.

That's when Oz Kalani leaned over and told us his philosophy on life.

"Lissen," he said, sighing and sounding slightly exasperated. "I'm gonna say this only once. In every person's life, there comes a moment where his life can change forevers. One chance. This *Hawaii Five-O* thing, this is it. My ticket out of here. Oz Kalani is a new man."

Days after *Hawaii Five-O's* Episode 21 was aired, CBS Television and the Diamond Head studio where the show was taped were inundated with hundreds of telephone calls asking about the young taxi driver. Who was he? When would we see more of him? How, you may be asking yourself, would your humble narrator know the inner workings of a major television production? How would he know that producers and executives were barraged with dozens of questions about Oz Kalani? I know, dear friends, because I made the majority of these inquiries. At Oz's request.

"Eh, Oz!" someone said, that day me and several of Oz's closest friends worked the phones like a bunch of crazed telethon volunteers. "You can do me a favor, or what? You can get me Jack Lord's autograph?"

"Shoots," Oz Kalani said.

"And ask 'em how he keep his hair so nice. Da thing never gets messy, you notice that? And even when da thing gets little bit messy, like if da wind blow 'em around, da buggah still looks shaka. You notice that? Kinda like Elvis. Oh, and ask 'em if I can borrow that big, black Cadillac of his to drive around. I get one date with Sassy Nancy next week. That car would impress da pants off her."

"I'll see what I can do," Oz Kalani said.

Believe it or not, Oz Kalani's plan worked. He had created the illusion of public demand. He was asked to do another *Hawaii Five-O*. Episode 32. "Beretania Street is a One-Way Street, Ewa Bound." Oz Kalani is a down-on-his luck boxer looking for quick cash. He joins an Asian heroin ring led by the international criminal Wo Fat. You remember the menacing Wo Fat? Bald head, thin moustache. Wo Fat's first order to Oz is, indeed, an evil one. Place poisonous blowfish meat on the Governor's inaugural dinner plate.

Oz's conscience, however, gets the best of him and he dutifully climbs the steps up to Iolani Palace and reports the vile scheme to McGarrett.

In the end, McGarrett and yes, Oz Kalani, capture Wo Fat at the old Oceania Floating Restaurant in Honolulu Harbor.

"I'll get you, McGarrett," Wo Fat says, perfectly sinister.

"Book 'em, Danno," McGarrett says, unruffled.

"Ho, awesome!" we said, once again watching the broadcast in the living room of Oz Kalani's Kuhio Park Terrace one-bedroom apartment. We cheered and clapped and popped open a bottle of Cold Duck.

"This is Big," Oz Kalani said, flushed and triumphant. "This is Da Big One!"

"No forget us, when you famous, ah?" someone said, maybe me.

"No worry," Oz Kalani said, with a wink that was, somehow, both reassuring and confident at the same time. "I'm gonna buy a big mansion and we'll all sit by da pool, eat poke and drink beer."

"Legend," someone said.

"Giant," another said.

"King," still a third said.

Everyone wanted to be like Oz Kalani. Not just because he was on *Hawaii Five-O*. Ever since we were kids, growing up in Kalihi. Oz Kalani was one handsome buggah. Tall, square chin, white teeth, body tanned from years of surfing off Canoes and Kaisers, brown eyes sweet as chocolate covered macadamia nuts. But it wasn't simply because of his looks that everyone wanted to be like Oz Kalani. It was because of his drive, his desire. Unlike most of us, he knew exactly what he wanted to do with himself. He knew exactly where he wanted to go.

Let me make the record clear, ladies and gentlemen. Oz Kalani was no overnight success. Whatever triumphs life handed him, he earned through years of hard work, focus and dedication. We all saw it. Even in the very early days at Kapalama Elementary School.

While the rest of us in the fourth grade played kickball and rode skateboard at Uluwatus, Oz Kalani scripted a ghost story. One day, during class, he acted it out for us. I don't remember much about the performance except it was supposed to occur in a grave-yard and once or twice, he turned off the lights and screamed. The lunch bell rang during Oz's play, I remember, but nobody moved from their seats. The ultimate compliment.

As the years went by, Oz nurtured his love for the stage. He played Brutus in a Farrington High School production of Shakespeare's *Julius Caesar*. Caesar was being played by our dork valedictorian and in the scene where Brutus stabs Caesar to death, everyone in the audience cheered and chanted Oz's name. "Oz-zie! Oz-zie! Oz-zie!"

At the University of Hawaii, Oz Kalani was Tony in *West Side Story*. He was the Man of La Mancha, the King in *The King and I*, Jesus in *Jesus Christ Superstar*.

But it was television that excited Oz Kalani most, and one show in particular.

"I gotta get on *Hawaii Five-O*," he told me, one day.

That was one thing we had in common. We were both big fans of *Hawaii Five-O*. I still am. I've watched every episode, remembered all the plots, tracked the numerous guest appearances by local celebrities. I'm a walking *Hawaii Five-O* encyclopedia.

Anyway, Oz Kalani submitted dozens of photographs and cover letters to *Hawaii Five-O* executives and one glorious day, he was called in to do a reading. The rest, as they say, is history.

Now, after his first two *Hawaii Five-O* appearances, Oz Kalani's future looked as bright as the white shoes and polyester pants Steve McGarrett sometimes wore. Rumors about Oz were everywhere. The producers at *Hawaii Five-O* appreciated Oz Kalani's talent so much, they planned to offer him a role on the series as a regular. Right up there with Danno, Kono and Chin Ho.

"Da deal is this," Oz confided. "Me and McGarrett, we'll be partners. Like Batman and Robin."

Another rumor circulating around Kalihi revealed that some big time Hollywood producer vacationing on Maui saw Oz Kalani on *Hawaii Five-O* and wanted him to be the lead in a film biography about King Kamehameha the Great.

Oz Kalani hired himself a mainland agent. The agent got him a role as an extra when the *Brady Bunch* came to town. The agent also got him a cameo on *Charlie's Angels*, the two-parter when the girls visited the islands.

Now, if life was fair, Oz Kalani would have become famous, a household name, a star of stage and screen, a legend. You'd have seen him thanking God, his agent and his family at the Academy Awards, holding up the golden Oscar statue after winning Best Actor. You'd have seen his picture on the cover of *Time, Newsweek, Life, People, Esquire* and *Rolling Stone*. You'd have seen film clips of him on the news, walking hand-in-hand with beautiful starlets in exotic locations. In a tuxedo in Cannes. Climbing out of a limo in Hong Kong. Dining out in a trendy Manhattan bistro. You'd have seen him as the Grand Marshal of parades. You'd have seen him sing the Star-Spangled Banner before the Super Bowl. You'd have seen his star on the Hollywood Walk of Fame.

If life was fair.

Alas, Oz Kalani was never asked to be a regular on *Hawaii Five-O*. He would not play Kamehameha on the big screen. And after awhile, the phone stopped ringing and the offers stopped coming. The letters and photographs he sent out in the mail returned unopened. The well appeared to be running dry.

"What happened to your agent?" someone asked.

"He's trying," Oz said. "He says no worry."

Now, no one loved Oz Kalani more than Yours Truly. But I must confess to you that during this dark and frightening period in his life, Oz Kalani became a royal pain in the you-know-where. Take going to the movies, for example.

"You call that acting?" I remember him whispering during a feature at the Cinerama one night. "I can do better than that clown." He memorized lines during the movie, leaned over to me and recited them. "How's that? Good, ah? Better than that bastard, ah? Da buggah's getting all kind awards. He's a millionaire. Wahines all over da place. Jeez."

When we saw the *Godfather*, Oz Kalani said he could give shooting lessons to the Corleone family.

"But they're all gangsters," I said. "They already know how to shoot."

"You just don't understand da acting business," Oz said, rolling his eyes.

During *Jaws*, Oz wanted to help Quint, Brodie and Hooper kill the great white shark.

"I come from a long line of fishermans," he said. "If I was on that sorry ass boat, I'd shove my tree prong spear right into that shark's eye. Dead meat, brah."

Oz wanted to be the first Hawaiian in space after watching *Star Wars* and *E.T.*

"Who's this Darth Vader clown?" Oz Kalani said. "You think he scares me? He's nothing. A panty. Half da boys at K.P.T. could knock him out."

And when we saw *Rocky*, Oz Kalani wanted to beef the Italian Stallion. "I can be da Scrapping Hawaiian," he said. "I'd give that bruddah dirty lickings."

Yes, sadly, Oz Kalani was becoming angry and disgruntled. But he had a point.

"There's no good scripts for us local guys," he'd always say. "No good parts. You know that. I know that. My useless agent knows that. And you know why that is? Because da big wig mainland executives, they don't care about Hawaii. They come here, go Waikiki Beach and Pearl Harbor. But they don't really care about da Hawaiian peoples."

Sadly, Oz Kalani and I started drifting apart. I'm not sure why. It didn't happen in a day. It was a gradual thing. We just saw less and less of each other. Before I knew it, a year had passed. Then two. Then three. One day, I called his home. A recorded voice said she was sorry but I had reached a number that was vacant and no longer in service. I asked around. No one seemed to know what happened to Oz Kalani. It was as if he had disappeared from the face of the earth.

As for me, fate led me down the improbable path of Animal Medicine. I became, of all things, a veterinarian. One day, I treated a Doberman afflicted with bad breath. On top of my usual fee, the Doberman's grateful owner gave me a lifetime membership to the Ikaika Fitness Center.

I was not what you'd call a health freak. I readily admit I could have gotten a little more exercise, maybe trimmed a pound or two off the midsection. And while a number of friends and acquaintances had turned to tofu, stir fry and salads, I clung to old favorites like New York steaks, chili burgers and kalbi ribs. And while others warned me about the health risks, I heartily enjoyed cups of strong coffee, a Chivas Regal after a particularly hard day, and an occasional Cuban cigar.

Still, I decided to check out the Ikaika Fitness Center and, yes, I was impressed. Heated pools, saunas, Jacuzzis, racquetball courts, basketball courts, rows and rows of exercise bicycles and Stairmasters, dozens of fitness machines and free weights.

My first day there, I saw a beautiful girl in skintight leotards standing in front of a mirror curling tiny dumbbells, one in each hand.

"Very good, sweetie," a huge guy next to her said. Obviously an instructor. And then it hit me. The pecs were bigger, the quads more expansive, the biceps and triceps more defined but—of course— the instructor was none other than my dear, long-lost friend, Oz Kalani. But I had to be sure.

"Excuse me," I said, tapping the instructor on a massive and very hard shoulder.

"Just a second," he said, not turning around. "You wanna work out? Call me." He handed me a business card.

Oz Kalani, Personal Trainer

"Oz," I said. "It's me."

He turned around and when he finally realized who I was, his eyes opened real wide and he hugged me. After the girl's workout was finished, Oz invited me to the lounge on the first floor of the gym. The Ikaika Bar. I was looking forward to a beer. Oz Kalani ordered two zucchini and broccoli shakes. The guy gave it to him for free. That was no surprise. An autographed photograph of none other than Oz Kalani—pumped and smiling—hung on the wall, behind the cash register.

"Damn, it's good to see you," Oz said, as we sat on a terrace overlooking a Jacuzzi. He sized up my body in that unique way guys who lift a lot of weights like to size up other people's bodies. "So, what you doing with your life now?"

"Me?" I said, touched by his interest, to be honest with you. "I'm a veterinarian."

"Oh yeah?" Oz said, very impressed. "Awesome, brah! Whoo, I admire you guys! So what? You don't eat meat? How about chicken?"

"No, no," I corrected. "I'm a *vet*erinarian. Not vegetarian. *Vet*erinarian."

"Oh," Oz said, nodding. "But what about seafood? Fish and stuff ..."

"No," I persisted. "You see ..."

"Eh," Oz said, apparently tired of the subject. "I'm glad you're working out. Shape that body of yours. Sculpt it da way an artist carves art out of one slab of marble."

"This is my first day," I said.

"It's so easy," Oz Kalani said. "Keeping fit. This is da only body you'll ever have. You better take care of it."

Oz Kalani explained how he was a personal trainer, working out one-on-one with politicians, celebrities and businessmen.

"Uh," I ventured. "What happened to your acting career?"

"Oh that?" Oz said, waving at two girls daintily dipping their toes in the Jacuzzi. "You've heard those stories about some actor who worked as a waiter or gas station attendant. Then one day, he's what-you-call discovered? That's what I'm doing. Only thing, I'm a personal trainer. I'm just passing time, waiting for da call to come. Da Big One. Then boom, my life will change. That's what my agent in Los Angeles says. He tells me, 'Be patient. Things are gonna happen.' And I believe him."

During the next several weeks, I visited the Ikaika Fitness Center every Monday, Wednesday and Friday after work. Oz Kalani was always there. As I curled, pressed, squatted and benched,

I watched Oz assist nubile lasses as they stretched their hamstrings and looked lovingly in his eyes. I watched him cheer on sweaty, out-of-shape executives struggling on exercise bicycles. And I watched Oz diligently take pencil to clipboard as he charted the weight training progress of young college students hoping to impress girls in Hamilton Library with the size of their shoulders and chests.

Oz had a fast, breathless, machine gun-like way of dishing out encouragement. *C'mon!Youcandoit!Pushpushpush!* And all the while, he wore a tight polo shirt—with the handsome Ikaika Fitness Center emblem, available for $29.95 at the front desk—shorts, Nikes, and shades hanging down from a string around his neck. Sometimes—on bad hair days, he explained—he wore a baseball cap sporting the insignia of a winning athletic team or the logo of a successful designer footwear manufacturer.

One day, though, Oz wore something new. Something I hadn't seen in ages. He wore the look of hope, a blissful sleepwalker enjoying the greatest dream of his life. And that afternoon, over Watercress smoothies and no fat, no cholesterol energy bars, I heard Oz Kalani's familiar refrain.

"This is Da Big One," he said.

"Da what?" I said, not sure I'd heard correctly.

"Da Big One," he repeated. "Remember how I used to say one moment can change da course of your entire life?"

"Yeah," I said, the understatement of my life.

"A producer guy just offered me my own exercise show. Can you believe that? We start shooting tomorrow. I want you to be in my first show. You'll stand right next to me. Stretching, doing jumping jacks, lunges, da works."

"Who's this producer guy?"

"One of da students in my Tuesday, Thursday aerobics class. They call him Da Kid. He said we'll start locally. But who knows where this will lead? Maybe I can go national, have my own exercise videos. Then some big time buggah will discover me. My dreams are coming true."

"Da Kid?" I said.

"Yeah," he said, with a wink that reminded me of the old, confident Oz Kalani I used to know. "You know these Hollywood guys. They give each other all kind funny nicknames."

I have to admit. I was pretty excited that night. I couldn't eat well. I hardly slept. After all, unlike the extremely photogenic Oz Kalani, I had never been on TV before. How much mousse should I put in my hair? Would I sweat too much?

Words can't describe the surprise waiting for me the next day when Oz Kalani took me to the set of his exercise show. Maybe I was naive. I was expecting us to tape at a beach or the grounds of a lush resort. Instead, Oz Kalani drove me to the employees' parking lot at the Ala Moana Shopping Center.

"This seems like a weird place to tape an exercise show," I said.

"You're always so skeptical," Oz Kalani said, slightly annoyed. "Look at all da exercise shows on TV. They're either working out in some fancy studio, or at some nice beach or golf course. Da Kid, he's sharp. He wants us to be different."

"Whatevahs," I said, shrugging.

And, yes, words can't adequately describe the surprise when Oz Kalani introduced me to the big-time producer named Da Kid. Instead of some forty-something-year-old executive type with dark glasses and a pipe, I wound up shaking hands with, well, a kid. A sixteen-year-old stock clerk on his lunchbreak from an Ala Moana store.

"Are you Da Kid?" I said.

"Yes," Da Kid said.

"We're shooting Oz Kalani's exercise show in a parking lot?"

"Yep," Da Kid said. "And we better hurry up. I only have twenty minutes before I need to be back at work."

Oz took off his warm up jacket, revealing skintight bike shorts as black and glossy as Steve McGarrett's hair. Da Kid positioned Oz and me just slightly left of a Toyota Tercel and an Acura Integra.

"If you like," Oz Kalani said. "I can sing, too. I have a pretty good voice. I could have done duets with Frank Sinatra. I could've been da Fifth Beatle. Or would you rather hear my Elvis?"

Da Kid whipped out one of those home video cameras you use at surprise birthday parties and baby luaus and Oz took us through his workout regime. A group of onlookers slowly gathered, making me quite self-conscious, as you can imagine. We got through some stretching and light aerobics when disaster struck. Several burly security guards informed us that we were on private property and just as quickly, kicked us off the aforementioned private property. Tears streamed down my face.

"Eh," Oz Kalani said, putting a consoling arm around me. "Don't cry for me, pal. I'll be all right."

I didn't have the heart to tell Oz that somehow, my cursed mousse had mixed with my sweat and run into my burning eyes.

"I always thought my destiny was to be somebody," Oz said, watching a Nissan Pathfinder squeeze into a parking stall clearly labeled 'compact.' "I always thought I was gonna do Big Things. Put Hawaii on da map. Now, for da first time in my life, I'm not so sure. Maybe I've been wrong all this time."

Oz Kalani was not at the Ikaika Fitness Center the next day. Nor did he make an appearance the next day. Or the next day. It was as if, once again, Oz Kalani had disappeared from the face of the earth. For a while, rumors about Oz Kalani circulated among the members of the Ikaika Fitness Center. He had received an offer to serve as Chief Trainer at the exclusive—and rival—Hawaii Club. Others said he was in Japan, personal therapist to sumo wrestlers. Still others said he was in Hollywood, signing a contract to star in an action thriller to be shot on location in Kakaako.

Recently, I was at the Ikaika Fitness Center and there—before my very eyes—Oz Kalani made his triumphant return. Sort of. Actually, they were running an old rerun of *Hawaii Five-O* on the TV. And there was a much younger Oz Kalani, with so much hope and promise written on his eager face, pointing out the way a mad bomber had run to Steve McGarrett. I wanted so bad to hear Oz Kalani's voice one more time but the clanking of the weights in the Ikaika Fitness Center drowned him out, kinda like the way you lose track of sound when you stick your head underwater.

THE HOUSE ON
ALEWA HEIGHTS

NOBODY EVER GAVE US A chance.
   I don't know when I came up with that conclusion, but I know it couldn't have been too long ago. Maybe it was the day I got fired from Mackey's Service Station over on Beretania Street for arguing with a customer. Two years, three months I worked for old man Mackey—changing tires, checking oil, wiping windows, scrubbing toilets, and pumping gas—and he fires me in five minutes, no questions asked, because I argue with a guy about his transmission. Mackey just looked at me while I was on my lunch break, shaking his head slowly and telling me to finish up my sandwich and go home and don't come back because I was nothing but a troublemaker and people like me would run him out of business.

Maybe it was the day I got arrested over at Kapiolani Park for getting into a fight I didn't start. Couple of drunk bastards complaining about me making eyes at their wahine, some tall haole girl in a white, cotton dress. I spent that night in jail, lying awake and listening to thirty or so half-dead people moaning and swearing themselves to sleep. I know I'll die before I ever forget that smell of booze, crap and vomit that, through the years, had soaked into every crack of that damned cell.

I really don't know when it was that I came up with the conclusion that nobody gave a crap about me. I remember this guy I went to high school with, Peter—Peter Rodriguez—saying that the only way we'd ever get anything was to take it, to steal it. I used to hate it when he said stuff like that. I remember the first day he said it, too. We were at Diner's Drive Inn on King Street, a little ways past Farrington. Farrington High School. That's where I, what you call, graduated from.

Anyways, the three of us, we cut out of our general math class, shot a couple rounds of pool, and headed over to Diner's. There was Peter, the guy I was telling you about earlier. He was the most quiet of the Three Stooges. Three Stooges, that's us. All the girls who knew us at school used to call us that on account of the fact that we always stuck around each other and did stupid things. Like a bunch of clowns.

Peter was also the biggest one of us. Hell, he must have been a ways over six feet, and well over two-hundred pounds. He had short, brown hair, and a dragon tattooed on his shoulder. I remember telling him it was the stupidest thing I had ever seen in my life. Peter's body was big and lean, not just fat like a lot of guys who lift weights. The cuts on Peter's body, especially his forearms and his stomach, reminded me of those boxers I see on television. Peter-boy, he was always talking about going back to surfing. He used to be a damn good surfer. He had all these pictures that he tore out from magazines attached to his folder with black electrician's tape. And you should have seen his room. The whole place was covered with surfing posters and calendars with tide charts and moon phases and all. But that was a long time ago. People who know what they're talking about say that Pete could have been one of the best. One day, though, he just quit. When everyone asked him why, he wouldn't smile or anything. "Too damn crowded out there." That's all he said. Just like that. "Too damn crowded out there."

The second guy over at Diner's that day was Tommy, Tommy Akina. Tommy was born on Kauai. Kapaa, I think. Tom, he had long brown hair—almost to his shoulders—and a thick moustache. We used to call him "Mr. Once-A-Week" because that's about how often he shaved. Tommy had a girlfriend named Trisha. Trisha was real nice, May Day Queen and all. It was amazing that Tommy could get a girlfriend like Trisha because old Tommy, he hated everybody. Trisha, she was a laid-back girl, friendly and stuff. Tommy was the exact opposite. The kind of guy who yelled at people walking down the street, just to start a fight. He'd steal quarters from the kids walking to Kalakaua Intermediate School. He acted like a tough bastard, always talking about fighting and killing. He talked about that kind of stuff so often that it didn't bother me too much after a while.

Me, you can call me Junior. That's what everybody else calls me. My last name is Japanese, because my father's father was Japanese. If you looked at me, though, and heard my last name, you'd probably laugh. The only thing Japanese about me is Grandpa, and all I know about him is that he fished a lot and did a lot of kendo. Most people don't even know my real name, which is okay with me. To everybody, I'm just Junior-boy. I don't know what I can tell you about myself. I like music—Hawaiian music. I play the uke and the twelve-string guitar. I always wanted to be like Gabby—Gabby Pahinui. Pete and Tommy, they used to like Hawaiian music too.

I remember that day at Diner's like it was yesterday. I had a katsu plate and a large Coke. I'm the smallest of the Three Stooges— about six feet—but I always eat the most. At school, I used to buy three or four cafeteria lunches. A quarter could take you a long ways back then. All three of us, we played football. Pete and Tommy, they were on the offensive line. Tommy made first-team all-star. Had his picture in the paper and all. Me, I was the tailback. Those were the best times of my life. My senior year, I almost cracked eight-hundred yards. Nobody asked us to play college ball, though. I played in the high school all-star game over at the stadium. East vs West. I had a bad game that day.

Anyway, that's how it was the day Pete first said that the only way we could get anything was to steal it. I shook my head and said that stealing was no good, that we all had an equal chance to do something with our lives. Pete, he laughed and called me a dreamer. Tommy, he just looked away as if he was sick or disgusted or something. Pete started talking about this house up on Alewa Heights, way past the park and the graveyard. He was saying something about hearing from a friend that the family up there left the house empty every Thursday night from about seven to midnight. I remember Pete talking real quiet because he didn't want anyone to hear. He asked if we wanted to go check out the place—look at the windows, doors, locks, neighbor situation, that kind of thing. Pete, he talked as if he had done this kind of thing every day, but I knew he hadn't. All talk. The only thing he had done was lift a couple of car stereos. People would park their Celicas and Oldsmobiles near the school to play tennis. You know where I'm talking about, right past the overpass on Houghtailing Street. Pete could pick the lock and unscrew the stereo in a couple of minutes. I remember that by the time I lit up a cigarette, Pete he was putting the screwdriver away.

"So what?" Pete said. "How's Thursday night sound?"

"Shoots," Tommy said.

Both guys looked at me.

"Nah," I said, shaking my head. "I don't wanna steal. I don't wanna go back to jail."

"Eh," Pete said. I could tell he was getting pissed. "If I thought we was gonna get caught, you think I'd be stupid enough to even say anything? You think I wanna go to jail?"

"Still yet," I said, soft, looking at the table.

"We all need the cash," Tommy said. I looked at him.

Right here, Pete, he went nuts. He slammed the table with his fist. "What the fuck is your problem?" he said, yelling. "Why you gotta be hard head? What the shit these people ever did for you?" I don't know if I ever saw him that mad. I didn't say anything after that. I didn't want to steal but I was too damn scared to open my mouth. He said come Thursday night, he'd pick me up at eight. I felt like hell.

* * *

I remember when Pete and I were kids over at Kalihi Elementary.

He was always the guy wearing pants with holes at the knees. His clothes had a musty smell because he went fishing a lot, but his parents never washed his clothes. My mom ended up washing his shirts and stuff several times. Peter-boy, he was a born fisherman. That's because all his father ever did was fish. Pete and his dad, they'd walk up Kalihi Stream—way, way up, past the taro plants and banana trees that the old Filipino men grew—where the water was cold and clear. They'd carry a couple of scoop nets and a plastic bucket and look for medaka and opai. Then, on the weekends, they'd drive over to Kaena Point and cast for papio using what they had caught in the stream as bait. Pete always talked about his father. I never understood why.

Once or twice, I went fishing with Pete and his old man. I remember riding in the back of his old, beat up pick-up truck. He'd drive us over to Waianae, or Sand Island, and we'd cast our lines and talk about the ten-pounder out there with our name on it. Pete always had the luck with the fish. Me, I never caught anything, except maybe a puhi or a stickfish or something. Once, near Honolulu Harbor a long time ago, I caught a small weke. While we were fishing, Pete's dad, he would stand around, drink beer, and look out into the ocean. Then he'd take out his parlay sheets and ask us if we thought the Vikings could beat the Dolphins. Pete's old man was always betting. When he won big—like he did on a 49ers game a while back—he'd throw a big party and invite everybody.

I remember a party they had once. They covered the front of the garage with a thick canvas, and a good thing too, because it rained hard that night. I was sitting down, talking to Pete and Tommy. Pete kept on telling us to eat up, that there was plenty of food. My plate was already full—cone sushi, shoyu chicken, pipikaula, couple pieces of roast pork, noodles, teriyaki meat, shrimp tempura, the works. And while we ate, we sipped beer and picked on the tako poke and sashimi they had lying around on the table.

All of a sudden, Pete's father comes into the garage. He wasn't wearing a shirt or anything, just a pair of underpants. He was drunk as hell. His eyes were blood red and he was breathing hard. He stumbled over a cooler and knocked it over, spilling ice all over the garage floor. He looked at Peter and said something like, "Where the hell is your mother?" I'll never forget how quiet that garage became. All the voices and laughter and stuff, it just died. "I said where the hell is your mother?" He was yelling.

"I don't know," Pete said.

His dad, he picked up one of those big knives that we were using to chop up the pig. He walked over to Pete, holding the knife and waving it around. "She must be talking to that Cabral bastard again!" he said. He was standing so close to us that when he talked, I could smell the whiskey on his breath. "Turn my back on that wahine for one second, and she off, running around!"

Pete shook his head and began talking to me and Tommy about this guitar he wanted to buy, the kind with two holes like the Beamers used.

"Eh, boy!" Pete's father screamed. His yelling shook me up, like if someone wakes you up in the middle of the night with a scream. "Listen when I talk to you! You like me kick your ass?"

He pounded the knife into the wooden table in front of us. It stuck with a harsh, dull thud, and faced straight up to the light bulb above our heads that dimly lit the garage. I remember the shadow of the knife slicing across my hand and curling around my fingers like one of those earthworms I see when I'm digging up the back-yard. Pete's old man began whispering to himself, like a child trying to remember his spelling lessons. I stole a quick, uneasy glance at Peter. I thought he was about to kill his own father.

* * *

Eight-forty. Late as usual. Pete is always late. I was sitting on the grass in front of my place. I live up in Kalihi Valley, almost near the end of the road, where the mornings are always cold. I remember looking into the stars that night and listening to the crickets in the grass. I was thinking—no, hoping—that maybe Pete had forgotten. Then, after a couple of minutes, I heard his car coming up the street. He had a Nova, a four-door job with a loud, rattling noise because he had done something to the engine. He pulled over and Tommy unlocked the door. I pushed away a box of Kleenex and a dog-eared copy of *Surfer* magazine and got into the backseat. The vinyl of the seats felt cold. I remember noticing that the car smelled like Brut. You know, the cologne. Pete and Tommy, those guys loved the stuff, ever since football days. You should have smelled the locker room after practice. It was like somebody spilled a bottle on a pile of wet, dirty laundry. Pete and Tom talked in the front seat but I couldn't hear a word they were saying on account of the fact that Pete was blasting his stereo and the speakers were right behind my head. Led Zeppelin.

Tommy looked back at me and said that Pete wanted to drive through town and check things out. I shrugged "whatevers" and watched the tassels from Pete's brother's graduation cap dangle from the rear-view mirror. He was the only guy I ever knew who did that. We drove up School Street and I looked up at the lights of Kamehameha Schools, high up on the hill.

After about ten minutes, we parked the car somewhere near River Street. The air near the river smelled like old, brackish water. As we walked closer to the buildings—past the alleys and over-flowing garbage cans—the air began to smell like piss. Hotel Street is a dirty place, but I always liked the lights. The way they blinked on and off, the neon signs coloring the sidewalks and bathing the streets in reds, blues and greens. We walked into one of those places where you put a quarter into a machine and watch some X-rated film for a while. The place had a funny smell, like cheap perfume. I could hear a fan blowing somewhere. It was a terrible place. Thank God Peter-boy had only one quarter.

We walked outside. I looked up at the old, wooden buildings and at all the windows above the pawnshops, pool halls, bars and movie houses. All the windows were closed. Every one. And the curtains were all shut tight. As if the people living up there were afraid of seeing something outside on the sidewalks, or afraid of people on the sidewalks seeing something in them. I don't know.

On one or two of the windowsills, there were small plants growing out of old, tin coffee cans. We kept on walking. I stepped on a piece of gum and it stuck to my slippers.

A couple of prostitutes stood around a street sign. Pete started talking to them. I heard him ask them their names. I sorta just stood there with my hands in my pockets, looking around as if I was lost or something. I heard the sound of laughter and the click of billiard balls from a pool hall across the street. I used to be a pretty good pool player when I was a kid. I raked in a couple of dollars from the old men who wouldn't let themselves believe that some stupid kid could beat them at eight-ball. Tommy lit up a cigarette. Every now and then I heard a car horn blast. A couple of voices followed, swearing. I looked at the two girls. The light from the streetlamps made their skin look pale and thin. One of the girls was tall. She wore a shiny, black dress. There were faint streaks of gray in her dark-colored hair, which grew past her shoulders in curls that reminded me of a poodle. The older one was short and fat and wore a red dress. Her hair was almost a bright orange, and she had a large mole on her neck, just in front of her right ear. It's funny. You see all these movies on TV about a girl who's a whore and all, but inside she's really supposed to be a nice, simple girl. I've never yet, in all my life, met a prostitute who was inside, just a nice, simple girl.

After awhile, Pete turned around. The girls left in a blue pick-up truck. "Let's talk about this Alewa thing," said Pete. Tommy smiled and threw his cigarette to the ground. We kept on walking till we came to this bar. I forget the name of the place. We walked inside. It was dark and cloudy with cigarette smoke. Two or three people were watching TV, laughing at the news. We sat at this table in the corner, next to a couple of well-dressed Korean-looking girls. Whenever I go to a bar, the first thing I do is check out the girls. Pete ordered a pitcher of beer. We drank Oly because that was all they had. We finished the pitcher in a few minutes and ordered another. The waitress asked us if we had the money. She said it nice though, so Peter sighed and took a crumpled ten-dollar bill out of his pocket. The waitress smiled and walked away.

* * *

Christmas morning. I must have been six, seven. What kid doesn't have a memory about Christmas from about this age? I spent that Christmas Eve sleeping over at Tommy's. We promised each other we'd stay up all night. That we wouldn't fall asleep until we saw Santa Claus. I remember sitting outside drinking some hot chocolate, looking at the sky and thinking about all the questions I wanted to ask old Santa. Tommy pointed to every star, wondering if that was him.

The next thing I know, I'm inside the house and it's morning. Christmas morning. I remember a bunch of blankets around me. It felt very warm. I moved my arm and I remember hitting something. I looked and there was this big box—wrapped in bright, pink paper and a green ribbon—with a card that read, "To Junior-boy, From Santa." I couldn't believe it. I opened it up real quick. Inside there was a basketball, the leather-looking kind that the pros use. I swear I couldn't believe it. I ran outside and looked for Tommy.

Tommy and his mom were in the yard. His mom was hanging the clothes on the line. She wore a gray nightgown. The wind made a dull sound as it blew through the thick, wet laundry. Tommy was sitting down next to the washing machine, pounding a roll of paper shot with a rock. Paper shot is the thing you put into toy guns. You fire the gun and it makes a loud sound, like a firecracker. The thing is, Tommy and his family couldn't afford to buy Tommy the gun, so he just hit the paper shot with a rock. The pressure or something made the caps explode. The air smelled like fireworks on New Year's Eve. Tommy smiled when he saw me and asked if I'd seen Santa Claus. I shook my head and Tommy laughed. He'd fallen asleep, too. I remember him saying, "Mom, did you see Santa?"

"No, Tommy," she said, with a smile. "I was sleeping."

Tommy was trying to spin the basketball on his finger. "I wonder what time he came to our house?" he asked, looking directly at me.

"Ten o'clock?" I guessed. That was as late as I could imagine.

Then Tommy, he sorta looked at his feet. "I wanna be like Santa Claus," he said. "I wish I was him."

"Why's that?" his mom asked. She really had a nice smile.

"Because," Tommy said, "he gives things to people and makes them happy. Because he knows how to be good." Those were his exact words.

* * *

I remember thinking how the moon looked like a shiny silver dollar high in the sky. The moon was full—or almost full—and it gave the night a silvery, almost holy, glow. Pete's Nova slowed to a stop high up Alewa Heights. The engine made a lonely tic-tic sound in the deep quiet of the night. I could see the lights of the sleeping city below—from Waikiki all the way over to Aiea and Pearl City—and I remember thinking how they glowed and flickered like the lights on Tommy's old Christmas tree. Now and then, a jet from the airport shot up into the sky and disappeared in the midnight-blue clouds. I had been up Alewa Heights a million times but I'd never seen it like this.

"That's the house," Pete said. He spoke in a low whisper and I could hear the sound of the wind blowing through the leaves of the ironwood trees at the top of the hill. The house was a one-story job on the makai side of the road, right at the edge of the hillside looking over the blackness of Honolulu Harbor. The blinking lights of several ships occasionally broke the darkness of the horizon like a pulse. The house had a front door and large plate glass window facing the street. On the roof was a weather vane, a rooster or something. When the breeze picked up, the rooster pointed directly at us. For some reason, the porch light had been left on.

"How do we get in?" Tommy asked.

"There's a door in back," Pete said. I kept on thinking how stupid we were. "I'll pick the lock."

I kept on remembering how everybody said we were bad, good-for-nothing, and how we wouldn't amount to anything. Up till now,

I didn't know if we were bad. I guess I really still don't know. It's more like something else. Maybe we're just frustrated or something. All we want to do is belong. But I don't know where. I don't know anything anymore. I guess I can only speak for myself. We ain't bad people. Pete's always helping his mother with the house. Polishes his grandfather's car. Waters the plants. Maybe we're just lonely. The three of us, we're the loneliest people in the world.

Pete sniffed. "Cold up here, boy."

"Just like the times we used to go camping," Tommy said.

We started talking about how we used to drive up to Makapuu and sit on the beach and play guitar until the sun came up. Pete, he kept on saying that he taught me how to play the guitar. All he ever did was loan me a pick. And I had to return that thing the next day, too. Pete, he could be a pretty persistent guy sometimes. Old Tommy, he used to have a Martin uke. I don't know what he did with it. So we'd get together and play Hawaiian music. I would have sworn back then, under the stars and all, we sounded like the Makaha Sons. Tommy kept all the music in this old, manila folder. His sheet musics were crumpled up and dirty-looking, and the print was always faded. Once in a while, if the beer put Tommy in a good mood, he'd bust out his harmonica and go solo. That harmonica is the loneliest sounding instrument I know. God, I miss those days.

Nobody talked about Alewa Heights for a while, and I thought that was a pretty good sign. Tommy brought up the subject of football. None of us had touched a football in almost a year, except a couple of games with the neighborhood kids, but you wouldn't know it listening to us talk. Pete started wondering what happened to some of the other guys on the team we used to play with—guys who we'd graduated with. Several of the guys I knew were up in college. This other dude, Jacob, was a mechanic and he was running his own place. It's funny, because it was through football that I got all the headlines and stuff, read my name in the paper every week. Yet, nowadays, I don't like to talk about football too much. It's like talking too much about a dead friend.

I kinda hoped they had forgotten about the stealing crap but I knew they hadn't. Those guys. They never forgot anything. After awhile, Tommy lit a cigarette and said, "So, what about the house?"

When the breeze blew, the cold air smelled like ginger.

"What you think, Junior?" Peter looked at me.

I tried to think of something to say. "Stealing," I said, after awhile. "That's no good."

Pete turned away, disgusted.

"My father … your father … they'd kick our asses if they knew what we was doing," I said, struggling for words. "You cannot just go inside somebody's house and take something that ain't yours."

"What you like do?" Pete said. "Starve to death? Be poor all your life?"

I didn't say anything. I didn't feel like saying anything anymore. I just turned and looked at the house. There was a large mango tree in the front yard, and a swing made of wood hung from the tree. On the sides of the house were ti leaves and a pair of avocado trees.

"What if we get caught?" Tommy asked.

"No ways," Pete said. He wasn't smiling. "No ways."

"But what if?" Tommy said. "Just what if?"

Pete opened the dashboard of the car. I remember the little light in the back of the glove compartment didn't go on. Among a flashlight, State of Hawaii roadmap, crumpled candy wrappers, rolling papers, and three packs of Marlboro cigarettes, lay a shiny, black .38.

* * *

I've talked about this thing so many times, to so many different people, and all I can think about is how stupid we were. Sometimes, when I'm lying around, I see the whole thing, all over again. Right in front of my eyes, like a play or movie or something. Still, it's gotten to the point that I don't know if what I'm remembering is true or not. Some of the things are clear, too damn clear. Other things, I forget. I still hear Pete saying that nobody would ever give us a chance, and the more I think about it, the more I start to believe it. I've left out a lot of stuff, mostly because I didn't feel much like talking about it. Some of it was hard to put into words. After awhile, it was like I was writing about something that never really happened. It was like I was getting numb. But I took your suggestion and just tried to be myself. I read it over several times, trying to catch all the spelling errors and putting all the verbs and commas and stuff into the right places. I even tried to copy the way the guys in the books you make me read talk. I don't know what's going to happen to Tommy now, but anything is better than what happened to Pete. I guess I learned something. I guess we all learned something. But God, did we learn it the hard way. But I should have known, because like I said, nothing ever came easy for us. Don't ask me to finish the story, because I don't think I will. All I can say is that I would give anything in the world to have that night back again. Then, what I'd do is I'd grab it by the throat and tie it up tight in a plastic bag and get in a boat and sail out into the middle of the ocean and throw the bag over the side of the boat and wait for it to sink to the bottom of the sea.

But I guess things ain't that easy. Nothing really is.

An Early Death to A.M.

Today is pretty much a special occasion.

Every Saturday, ten teams from across the island meet at public parks or elementary school fields to play football. I guess you can call it a league, seeing as we all signed up for it and have rules and rosters and a playoff thing at the end of the season. But it's all informal as hell, no big deal. No dues, no helmets, no uniforms, no team names. We don't make headlines in the morning paper. Not even fine print. The only press we get is word of mouth and the only reward comes when you see someone you played against and maybe he'll remember your name and want to shake your hand.

Last summer, my Kalihi team went 8-0-1, running over everybody and winning the championship. It was a good season, but that one tie—against the strong Waianae team—was the kind of thing that keeps you awake all night running plays in your mind over and over again. Today, after a year of waiting, we have another crack at them. That's why today is pretty much a special occasion. Waianae vs Kalihi, the two bad boys of Oahu. Like two heavyweights going at it in the last seconds of the fifteenth round. Or better yet, two wrestlers in a grudge match gouging, choking, scratching in a shower of warm beer and boos and perspiration and spit. Waianae vs Kalihi. It has a mean ring to it and I like it a hell of a lot.

I'm a running back. The best in the league, pal. Ask anybody. They'll tell you, "Almo, he's number one." That's what my friends call me, Almo. My real name—the one on my driver's license— is Alexander Molina, but my friends cut it short and just call me

Almo. I've played football all my life. Until high school that is. Used to play every chance I got when I was a kid. You should've seen me over at Kalakaua Intermediate playing intramural ball. People used to tell me I'd go places, that I'd play pro ball one day. Maybe that's why I always wonder what it'd have been like to carry the football for my old high school team, the Farrington Governors. Seven years next June since I've been out of high school and I still think about it. Some nights, I can't sleep, wondering about what could have been, asking myself if I could have cut it. I guess maybe guys like me, we never grow up. But hell, everybody wonders about something, some decision they made in life. Right?

Today's the first game of the season and we're at Kapalama Elementary School, on School Street, waiting for the Waianae team to show up. Even though you have to leave your car at the big shopping center across the street because the parking lot is chained on weekends and you have to move the tetherball poles off the field, Kapalama is a nice, well-kept place to play.

I'm stretching out my calves when our quarterback, Robert Kane, comes over and sits down. Robert is a Hawaiian dude, a rookie cop. Handsome bastard, with a square chin and sassy brown eyes. He throws tight spirals with a worn leather football ten yards in the air. His elbow is crisscrossed with scars. "Almo-buddy," he says. "Long time no see. How's everything? How's the job going? You a millionaire yet?" Robert tosses the ball to me. My hands cover half the ball. I have very big hands.

"You kidding?" I say. "I'm barely making ends meet."

"Same old Almo," Robert says, smiling. "Always finding something to worry about."

I'm an accountant, CPA. Wilcox, Brooks, Vance and Register. I work in an air-conditioned office in downtown—the 24th floor of the Pacific Tower in Bishop Square. Fifty, sixty hours a week. I've been asking myself recently, I mean really asking myself, if this is the way I want to spend the rest of my life. Don't get me wrong, the money's okay. I just don't know if it's worth it. It's funny because when I look back, I always wanted to be a businessman. In high school, I was vice president of FBLA. Future Business Leaders of America. I worked two jobs to pay my way through college. While everyone was screwing around at the university—drinking, dancing and running around—I worked part-time at First Hawaiian Bank and stayed home studying. I wound up with a 3.9 grade point average, double majored in finance and accounting, and graduated with honors. Yeah, it seems like my whole life, I wanted to be a businessman.

"Cheez, Almo," Robert says, rolling his head around and loosening the muscles in his neck until the bones popped. "We hardly see you around nowadays."

"Busy like hell," I say. "This is my first day off in three weeks. Fifteen-hour days. Saturday, Sunday, everything. Just finished auditing Matson."

"So what?" Robert says, changing the subject. "How many yards are you running for today? Four hundred?"

"Oh yeah," I say. "At least."

Four hundred yards might sound like a whole lot but it really isn't. One game I had like five-hundred something. The way we play football here is very different from, say, the way they play it in high school or college or the pros. I mean, the rules are pretty much the same—four downs to make ten yards—but like I said earlier, it's less sophisticated, informal as hell. No coaches, no game plans. Just a few running plays and a few passing plays, the basics.

"Eh," Robert says, spinning the football on his index finger the way basketball players do with basketballs. "You heard about that new psycho guy on the Waianae team? They call him Kaku. Defensive line. The bastard is a mean dude. Big sonuvabitch. And the way he hit. Like a fricking Mack truck. I seen him play the other week against Nanakuli. Scouting, ah? Kaku, he hurt all four running backs. Gave one guy a concussion. The Nanakuli guys had to forfeit the game. They didn't have enough people to finish. That was Kaku's plan, I think so ..."

"He doesn't belong here, playing with us," I say.

"Be careful out there, Almo," Robert says. "I understand the buggah's been talking about you. You the marked man. Kaku, he's gonna try and take off your head."

A flatbed truck and a VW van with tinted windows pulls up into the big shopping center parking lot across the street. The Waianae team. A couple of guys—huge-ass bastards—jump out of the van, carrying coolers and canvas sacks full of footballs. They run across the street towards us, laughing and whooping and howling as they jaywalk and yell at the cars speeding by them. I pick out Kaku immediately. He's the biggest guy on the team, maybe six-four, six-five, and easily three hundred pounds. His body is smooth—not defined and cut up with muscle—and when he runs, his belly jiggles and the skin around his biceps and thighs shake like guava jelly. Still, just by looking at his face, you know he's strong and you know he's mean. He has the face of an angry tiki, with no hair on his eyebrows and a sharp nose with wide nostrils. He wears a goatee and a thin moustache and is almost bald because he shaved his head. His teeth are sharp and jagged and the ones in front are covered with gold. I ask Robert why they call him Kaku. Kaku is Hawaiian for barracuda. Robert says no one knows his real name so everyone calls him Kaku because of his gold teeth and a large, bruise-colored tattoo of a barracuda on his back.

Our team slowly gathers around me and Robert. One of the guys is eating a strawberry Danish. I feel small. I'm one of the smallest guys on the team, 5-9, 185. I said earlier that it's an informal league, but let me take that back. It's as informal a league as pride will allow. I mean, yeah, the end zones are a pair of traffic cones someone working for the telephone company ripped off, and the sidelines are assorted rows of kamaboko slippers, Bic lighters, Marlboros, and bags of potato chips, but when you get down to the bottom line, everybody is out there to win. I mean, what else is there? No one wants to bleed and sweat and eat dirt for three hours and go home a loser. In fact, to a lot of these guys, these Saturdays are as big as any damn Super Bowl.

We start the game with a coin toss. I tell Robert to call tails but he calls heads and it's heads and we get the ball first. We have a referee to make sure everything is on the up and up, Jimmy. Jimmy worked at Dole pineapple for fifteen years and keeps himself in good shape by running in marathons and eating more sweetbread and Portuguese bean soup than anybody I know. He has a tough job, Jimmy does. For one thing, no one wears uniforms. On good days, we might all show up wearing the same color t-shirts. That was about it. He must have a helluva time telling everybody apart.

All of the Waianae guys come over to shake my hand, even Kaku. He's wearing a tight gray gym shirt and black shorts. He has pads on his knees and forearms and tape on his fingers and toes. He's scowling because the sun is in his eyes, and he keeps opening and closing his fist. He spits on the ground and shakes my hand without looking me in the eyes. Kaku is the only barefoot guy on the field. One of the Waianae players, I think he's a split end, turns to me and says, "Take it easy this time, brah. Give us chance."

I must have thought about the last Waianae game at least a thousand times. It was over at Perry Park in Kalihi Valley. It had rained the whole weekend and the ground was soft and muddy. The air was full of the smell of rotten mangoes. Toads sat on the grass and Jimmy had to get a broom and chase them off the field. Sometimes Jimmy hit them on the head and the toads bled white blood, like paste. I ran for five touchdowns that day—five touchdowns—but all we did was wind up with that lousy tie. One of the Waianae guys, he isn't around anymore, was a dude I used to play intramural flag football with back in the old days at Kalakaua Intermediate. I forget his name, Brad something. After the game he came over and shook my hand. "Eh, Almo," he said. "Jeez, you still got it, brah. So, what you up to nowadays? Haven't seen you since, what, eighth grade?"

"Me, I'm doing okay. I'm an accountant."

"Me," Brad said, "I farm. Jeez, I was watching you and thinking, 'eh, that looks like the same Almo I used to hang out with but damn, he talks and acts different now.' Alexander Molina talks like a haole now. Never thought I'd see the day ..."

"Yeah, I'm a CPA. Wilcox, Brooks ..."

"Eh," he said. "I wanted to ask you, brah. How was it playing high school ball? I always used to look for your name in the sports pages. Alexander Molina. Farrington. But damn, I never saw nothing."

"I never played high school football."

"What the hell you talking about? You nuts, or what? Remember the game against Stevenson? Intramurals? Four touchdowns? The guys from St. Louis and Punahou and the other private schools was all lining up to recruit you. You was all set up, brah. Not hard, wondering if ..."

"I tell you," I said. "Sometimes it is. Always wondering, you know? When I watch games on TV or at the Stadium, I shake and juke in my seat. I get a funny feeling in my hands, an itch. When I think about how it was carrying the ball ..." I shook my head. "People I don't even know calling me by name and saving me a space in the lunch line, girls calling me up asking me to the YMCA dances. Everybody wanted to be Almo's buddy ..."

"Even what's his name, the Farrington coach, talked to you, ah?"

"Yep. Coach Freitas."

"What you told 'em?"

"I told him the same thing I told everybody else. I told him no."

Nobody can kick the ball off if their life depended on it so the game usually begins with one of the guys—usually the quarterback—throwing the ball as far as he can. We used to start with a kick-off because we wanted to look official but more often than not, we'd end up kicking the ball into the street or knocking some old lady going to the supermarket on the head. I'm usually the return man, the guy waiting in the back to bring back the kick, throw, whatever, but they never send it my way. So Kyle, the other running back, gets the ball and takes it to about the thirty. The thirty-yard line is a pile of socks and a bag full of homemade brownies.

On the first play of the game, I take a pitch and gain maybe eight yards before the linebacker catches me from behind and tangles up my ankles. The play went to the right side and if Hector and

Benjy had held their blocks for just a half second more, I would've been gone. Hector drives tourists to Sea Life Park and the Pali Lookout and raises pigeons in his free time. Benjy, he works for a tire company doing tune-ups and oil changes. He's the only guy I know who has ever bowled a 280.

On second down, I take the handoff and try to turn the corner but the Waianae safety—a shifty Filipino guy—comes up to the line of scrimmage and closes off the outside so I have to go back inside and settle for a yard. The next play, third down, Robert tosses me a swing pass and Art, one of our wide receivers, makes a great block downfield on the cornerback and I run it all the way down the sidelines for the touchdown. It was a smooth play. I caught the ball and had one of the linebackers—a big Hawaiian dude with the eyes of a pissed off bulldog—one on one. Just the way I like it. Nobody catches Alexander Molina in the open field. Nobody.

I love those short pass plays that take you outside, where there's not so much traffic and you have more room to work with, more room to maneuver. I remember one game I had back in intramurals. I must have been in the eighth, ninth grade. We went over into the valley and played Dole Intermediate. Whenever Kalakaua and Dole got together, it was always a pretty big deal. Bragging rights of Kalihi, and all that. There was always an extra squad car or two around during those games. Anyway, it was 14-14 in the second quarter when our quarterback, Orlando, tossed me the same pass. I broke the play for sixty yards and a touchdown. Turned the game around. We beat Dole 28-14 and, on the bus, everybody sang and chanted my name. When we got back to school I got a message in my accounting class on a green slip of paper saying that the varsity football coach, Simon Freitas Jr., wanted to talk to me.

After school I headed across the street to the Farrington High School gym. The coach's office was in the corner of the gym, next to a water faucet and the entrance to the locker rooms. Above the entrance to the locker room was a clock in a metal wire cage. I knocked on the coach's door and heard a chair squeak. Then Coach Freitas opened the door. "Alexander," he said. "Thanks for coming by."

He shook my hand and I walked into the office. The coach was a big man, bigger than he looked on television. He must have been pushing three hundred pounds. He had short hair and a dark, sunburned face. There were wrinkles on his forehead and gray bags under his eyes. He wore an FHS t-shirt that looked a size too small, shorts and Adidas high-tops. The air smelled like Vitalis. Coach Freitas asked me to sit down and I did.

There were file cabinets and electric fans all along the walls of his office. On the tops of the cabinets were bronze trophies and koa bowls—dusty as hell—and yellowed newspapers in picture frames hung on the walls. One headline read, "FARRINGTON WINS HONOLULU DISTRICT" and there was a picture of the coach being hoisted up on his team's shoulders by his smiling players. Another said, "GOVS' MATAFAO VOTED LINEMAN OF THE YEAR." Also hanging on the walls were official team photographs displaying the players with groomed hair and smiling faces sitting on bleachers in maroon-and-white numerical order. Homecoming ribbons dangled from a bulletin board, neglected and speckled with staple holes and cockroach crap. On a chalkboard in a corner of the room, several passing plays were diagrammed in messy x's and o's. On a chair next to me was a cardboard box full of neatly folded mesh football jerseys.

"Nice game today, Alexander," Coach said, leaning back on his chair and resting his hands behind his head. The chair squeaked loudly. The coach had the kind of strong and deep voice that made your guts tighten up. "Dole is supposed to have a strong rushing defense. But you went through them like a hot knife through butter. You did a helluva job. Especially that run in the second quarter. You get good speed, good eyes, good brains. And the most important thing is you get the instincts. You know what I talking about? The instincts? That's the most important thing. The instincts. Something you cannot teach. Something you was born with, something you was meant to do. If you get the instincts and the desire and the discipline, boy, you can go a long way. Alexander, I want you to play varsity ball for us this year."

"I don't know, Coach," I said, swallowing hard. The coach watched my eyes.

"Yeah," said the coach, shifting in his seat. "I talked to some of your teachers. They tell me you put a lot of time into the books."

"I need to get the grades, Coach. I want to go to college. Be a businessman."

"Look, Alexander." He sat up and played with a paperweight on his desk. He turned the paperweight over and glitter began to fall like snow upon a plastic castle. It seemed like an odd thing for a football coach to have on his desk. "Certain people are made to do certain things. The secret to life is finding which of these things is right for you. Get planny people out there spending their whole lives looking. You blessed with a special talent, a gift." Coach scratched the back of his head. "Alexander, you ever been to a football game before? I mean a real game, with the pads popping and the helmets banging and the crowd going crazy?"

"No, sir. Only on television."

The coach's fingers tapped on piles of unopened magazines, cardboard-colored envelopes, telephone messages, and several copies of the campus newspaper.

"I see," he said. "I see."

I looked out the window. Below the corrugated metal roof of the shop building, three guys stood around a Pontiac, pumping the gas pedal and listening to the rumblings from the engine block.

"I tell you what," said Coach. "There's a game going right now. Moanalua and Radford. Junior Varsity. Let's go check 'em out. Then you can see what real football is all about. Get the blood to start pumping and the hands to start itching. Then you can make up your mind. Sounds good to you?"

"I have a finance exam tomorrow," I said.

"No worry," Coach said. "I'll have you home with planny time to hit the books."

We're all huddled around Robert. We have the ball and an early 7-0 lead. A group of children, maybe five or six of them, sit on top of a chain-linked fence and watch us play. Robert has his hand open

166

and traces a play on it with his right index finger. He reminds me of a palm reader. "Almo," he says. "This one, you go up the middle."

I nod and we clap and break the huddle. The children on the fence clap and cheer. I have to smile. We line up in an I-formation. Kaku is staring right at me. He's standing up, his knees bent and his massive arms dangling limply at his sides, his fingers opening and closing, opening and closing. He's perspiring and the sweat rolls down his face and goatee and falls to the ground. His mouth is slightly open and I can see the gold caps on his sharp teeth. I look into his black eyes and I realize, hell, he knows the play is going to me.

"Go!" Robert says. "Go!" He takes the snap and I push forward towards the line of scrimmage and take the handoff and I see Kaku out of the corner of my eye and I try to put my shoulder parallel to the ground to stick him with the hard collarbone but he and some other dude high-low me, one guy taking out my legs and Kaku nailing me with his forearm into the soft spot below my rib cage. I fall on a dirt patch on the ground and tear my elbow open. Kaku's boys whistle and howl. "Yeah!" one guy says. "WHOOOWEEE!"

I try to get up but Kaku walks over and pushes me back down to the ground. "You ain't so tough," he says, looking me straight in the eyes. "You ain't so fast! Where's the tough Alexander Molina I've been hearing so much about? You nothing, brah. You NOTHING!"

I get up and walk back to the huddle. I have to hold my breath because my lungs hurt. When I walk, a sharp pain shoots from my diaphragm to my legs.

"Whew," Robert says, dusting me off. "You all right, or what?"

"Yeah," I say, running a finger from my eye to my temple. "Give me the ball again."

"You stay away from Kaku. The buggah is crazy. He no belong ..."

"Give me the ball again. Block Kaku and I'll shove it down his throat."

And we line up again. This time the children on the chain-linked fence don't cheer. Kaku looks at me and smiles. He twitches his fingers and the cords in his forearm dance. I take the pitch and I see Kaku again but this time he tries to hit me straight up and I lower my shoulders and accelerate into that bastard until bang, I blast my elbow into his jaw and I hear his teeth grind against each other. He swears and misses the tackle and it becomes a footrace between me and the shifty Filipino safety, which I win. Touchdown, 14-zip. The children jump off the fence and cheer. Kaku stands up watching me, his hands on his hips. He swears and spits on the ground. I walk over to him and wave the football in front of his face. He slaps it away. Several of his boys have to hold him back. "You ain't so tough, Molina!" he screams. "Come my way again, bastard! Come my way again, Molina, and I'll kick your yellow ass!"

One weekend after a game on the North Shore last year, the Haaula team invited me and Robert over for some beers and lobsters. We sat outside on a patio shaded by a coconut tree listening to the ocean. In front of us, on a checkered tablecloth, was a plate full of bright red lobsters. The Haaula dudes tore the lobster tail off and gave that to me. Then they put the rest of the lobster on a cutting board, with the legs facing up, and drove a cleaver right through the center, between the part where the legs connected. The brown innards of the lobster spilled out on the cutting board and the Haaula dudes dipped the meat into the liquid and ate.

"What high school you played ball for?" the man with the cleaver asked. His name was Scotty Akana but he asked us to call him Billy. Billy was sort of a big wheel because, three years ago, he was the guy who came up with the idea of the football league. He got his neighbors and his nephews and his calabash cousins in on it, and they hung up fliers on telephone poles and took out space in the newspaper classified ads. Billy licked the olive-colored liquid off his fingers and sucked on a lobster leg. "The way you run with the ball. Sheesh. Our boys couldn't catch you for nothing."

"Never did play," I said.

"Nah? Me, I played. Defensive end, Kahuku Red Raiders. Damn, you as good as anybody I seen, Almo." Then Billy looked at me and wrinkled his forehead. "Can I ask you a personal question?

How come you look like a local boy, but jeez, you talk like a librarian or something?"

"He's a businessman," Robert said, patting me on the back. "He has to talk like a haole. This boy makes hundred grand a year sitting on his ass counting money."

"Ho!" Billy said. "How you got a job like that?"

"Long story," I said. "See, when I was at UH, I met a guy named Robert Wilcox. He was the son of one of the partners in my accounting firm. Wilcox, Brooks, Vance and Register. We became friends and he got me the job …"

"So, you like what you're doing?" Billy asked. "Being a businessman?"

"On good days," I said, after awhile. "I'm busy as hell and the hours past too fast for me to think about what I'm doing to myself. On other days, bad days, I look out my downtown window and start thinking, damn, there has to be more to life than this."

"If you don't like what you're doing," Billy asked, "why don't you quit?"

The scrape on my elbow is really hurting now. It's throbbing so much that when I move my arm to scratch my nose or tie my shoelaces it feels like someone is sticking a nail in my cut and twirling it around. Kaku is yelling and pointing at me on every play. "C'mon, hotshot!" he says. "Run the ball Kaku's way! I'll crack your fricking skull, you bastard! You nothing, brah! You NOTHING!"

It's first down, maybe forty yards away from the Waianae end zone. Robert goes deep—a nice, tight spiral—but the ball bounces off Art's fingertips. Art is the quickest guy on the team. You should see how fast he hauls in his illegal lobster traps when he sees the Harbor Patrol.

On second down, Kyle takes a pitch and gets maybe five yards. Third and five. I run a crossing pattern over the middle and Robert fires me a bullet and I catch it and I don't see Kaku or nobody, just this wide open space in front of me, and I run and run—past the Bic lighters and bags of potato chips—until suddenly I feel my backbone snap and my legs shoot out from under me. At the same time someone sends a hard forearm to my face and something in my nose pops and I fall to the ground and, damn, I can't get up.

Kaku is jumping up and down and his teammates shake his hand and pat him on the back. Robert and some of the dudes on my team stand around me, sorta in a circle. "You all right, or what?"

"Yeah."

"Fricking cheap shot. Jeez, your face. You can play, or what?"

I shake my head and walk slowly towards the sidelines. My nose starts running something thick and warm. I feel for the side of my face and look at my fingers. Blood.

One of the kids sitting on the chain-linked fence comes over with a marsh pen and asks me to autograph his hand.

"You famous, ah?" he says. "You play pro football?"

"No," I say, trying to smile. "I'm an accountant."

"Accountant? What's that?"

"Someone who counts someone else's money."

The metallic taste of blood is ripe in my mouth. The kid stands next to me for a while, and then he walks back to his friends. Damn, it's hard to breathe. Every time I try to inhale, the blood in my nose goes down my throat and I have to spit it out. For a while, I try to watch the game. Then I stand up and leave the field.

"Where you going?" Robert calls, standing in the middle of a huddle.

"I'll be back," I say.

"You all right?" Robert asks.

"I'll be back."

I cross School Street and walk into a service station bathroom. It's small and dimly lit. The floor is wet. Water trickles in the urinals. I look into the mirror. There is a huge cut running down the left side of my face, from the eye to the chin. Like a blood red tear. I want to wipe the blood off my face but I don't have a napkin or Kleenex so I go into one of the bathroom stalls to get some toilet paper. I sit on the toilet seat and gingerly dab at the cut. I accidentally break the soft, fresh scab and the blood flows dark, almost black on the toilet paper.

The stall is marked with poems and dirty limericks and propositions and rude pencil drawings and phone numbers and Jim loves Glorias and religious messages and initials and hearts. And in every conceivable medium. Felt pens, ball points, chalks, colored pencils, crayons, model paint, and fingernail polish.

And then I see it.

On the right side of the stall, next to the roll of toilet paper. In black, fine-point marsh pen. *An early death to A.M.* That's what it reads. *An early death to A.M.* I try to tell myself that, yeah, A.M. is my initials but damn, there must be thousands of A.M.'s in Honolulu. But for some reason, something tells me this A.M. stands for Alexander Molina. I try to rub the writing off the wall, first tentatively and self-consciously, then more vigorously with anger and frustration. It won't come off. I wet my fingertips with spit and run my hand back and forth over the mark. The blood makes a thin rust-colored stain. *An early death to A.M.* Why the hell would anybody write something like that on a wall?

The next thing that comes into my mind is 'Who the hell wrote it?' I try to figure out the writing, place who could have done it. I think about all the memos at work I've gotten, the phone numbers and lunch invitations I've received on the flip sides of business cards, the signatures in my high school annual, the Christmas cards I've collected over the years. Was the ink fresh? Maybe Kaku did it, the bastard. I dab at my cut face. Kaku. That really could have been the best thing that happened.

A kid wearing blue jeans walks into the bathroom carrying a wooden skateboard with thick wheels and sandpaper nailed on top of the board. He looks at my face. "What happened to you, brah?" he asks. "Old man like you, you better take care."

"Who the hell are you calling old?"

"Relax, brah," the kid says, smiling. "Cannot take a joke? Jeez, you're one uptight dude. Sensitive buggah, ah?" The kid takes out a plastic bag from the back pocket of his jeans. "Like buy pakalolo? Good stuff. My cousin from Maui."

"Nah."

"You sure, Mr. Sensitive Buggah? A-1 stuff. Give you cheap. Take a whiff."

My arms are covered with little bits of grass, and when I flick them off, they leave lines on my skin that look like chicken feet tracks in sand.

"Nah," I say, again.

"Mr. Sensitive Buggah, you don't know what you're missing."

The grass at Moanalua High School was hard and yellow because it hadn't rained in a long time. Coach Freitas and I stood along the sidelines watching the J.V. football game between Moanalua and Radford. Watching a football game in person was an entirely different thing from watching it on television. Especially the sounds, the noises, from the pops of shoulder pad on shoulder pad—like the crack of a circus whip—to the banging of helmets to the grunting and the exhorting and the swearing. When the breeze blew, I could smell the perspiration and the medicine.

"They keep the field so neat," I said. "Looks bigger than on TV. More open space."

The Radford running back broke a tackle and carried the ball twenty yards to the Moanalua one. The Radford side of the field cheered loudly and stomped their feet on the wooden bleachers and threw shredded newspapers and cassette tapes into the air. The cheerleaders did splits and waved their pompoms high in the air and chanted, "Who's got the best team? We've got the best team!"

"You watch this now," Coach Freitas said, his big arms folded. "First and goal at the one. They're going over the right guard. See 'um, number 74? You watch."

The players lined up, pulling up their socks and adjusting the face masks on their helmets. The Moanalua cheering section on one side of the field chanted "Defense! Defense!" while the people on the Radford side of the field screamed "Touchdown! Touchdown! Rah! Rah! Rah!" The Radford quarterback called the signals—a mumble jumble of alphabets and colors and numbers—took the snap and handed the ball off to the fullback.

I could see the back's dark face shiny with sweat and his teeth clenched hard on his mouth guard and his eyes behind his facemask, the eyeballs darting around like fish in a bowl. Then I saw the Moanalua middle linebacker—thick with pads from neck to knee—stick his helmet into the Radford guy's back. The Radford guy fell forward and let go of the ball, which bounced out of bounds near our feet. Referees in black and white stripes blew their whistles and waved their arms in the air. The running back stayed down, rolling around on the grass and screaming. Coaches and trainers ran onto the field. Something about his arm looked very wrong. It took a while for me to realize that the forearm had been snapped in two.

By the time the ambulance took the boy away on a stretcher, the sky was a dark orange and people began to file away because they had to get home and eat their dinners.

Coach Freitas drove me home in his Valiant. When he pulled over in my driveway, he turned off the headlights but left on the parking lights. He cleared his throat and turned down the radio which had been playing Hawaiian music. "I hope that what you saw today—the injury—won't put you off to football. That's just part of the game. You have an amazing talent …"

"The angle of his arm …"

"You know, Alexander, in the next few weeks a lot of private schools will be knocking on your door asking you to carry the ball for them. And don't get me wrong, they got a lot to offer. But Farrington—Kalihi—this is your hometown. And there ain't nothing like playing in front of your own people. Your family, your friends. At Farrington, football is a big deal. They take it pretty serious. The community follows us and it's a nice feeling. Farrington, it's a school people tend to associate with football. And we play at Aloha Stadium. You ever been there?"

"No."

The coach whistled. "Nice place. Forty, fifty thousand. AstroTurf and a big fancy scoreboard. Nice fast track, perfect for a back with speed."

"Never ran on no AstroTurf."

"Alexander, come out to the practice field tomorrow. Three o'clock. Just run around little bit, meet the boys. Put on the pads, get used to the feel of the equipment. You gotta try, Alexander. I'm telling you, you gotta. For yourself."

"I guess."

"Cause if you don't try, you'll always be asking yourself, 'I wonder what it would've been like?' You'll never know what you're missing. See what I'm saying to you, pal?"

"I think so."

"Good. See you tomorrow, Alexander? Three o'clock."

"Yeah," I said walking out of the car and into the cool spring night. "Tomorrow."

An early death to A.M. Half of me is saying that A.M. could've been anybody—Alvin Medina, Alisa Mori—but the other half of me is asking why someone would want to see me dead? The cut on my face has made the whole left side of my cheek numb and stiff, like it's covered with dried maple syrup. I look at the writing again. Damn, I wish I knew who the hell wrote it. Maybe it's somebody at the office. There's one guy, a managing partner named Nelson McCabe, who gets on my ass. He's one of those pricks who'd rather catch his staff doing something wrong so he can yell at them rather than seeing them do okay. There's another guy, Richard, who'd do anything to take my job. New guy who wants to make a name for himself. It really can be so many people. That's the scary part.

"What the hell are you doing in here?" Robert says, coming in and unzipping his pants. "How's the nose?"

"Might be broken," I say.

"That was a cheap shot," Robert says, taking a leak in the urinal. "That Kaku, what a sonuvabitch. But ain't gonna be no tie this year. Halftime. We're whipping the bastards, 42-14. I think we have a good shot at defending our championship, go undefeated."

"Those Waianae guys can come back," I say.

"There you go, worrying again," Robert says. "All that business stuffs, being stuck in the office too much, I think so that's making you *pupule.*"

I pretend to laugh.

"I don't know what you're laughing about, Almo," Robert says. "I mean it. You think too damn much. That's no good, brah. Thinking too damn much, that shit can kill you." He moves to the basin without flushing the urinal. He washes his hands, soaks his head in the running water, and pulls his wet hair back with his hands. "Jeez," he says, looking at me one more time. "What are the guys at your fancy office gonna say when you walk in on Monday with that cut on your face? Well, I guess they know that you was—is—a hotshot running back …"

"They don't know. I never told them. They wouldn't understand."

"You're probably right," Robert says, walking out of the bathroom. "Oh, well. See you in the second half, brah."

"I'll be there."

I go back into the stall and put my head in my hands and sit on the toilet seat. The scrape on my elbow rips open. In the back of my mind something is saying that maybe the damn writing has disappeared, that I'd gotten hit on the head once too often and was seeing things. It's like watching a movie with a sad ending again and hoping things come out different the second time. But the dark ink is still there. *An early death to A.M.*

I don't remember the year anymore. It was a Homecoming game and the Farrington Governors were playing the Kaiser Cougars for the Honolulu District title. The stands were pretty full for a high school football game, maybe ten thousand. The band was playing and the cheerleaders screamed into large cardboard megaphones and made human pyramids and it was the first time, the only time, I had ever stepped foot on the AstroTurf field of Aloha Stadium. One of seventeen students carrying the Homecoming float from one side of the field to the other during the fricking halftime show.

"I hear you got accepted to UH," a guy named Tim said to me.

"Yeah," I said. "I'm majoring in business."

"Business?" Tim said. "You want to be stuck in an office the rest of your life?"

"Lemme see you say that to me when I'm making six figures a year and you're parking cars someplace."

"But just think, Almo," Tim said. "Three years ago—if you played your cards right—you could have been Alexander Molina, All-State running back. Coach Freitas never asked you again?

Especially after the tailback Santiago got hurt? He never asked you to join up again?"

"No."

"I guess those guys don't ask twice."

And we walked across the field, carrying a maroon-and-white float of tissue paper and plywood and Elmer's glue and chicken wire of a Governor in a top hat and long tailed tuxedo holding a Cougar over a pot with a banner saying 'Cook da Cougars.' The band marched on the field, forming squares and diagonals and playing the theme song from *Hawaii Five-O*. Girls held flags that waved lazily in the breeze. I felt like hell. I looked towards the sidelines and up past the brilliant floodlights and the scoreboard, imagining people in the stands listening to their transistor radios and fingering through their programs. "Fourth and inches. Alex Molina takes the pitch, breaks a tackle, breaks another tackle! Twenty! Ten! TOUCHDOWN! TOUCHDOWN! Alexander Molina, the 5-9, 185 pound All-Stater from Farrington! That kid is bound to go places!"

"Molina," someone said. "You're throwing us off! Left foot first! Then right foot! And hold the float up higher!"

I hoisted the plywood handle up higher. "Imagine," I said to whoever was next to me. I forget who it was. "Imagine if I had played. Look at this field." I stamped my foot on the AstroTurf. It was smooth and hard, like a well-paved parking lot. The last thing it felt like was grass. "I could do this track in ten seconds, maybe nine-five. Imagine if I had played. I could have gone places, babe. Like in the Kalakaua days. Intramurals. I could have ..."

"Shhhh," said a girl with thin eyebrows and braces who wore too much makeup. "They're announcing the Homecoming Court."

And I walked across the field without saying another word.

I run my finger over the cut on my face and head for home. The children who had been sitting on the chain-linked fence are gone. The sounds of Robert cheering, and the grunting of the barefoot Kaku with the tattoo and the golden teeth, and the clapping and swearing and laughing of the football game follow me on the sidewalk like a stray dog with nothing better to do, no place better to go.

A HIT MAN
NAMED LILIKOI

NERJOUS?

Me? Nah. Why should I be nerjous? I've done this hundreds of times. I'm a professional. My boss gives me the assignment, I do some research, and I finish the job. Easy money. Please, don't ever call me a hit man. I don't like the word. It sounds so, I don't know, barbaric. I like to think of myself as an assassin. Sounds more classy, don't you think? I know, I know. Only kings, queens, presidents, maybe a celebrity type, gets assassinated. The rest of us, we just get plain old killed. That's another thing. I don't kill people. I take care of them. I hate the word killed. It sounds so, I don't know, brutal.

"Howzit. I'm Pono. If there's anything you need, lemme know."

I knew you the minute I saw you, Pono. Pono the Male Model Flight Attendant. I'm on an interisland flight from Honolulu to Hilo. Pono the Male Model Flight Attendant is everything I'd heard. Six feet, tan, wavy hair. *Magnum P.I.* extra. Former Kramer's Man of the Year. Part-time model, full-time flight attendant. This is the guy I've been hired to, uh, take care of.

"Aloha. I'm Elvis. If there's anything you need during our short thirty-five-minute flight, please lemme know."

As if I didn't know who you were, Elvis Kawasaki. Another flight attendant. Little bit chubby around the middle, the beginnings of small-kine male pattern baldness emerging. Elvis the Male Pattern Baldness Flight Attendant is the guy who's hired me to take care of Pono the Male Model Flight Attendant. Can you believe that? Two rival flight attendants. Male Pattern Baldness versus Male Model. What the heck is this world coming to?

"Brah," I say, to Elvis the Male Pattern Baldness Flight Attendant. "What you said earlier? About the oxygen masks?"

"I said in the unlikely event of a change in cabin pressure, oxygen masks will be released from a panel above you."

"And what about the life jackets, bull?"

"Under your seat."

Before we go any further, please allow me to confess something to you right now. I *am* a little bit nerjous. Not because of the job at hand. That's duck soup. It's this plane thing. Here I am, thirty-something years old, and this is the first time I've ever been on a plane.

"How many emergency exits did you say this buggah had?" I ask.

"Seven."

Now, please don't hate me just because I'm an assassin. It's just a job. Nothing personal. Sometimes I think us assassins, we get a bad rap. It's the media's fault. I'm a human being, just like you. I have feelings. I do the laundry, I wonder what I'll cook for dinner, I worry about drugs, pollution, war. Maybe you might be wondering how I got into this hit man—assassin—racket in the first place. It was luck, really. But it was hard work, too. You see, ever since I was a sophomore at Farrington High School, I was one of those rare kids who kinda had an idea about what they wanted to be when they grew up.

I was always big for my age. One day, the teachers asked me to watch the cafeteria because we had a problem with folks cutting in the lunch line. So, my job was to stand at the doorway with my baseball bat, wearing no-shirt and barefoot. Nobody cut. Except my boys, of course.

After I dropped out of high school, I was lucky to secure myself a choice job. I started out as a doorman at Club Peach Fuzz, on Keeaumoku Street. Then I moved over to the Hairy Palm Cafe. One night, I had the chance of a lifetime. Who else but Dex Cartlage himself offered me a job to work for him? You've heard of Mr. Cartlage, right? What do the papers call him? Reputed underworld figure. How's that? I love it. Anyway, I drove Mr. Cartlage around, ran errands for him. And we've been together ever since. I know, I know. I'm lucky. Things just kinda fell into place. My rise up the career ladder was quick. To this day, I look back with amazement. Anyway, this morning, Dex Cartlage told me I was flying over to Hilo to take care of this Pono guy. Whatevers, I said.

Okay, I must make another confession to you. And you better not laugh, punk, or I'm coming after you the minute I take care of this Pono clown. My name's Lilikoi. Yeah, asshole, you heard right. Lilikoi. Yeah, like the fruit. You think that's funny, don't you? Do I have to go over there right now and slap your head? Lilikoi. How the hell did I get that name? My folks. They said the minute I was born, the whole hospital room smelled like lilikoi. Can you believe that? Don't ask me. That's what they say.

Now, can you imagine the trauma of growing up in Mayor Wrights Housing and telling people my name is Lilikoi? Can you imagine me playing middle linebacker for Farrington High School with a name like Lilikoi? Can you imagine me trying to hook up with some chick at Restaurant Row and when she asks me my name, I tell her it's Lilikoi? Can you imagine me benching in the gym and some bruddah asks me to spot him and I say shoots and he asks me my name and I tell him Lilikoi? That's the story of my life. All my other friends, they're blessed with regular-sounding names like Kawika, Rocky, Bully, Killer. Me, I get stuck with Lilikoi. No wonder I murder people.

Anyway, we're on an interisland flight from Honolulu to Hilo. While Elvis the Male Pattern Baldness Flight Attendant is pouring Diet Cokes and coffee, picking up crumpled napkins off the floor, catering to crying babies, all the wahine on the plane are checking out Pono the Male Model Flight Attendant. The two German girls across the aisle from me with the Fodor's Travel Guides. The Japanese girls with the Ralph Lauren blouses and the sun burned noses. Of course, Pono knows it. It's pretty disgusting, really.

Earlier, I asked Elvis how he wanted to take care of Pono. I figure he meant the usual way. Pop him with the bag over the head. Car bomb. Nah. My man Elvis, he had it all figured out. He was going to take Pono goat hunting on some remote stretch of land outside of Hilo. But Elvis said instead of bagging a goat, he'd bag himself a male model.

"Does this guy, Pono, hunt?" I asked.

"Are you kidding?" Elvis said. "The pretty boy? He too busy combing his hair to go out hunting."

"Oh."

"Deal?" Elvis said.

"Easy," I'd said.

The plane landed in Hilo in one piece. Then the three of us hopped into Pono's 4x4 and drove over to his house to change into our hunting gear.

"You hunt, brah?" Pono asked me, to make conversation.

"Me?" I said, sneaking a quick knowing glance at Elvis. *Winkwink. Nudgenudge.* "Small kine."

"I can tell," Pono said. "You look like a hunter."

But the minute we got to Pono's house, I started thinking, hell, maybe it was me and Elvis who were the ones in trouble. The first thing I saw when we pulled up in the yard was a bow-and-arrow target. And then when we walked into the house, the living room walls were covered with dozens of heads of unfortunate birds, pigs, goats, rams, even a bear and a lion. An arsenal of shotguns lay scattered on the floor, alongside bullets of every caliber.

"Uh, you hunt?" I asked Pono.

"Oh, yeah," he said. "Live for it. And I could tell from the first time I seen you, you was a hunter too. Instinct, I guess. I feel like I've seen you before. You did any modeling? Maybe we was on the same shoot together?"

Let me confess something else to you right now. I've never gone hunting in my life. I hunt only the two-legged animals, if you know what I mean. *Winkwink. Nudgenudge.* If I want to eat meat, I'll go to Safeway.

While Pono showered off the Liberty House smell of his cologne—a dead giveaway to the goats we'd soon be stalking—Elvis gave me his instructions. He came up with a secret code. When he uttered two words, Pono's fate was sealed. The signal? Haupia cake.

Pono emerged from the bathroom in military fatigues and a bandanna wrapped around his sun-streaked locks. I mean, he looked like a hunter.

"This better be good," he said. "I could've been cozing up to that British girl in First Class up at the Volcano House right now."

"It'll be good," Elvis said. *Winkwink. Nudgenudge.*

After sharpening knives and filling canteens with water, we were off. In about a half hour, we got to the hunting grounds. We passed through a locked gate and soon were driving on rough and dry lava fields. Every now and then, you heard the sound of the goats. Pono surveyed the landscape with binoculars like an army general studying enemy lines.

"You sure you didn't do any modeling?" Pono said to me. "I'm sure I've seen you somewhere. The bank commercial?"

"No."

"You should think about it," Pono said. "Lemme know. I can hook you up with my agent."

After a while, Pono knelt on the ground and opened his backpack.

"You guys hungry?" he said, his back to us. "I get choke food in here. Chicken, spam musubi, mahi ..."

"Haupia cake!" Elvis said, seizing his opportunity and giving me the fateful signal. "Haupia cake!"

"No," Pono said. "No haupia cake in here. Let's see. Hot dog, turkey, kal bi ..."

I quietly released the safety of my rifle. The back of Pono's head looked as big as one of those Mexican *pinatas*, filled with toys and candies.

"Eh," Pono said, turning to me all of a sudden. "Where you lift?"

"Excuse me?" I said, caught off guard.

"Where do you lift?" Pono asked. "You look like a man who works out a lot. Which gym do you go to?"

"Gym?" I said, putting the gun down. "I don't go to any gym."

"Really?" Pono said, stuffing his face with a spam musubi. "With those biceps? That chest? Dose lats?"

We hiked through the tall brush and suddenly saw a herd of goats run through the grass. Boy are they fast. If you blink, you'll miss them. But Pono did not blink.

"Saw one billy," Pono said. "Couple nannys."

"Hah?" Elvis the Male Pattern Baldness Flight Attendant said.

"That's hunter talk," Pono said, winking at me. "Only us hunters understand."

We tried to track the goats, with no luck.

"Where the hell did they go?" Elvis asked. "How disappointing."

"Life is about disappointments," Pono said. "You know that? I mean, think about it. You cannot understand what's good, unless you understand what's bad."

"Yeah," I say. Pono's getting philosophical during his final moments.

"Like I still can't believe they didn't pick me for *Baywatch*, you know? That bothered me for a long time. But whatevers. Life goes on."

And then came the ultimate. The clincher. The coup de grace. Pono turns to me and asks The Question.

"Brah," Pono the Male Model Flight Attendant says. "What's your name?"

"Lilikoi," I said, hands on the rifle. Laugh it up, punk. But there was no laughter.

"Lilikoi?" Pono said. "What a trip! That's my Dad's name."

Suddenly, we heard the goats again.

"Over there," Pono said, pointing to a ridge. "Let's go!"

We sprinted through the tall grass. The goats ran through the thick brush.

"Shoot!" Pono said, firing his rifle. A firecracker smell filled the air, along with the cries of goats.

"Yeah, shoot!" Elvis the Male Pattern Baldness Flight Attendant said. "Haupia cake! Haupia cake!"

I picked up my rifle and saw the back of Pono's head in my scope. I pulled the trigger. *Bang!*

"Yes!" Elvis said, clapping his hands and whooping like a guy in Las Vegas who's just hit Megabucks. "YES! Haupia cake! HAUPIA CAKE!"

When the smoke cleared, a goat—yes, a goat—lay on its side on a tuft of dry grass, a bullet hole right between its eyes.

"Ho," Pono said, running his hands through his male model hair. "Good shot, brah."

Pono slit the goat's belly with his hunting knife and with the skill of a surgeon, removed the organs with his bare hands and threw them into the lava field. Then he hung the animal from a tree by the legs and skinned it. Then, like a butcher now, he dissected the animal and tossed the meat into a bag, which he then placed in a cooler.

All right, all right. If you haven't figured me out by now, let me make yet another confession to you. I'm a fake. A phony. I ain't no assassin. I ain't even a hit man. I'm just plain old Lilikoi. I've beaten up a couple of people in my time. But that's about it. That poor goat was the first thing I ever killed in my life. I thought maybe I could pull this Pono job off. But I couldn't.

Anyway, that night, the three of us got together for a dinner of smoked goat meat, rice and beer.

"You wanna hear something really stupid?" Elvis confessed to Pono. "Me and Lilikoi here, we planned to shoot you today."

"I know," Pono said, not blinking a Male Model eye.

"You know?" Me and Elvis said, shocked.

"Sure," Pono said. "Another beer?"

"How the hell did you know?" I said.

"A hunter knows when he's being hunted," Pono said, handing me a beer.

"You dirty bastard," I said, seeing the light. "So when you asked me if I was a male model, asked me where I lifted because I look so buff, told me your dad was named Lilikoi, you were ..."

"Playing you like a ukulele?" Pono said, sipping his beer. "That's right."

"Haupia cake," Elvis whispered. "Haupia cake."

Elvis was right. It wasn't too late. I should get my rifle right now and, once and for all, send Pono to that Male Modelling Contract in the Sky.

"I've got it!" Pono said, snapping his fingers. "Now I know where I've seen you. Farrington High School. You were the guy watching the lunch line to make sure nobody cut. That was you, right?"

"Uh …" I said.

"Haupia cake," Elvis said. "Haupia cake."

"You was so macho," Pono said. "With the bare feet and the baseball bat. Everybody looked up to you. You was my idol. My hero. That was you, right?"

"Yeah," I said, failure that I am. "That was me."

Now, I'm on a flight from Hilo to Honolulu with a chocolate ulua from Big Island Candies on my lap. A peace offering for my short-tempered employer, Dex Cartlage. How the hell do I explain this fiasco to him? Elvis the Male Pattern Baldness Flight Attendant narrated how in just a few minutes, we'll be able to enjoy a complimentary glass of Coke or pass-o-guava juice, or opt instead for beer or wine for three dollars. Meanwhile, Pono the Male Model Flight Attendant is cruising with some Swedish tourist who says she'd love to buy Pono dinner tonight.

Looking out the window, I notice there are a lot of waterfalls on the Big Island. Dozens of rivers flowing from the mountains, carving their way through the landscape and tumbling to the ocean. Kinda like my miserable life, I guess. I was born and wound my way through Kalihi. Now Dex Cartlage was about to donate what's left of my sorry-ass, failure body to the sharks in the waters off Sand Island. Friends, if you're thinking of having kids or know someone who is, please heed these words of advice. Do yourself a favor. Take it from someone who knows.

Don't ever name your kid Lilikoi.

THE LONELY CHILDREN

THIS IS MY FIRST MEMORY. One of the first things I always remember about being a kid is riding my bike up Nuuanu Pali Drive, past the churches and the embassies, and checking out the mansion on the side of the mountain. That was the biggest house I've ever seen—three, four stories high—with fancy cars in the garage and an iron gate surrounding the entire place. The mansion even had a chimney—something I only saw in the movies—and in the wintertime, smoke puffed out of that chimney. There was a yard as big as a football field in the front of the mansion and a pool in the back. You couldn't see the pool from the street but I knew it was there because when I hiked in the mountains behind the mansion, I saw it clear. From so high, that pool looked like a tiny blue jewel.

I could spend hours just staring at that mansion, wondering what it'd be like to live in a house that big, wondering what kind of people were lucky enough to live in a place like that. Sometimes on Saturday nights, my dad took me and my mom out for rides in his old Dodge. I sat in the backseat and we drove past that mansion on Nuuanu Pali Drive. The patio always seemed to be lit up and we could hear soft music and people laughing and there'd be a whole line of limousines parked along the driveway with the drivers dressed up in black tuxedos all standing around outside. My dad would look back in the rearview mirror and say to me, "Whew, I wish I could take you folks home to something like that."

One morning, I rode my bike all the way up to Nuuanu Pali Drive and stopped in front of the iron gates of the mansion. I was about ten. I was carrying around this model airplane I'd just put together, an old P-51 Mustang that they used to fly during World War II. It was a nice day, with the sun shining high in the sky and the birds singing in the trees. The sky looked real blue and I started playing with the airplane, pretending the iron gates of the mansion were actually streaking bullets from anti-aircraft guns. The Mustang weaved through the bars of the gate, in and out. Va-ROOM! All of a sudden, the plane's wing touched the gate. *BOOM!* The Mustang was hit! I made her tumble towards the ground, like a plane on fire. Before I knew what happened, *auwe,* the plane slipped out of my hand and fell in the yard on the other side of the gate. I stretched for the plane until I could feel my face turn red, but it was just out of my reach, maybe an inch away. I had no choice. I climbed over the gate and was in the mansion's yard in no time. Jeez, it was strange in there. The grass felt soft under my feet, like a carpet. Even the air smelled different. It was like being in another world. I picked up my Mustang. Just then, a funny feeling came over me. I don't know why. I guess it was something building up inside of me for a long time. Instead of climbing back over the gate, I walked towards the mansion.

They had some big pagodas in that yard. Drops of rainwater made *plop plop* sounds as they fell from trees and ferns into a pond filled with koi. Somebody inside the mansion played the piano and I thought it sounded pretty good so I stopped and listened for a while.

I heard this dog barking but I didn't pay any attention to it. Little by little, though, the barking seemed to get louder. I looked over my shoulder and, jeez, this huge ass black Doberman came charging after me. I never ran faster in my life. I hopped over lawn chairs and hedges and bonsai plants. I didn't have the nerve to look back over my shoulder but I knew that dog was catching me up because its footsteps sounded louder and louder. Just as I was getting real tired and I thought about stopping and letting that dog tear me apart, I saw a tree. I ran towards it and jumped four feet in the air to reach the first branch. While I was on the tree, the dog was jumping around, barking like crazy. The fangs in its mouth were huge, but I figured as long as I stayed up in that tree, I was all right. Then, I couldn't believe my eyes, the dog started clawing its way up the bark of the tree.

The dog got closer and closer, its eyes looking at me like I was a huge Sizzler's steak. Just when the dog was a couple inches away from my leg, someone yelled, "Kaipo! Down!"

The dog didn't want to listen. It kept climbing towards me.

"KAIPO!"

The dog jumped down the tree and ran towards this thin boy in gray shorts. I looked at the sky and let out a sigh of relief. The boy looked about the same age as me, but he seemed way different from the kids I hung around with. For one thing, his hair was short and neat. And his skin was pale, not dark like the guys I surfed and fished with. It was like he never spent that much time in the sun. And he didn't have no scars and cuts on his legs, like he never fell off a skateboard or skinned his knees playing chase master in his life. And his shirt was tucked into his pants. On a Saturday.

"You can come down from the tree now," the boy said to me. That's how he said it. He even talked funny, like the people on TV. The boy had his fingers twirled around the dog's collar. "Don't worry about Kaipo," he said to me. "He's harmless."

I climbed down the tree. The dog started growling again.

"Kaipo!" the boy said, in a warning voice. The dog stopped growling. But the way the dog looked at me, I knew it was growling inside.

When I reached the ground, my legs were so shaky I fell down. The boy helped me up and dusted off my shirt.

"I'm Lawrence Kalapa," he said. "What's your name?"

"Bret," I said, not used to telling strangers my name. I thought he was going to call the cops on me. After all, here I was, some strange kid walking around on his property. Instead, Lawrence smiled and offered to shake my hand. Yeah, I was a little bit confused.

"It's a pleasure to meet you, Bret," he said.

"You live here?" I said.

"Yep," Lawrence said. "Me, my mom and my dad."

Lawrence offered to show me around. We walked past the tennis courts with machines that automatically served balls to you. He showed me a row of statues carved out of stone, and he pointed out the large swimming pool with two diving platforms. I'd never swam in a pool in my life.

Afterwards, me and Lawrence sat on these lounge chairs around the pool and sipped lemonade.

"Your house is huge," I said. "A hundred families could live here."

"Yeah," Lawrence said. "Sometimes I wish a hundred families lived with us."

We didn't say anything for a while. I listened to the birds in the trees. When the day was over, I must admit, it was hard riding my bike back to my house in Kalihi. All I could think about was what it'd be like to live in Lawrence's mansion, play in his big yard, swim in his pool. It kinda bothered me. I had never felt that way before.

* * *

That's pretty much how I remember that first day too. I was sitting outside, reading a Dickens novel. *David Copperfield.* Mom was playing the piano. Dad was at work, where he usually was on the weekends. All of a sudden, Kaipo starts barking like crazy. I figured he was chasing a cat around or something. Instead, I see a boy in one of our trees, hanging on for dear life. Bret was about my age. We were about the same height and all, too. The thing about him was that he looked like one of those kids who ran faster than anybody else in class, who could throw the dodge ball farther, the boy who was always picked first when choosing up sides for football or basketball.

Now, Kaipo wasn't really climbing up the tree the way Bret says. He was actually sorta hopping up and down on his hind legs. Kaipo wouldn't harm a fly. He was a scaredy-cat, to be honest with you. I told Kaipo to hush up and he did and Bret eventually came down and I showed him around the property. I never thought about calling the police or anything. Bret didn't seem like the kind of guy you called the police on. Something about the way he looked, the way he acted. He just didn't look like someone who could hurt you.

Strangely enough, Bret and I started hanging out a lot. I don't know how it happened. Here we were—so different—from two different worlds. I went to Punahou. He went to Puuhale Elementary, over by the prison. But we got along so well. I guess we were young—both ten—and when you're that age, maybe that's all that really matters.

I remember the first time I went over to Bret's place. His dad was a truck driver for the city and his mom worked in some bowling alley coffee shop. They rented a small house near Sand Island. It was in the warehouse district, a dry area where the grass was as brown and stiff as the stalks at the end of a broom. That day we went over to Bret's place, the sun was directly overhead and the air felt thick and warm, like when you stick your face in front of an oven that's been baking something for an hour.

Bret's place was very small and very dark for some reason. All the windows pointed away from the sun, it seemed. In Bret's room, there were maybe fifty model airplanes hanging from the ceiling with fishing line, suspended in air like they were flying. They were all beautifully made, down to the last detail. From the decals on the wings, to splotches of dirt on the landing gear, to the intense frowns painted on the faces of the tiny pilots.

"That's a Spitfire," he'd say in his Pidgin English, pointing to one of the planes. "A British fighter. And this here, this is one Corsair."

"You made all of these yourself?" I asked.

"Yep."

"Wow!" I said. "You can't even see the glue marks."

There was another project on his desk, half finished and lying on a piece of newspaper. In an old shoebox was an assortment of vials, bottles and tools: paints, thinners, brushes, tweezers, pocket-knives, sand paper, putty, a magnifying glass.

"I love airplanes," Bret said. "One day, I'm gonna be a pilot. Eh, you know what? Sleep over here tonight! You can help me finish my Stuka!"

I sneezed. My nose began to run. It was my allergy. I was allergic to a hundred things. I looked over the room. I figured it was the dust.

"You hungry?" Bret said. He walked over to the kitchen and opened the refrigerator. The light had burned out. "I think so my mom making spaghetti tonight. We usually eat spaghetti on the weekends. You like spaghetti? Sleep over! Going be good fun! What you think?"

"I think you need a new bulb," I said.

"What you mean?"

"Your refrigerator light's burned out."

"Hah?" Bret said. "You mean supposed to have one light in there?"

Bret took out a loaf of bread. I'd never heard of people leaving bread in a refrigerator before. He took out four slices and made peanut butter sandwiches. He handed me a sandwich and I bit into it. The bread was hard and cold and had a strange taste.

"Oh, oh," Bret said, making a face. I looked at my sandwich. There were little dark green splotches on the skin of the bread. "No worry. Just peel off the junk part." And that's what he did. He picked off some of the mold and continued eating his sandwich. "So what?" he said. "You like sleep over tonight?"

"Uh, it sounds nice," I said, looking at my sandwich. "But I think I have to go out with my parents tonight. We're going out to dinner."

"Oh. Well, maybe some other time."

I felt so bad. I can still see that look Bret had on his face. I knew he was disappointed.

* * *

I never met anybody like Lawrence Kalapa in my life. For one thing, he wasn't interested in sports ~~like regular kids~~. Instead of playing ball or going to the beach, he went to the library and read books. I've never stepped foot in a library my whole life. And Lawrence, he was very clean, very neat. His skin smelled sweet, like somebody who just walked out of the shower. You got the impression he took three, four, maybe five baths a day. And his dad. Jeez, he was like some big-time politician or something. Lawrence took me to City Hall and showed me a picture of his old man hanging right up there on the wall. Damn, that was amazing.

One afternoon, I took Lawrence up to Kalihi Stream and we hiked up to this place where the water is ice cold and clear. The stream was flowing quick so I knew it was raining hard in the mountains. Lawrence had never gone fishing before. He didn't have any poles or equipment or anything so I brought over an extra rod and reel for him, a bucket, my tackle box and some bait. We sat on these huge rocks in the middle of the stream. I told Lawrence to watch out because the rocks were covered with moss and you could hurt yourself bad if you slipped and fell in the water. Then I helped him bait his hook because every time he did it himself and he cast his line out, the bait fell off the hook before it hit the water. Lawrence was complaining about the mosquitoes biting him—for some reason, they only bit him, not me—when all of a sudden, his pole started jerking big-time. "I've got something!" he said, all excited. "I think I've got something!"

"You're probably snagged," I said. "Lemme see." No ways Lawrence could have caught a fish before me.

"No," he said, yanking on his pole. "I think I've got something, all right."

Lawrence started reeling in his line. The pole was bending so sharp, I thought for sure, the buggah was going to bust. Then, boom, something pulled at the line and before I knew what happened, Lawrence slipped off the rocks and fell head first into the water.

I reached out my hand and pulled him out. He had a cut above his left eyebrow and a thin line of blood spilled down his face. That was the first time I saw Lawrence bleed. It was a scary feeling.

"You all right?" I said.

"I'm okay," he said. "My head hurts a little. But I'm okay."

What really amazed me, though, was that he was still holding onto that fishing pole, which was good because my dad would've kicked my ass if I had lost it. I took the pole from Lawrence and, after about a fifteen-minute fight, pulled in this huge catfish. Foot long, with whiskers thick as octopus legs. The meanest looking catfish I'd ever seen. Now, I've seen a lot of catfish in my time. Most of them are dark and dead looking. But this one was different. The buggah had a fire burning inside its eyeballs. It actually looked pissed at us for pulling it out of the water. I don't know how to explain. It just looked so full of hate.

"I don't like it," Lawrence said, shaking his head and wiping the blood from his eyes. His hair was wet and when he shook his head, the water splashed into my eyes. "Throw it back, quick!"

I wrapped my hands around the body of the catfish and took the hook out of its mouth. All the time, its eyes never left mine.

"It's ugly!" Lawrence said. "Throw it back, Bret!"

"It ain't ugly."

"Yes it is! Yes it is!"

It started raining real hard. I put the fish in a bucket full of stream water and me and Lawrence went home. Lawrence's shirt was dripping wet and he was shivering.

"Why do you want to take that ugly thing home?" Lawrence asked.

"I don't know," I said. "How's your head?"

"It's okay," he said. "Why? Is it still bleeding?"

"No."

"Oh," he said. He almost sounded disappointed that the cut on his left eyebrow wasn't bleeding anymore. Lawrence sneezed. "Thanks for pulling me out of the water. You saved my life."

"Forget it," I said.

"Bret," he said, sneezing again. The bucket with the catfish was getting heavy. "You know why you and me, we get along so well?"

"No," I said. "Why?"

"I've been thinking about it," Lawrence said. He sneezed one more time. "You and me, we'll never fight. We'll be friends forever. You know why?"

I shook my head.

"Because we have something in common. Something important."

"What?"

"Bret, we don't have any brothers or sisters," he said. Just then, a plane passed overhead. A Hawaiian Airlines DC-9. Va-ROOM! "You know what people call us? Only children. We're only children, Bret." He was shouting, trying to be heard over the plane's engine. "You and me, we're only children!"

"*Lonely* children?" I screamed back, trying to figure out what the hell he was talking about. Lawrence nodded and the plane disappeared into the sky. Lonely children. That's what I heard.

When I got home, I filled this old porcelain bathtub in the backyard with water. After the sun warmed the water up, I gently placed the catfish into the tub. It swam around for a while and then it stopped and didn't move at all. I put a wire covering on top of the tub so the stray cats in the neighborhood couldn't get at the fish. By the end of the month, the catfish had grown almost half as long as the bathtub and about as thick as a telephone book. One day, Lawrence came over to the house and I showed it to him.

"It's ugly!" Lawrence said, coughing into a handkerchief. He caught a cold from the time he fell into Kalihi Stream and still couldn't shake it. "It's too big! It's a monster! Get rid of it!"

"My dad says it'll get bigger," I said.

"It's ugly!" Lawrence said, coughing until his face turned red. "I wish it were dead!"

"Don't say that, Lawrence," I said, shaking my head. "No good, brah! If you say stuff like that, you'll get *bachi*. Bad luck."

"I don't care. I wish it were dead!"

Sure enough, the sound of Lawrence's cough started to change as the days went by. It got more hoarse, like the cough of an old and sick man. He told me to put my ear against his chest. When he inhaled, it sounded like pouring rain inside his lungs. One day, Lawrence started coughing hard. He cleared his throat and spit out a hard round ball of blood.

"You know why you sick, ah?" I said. "It's because of the fish. You talk bad about the fish so the fish, he don't like you."

"Don't be ridiculous," Lawrence said. But he started coughing again and brought up another ball of blood.

The next day, he called me up and said he had to stay home from school. He said he had a 104-degree fever. The next day, they had to take him to the hospital in an ambulance. Meanwhile, the catfish just seemed to get bigger and bigger. It never moved—you could hardly tell it was alive—except for a small wave of its fin every now and then, or an air bubble escaping from the side of its mouth. I couldn't understand why it hated Lawrence so much.

One evening, I walked outside and watched the catfish. I figured it'd be dark in about a half hour or so. I took the wire covering off the bathtub and stuck my hand in the warm water. I pulled the plug at the bottom of the tub and the water sucked out and spilled on the grass. A warm, salty smell filled the air. The catfish started jumping around like crazy and then it turned over on its back, its white belly pointing towards the sky. I put my left hand on the fish and held it down against the bottom of the tub. Its skin was smooth, cool, slippery—like the feel of a dead chicken you prepared for dinner. The fish moved under my hand—sensing, maybe, that something was terribly wrong—and I held it even tighter. I came down fast with the hammer and the fish's head exploded like crazy fireworks and covered the mossy sides of the porcelain bathtub with thick red blood and brains.

* * *

Dr. Miho said I had bronchitis and pneumonia, both at the same time. He showed me X-rays of my chest and pointed out these white spots in the air passages of my lungs. There seemed to be hundreds of them, like stars in the night sky. Dr. Miho said each spot was a ball of mucous that had hardened, and I was lucky they had all been separated. He said if the mucous had all congregated in one area of my lungs, I wouldn't have been able to breathe and could have suffocated. Dr. Miho gave me antibiotics and a syrupy medicine I had to drink three times a day. The medicine tasted awful and, more than once, I dumped it into the toilet. The pills were big and hard to swallow and they left behind a taste like the moldy bread I had eaten at Bret's house that one day. I stayed home from school and spent the time listening to music and reading, Dickens mostly. In about a month I was okay, but I had lost twenty pounds.

Dr. Miho was a family friend. My dad and him were old college buddies. While I was sick, I had to go visit him once a week. But I didn't mind. In fact, I actually enjoyed going to Dr. Miho's office. See, every day after school, Dr. Miho's daughter Julie took the bus to her dad's office to wait for a ride home.

Julie Miho was the prettiest girl I had ever seen. Big brown eyes, hair that came down past her shoulders, and bright red cheeks. From the first time we met, we hit it off. Yeah, in a way I was a little disappointed when I got well because I wouldn't have to go to the doctor anymore and my chances to see Julie went out the door. Once in a while, though, we'd have parties at the house and Julie and her folks would come over and we'd talk. That was the only times I got to see her.

Julie talked about her family a lot. I have to admit, I envied her. She had a big family—three brothers and two sisters—and they all seemed close. Julie said they all got together every Sunday and spent their afternoons at Bishop Museum or having picnics at Moanalua Gardens.

Every night, before I went to sleep, I imagined me and Julie getting married. I believed, if I thought about it hard enough and often enough, that maybe one day it'd happen. I even wrote out our wedding invitation, in my best handwriting, on a piece of paper:

Lawrence Kalapa and Julie Miho
Request the honor of your presence
At their wedding …

I kept the piece of paper in my wallet and carried it with me everywhere. I had turned eleven and would've given up everything I had just to be able to hold Julie's hand.

Shortly after I got well, Dad received a job offer on the mainland and we left for New York City. It all happened pretty quickly and I didn't get the chance to tell Bret goodbye. It's sad how people fall out of touch with each other, but that's the way it is, I guess. I mean, look at the world. It happens every day. Anyway, every time I thought of Bret—which was pretty often, for a while—I remembered the way he pulled that ugly catfish out of Kalihi Stream and kept it in that old porcelain bathtub in his backyard.

The night before we left for New York, my folks threw a huge pool party at the house. Hundreds of people showed up, including Julie and her folks. Julie gave me a going away gift, wrapped up all nice and neat. She said it was just something small and she asked me not to open it until I was on the plane. I thanked her. Then we sat down on lounge chairs by the pool and talked. I still remember the way the lights from the house reflected off the water and sparkled in her eyes. Since I figured I'd never see her again and had nothing to lose, I told her she was the prettiest girl I'd ever met. She shocked me when she said she did not think of herself as being pretty.

"You're so lucky," Julie said. "Moving away like this. Seeing new things, meeting new people …"

"I don't know if I want to leave Hawaii."

"Are you serious? Think of it as an adventure."

"An adventure?"

"Yeah. Absolutely. Leaving Hawaii. I think that's so cool. I'm a little jealous, to tell you the truth."

"You are?"

"Yeah. While you're walking around the streets of New York City, I'll probably be stuck working in my dad's office. Answering phone calls, scheduling patients, filing records …"

"Will you grow up and be a doctor like your dad?"

"That's what he wants," Julie said. "But I don't know if I can be a doctor. I can't stand the sight of blood. In fact, I …"

"Julie," Dr. Miho said, walking over to us with a glass of wine in his hand. "I want you to meet some old med school buddies of mine."

Julie rolled her eyes to the ceiling and joined her father. The next day, I sat in the plane with Julie's gift on my lap. In a way, I didn't want to open it because she had wrapped the package so pretty. But about an hour after we took off—miles above the Pacific Ocean—I carefully removed the wrapping paper and opened the box. Inside, she had given me a scarf and a teddy bear. On a tiny card, she wrote:

> *Dear Lawrence,*
> *Here are two things to keep you warm.*
> *Love, Julie*

I couldn't hold back the tears. I pinched the skin between my eyes until it hurt. I thought about asking the pilot to turn the plane around. I was getting farther and farther away from her.

* * *

Dad gave me dirty lickings for what I did to that poor catfish. He caught me washing the bloody hammer with a garden hose and called me every name in the book—stupid, crazy, psycho. Then he took off his belt and wailed on my butt until I couldn't sit down for three days. When my ass could finally tolerate sitting on my bike seat again, I pedaled up to Lawrence's mansion. I wanted to see if he was all right, needed to see how he was doing. But everything about the place was different. The cars in the garage, the toys in the yard, the kids swimming in the pool. It didn't look like a place for lonely children anymore.

Days, months, years passed. I got a job loading luggage and cargo and stuff onto planes at the Honolulu International Airport.

Some of the guys I worked with loved being around airplanes, like me. For others, it was just a paycheck. Anyway, after work, I'd sometimes go to this bar in Kalihi called the Tuxedo Lounge. The place was pretty much a dive. But one night, I sat at the bar and saw a pretty girl clearing a table and placing the empty beer bottles on a tray. When she finished, she looked up and I don't know if it was my imagination or not, I thought she looked at me and said, "Hi."

I guess it wasn't my imagination because, after a while, she walked over and introduced herself. Her name was Avis. She asked me what my name was and I told her it was Bret. Avis was tall and thin, with brown shoulder length hair and very long legs. I figured she was about my age, maybe a little older. It was hard to tell what nationality she was. She could've been from anywhere, really. A little Asian, a little haole. The thing that struck me first was her eyes. They were big and brown and when she smiled, she looked confident and scared, both at the same time.

"Can you help me with this?" she said.

Avis wore one of those camisole things. The problem was the strings in the front of her outfit had been tangled into tight small knots. I felt a little uncomfortable about it but she asked me again and I wiped my hands on my pants to get rid of the moisture on my fingers from my beer bottle and I began working at the knots. Of course, I couldn't ignore Avis' smooth skin beneath the camisole, but I tried like hell not to stare or touch her. The knots were very small and I didn't know if I was making things worse or not.

"How'd you get it like this?" I said, not having anything else to say. I realized I sounded like Mom when I was a kid and I got my shoelaces all tangled.

"I don't know," she said, her eyes down, just like an eight-year old would've done.

Once in a while, either she or I moved and my hand brushed against her skin. It felt very soft and very warm, like freshly baked bread.

"I think you've almost got it," Avis said.

"Yeah," I said, feeling relief and disappointment at the same time as the knot loosened. The camisole came loose and before it slipped off her shoulders, she caught the strings and tied them into a neat bow.

"Thank you, Bret," she said, looking a little embarrassed and a little shy. I didn't know if she had done this trick a million times or not, and at the time, I didn't care.

"No problem," I said.

Me and Avis wound up sitting in a dark booth. Sometimes, Avis' hair brushed against my face and tickled. It smelled very nice. I wound up ordering another beer for myself and a twenty-dollar glass of cranberry juice for Avis.

"Thank you," Avis said, touching her glass to my beer bottle, just lightly enough that it clicked softly.

"You're welcome," I said. "Are you from here?"

"No. I'm from San Francisco. Born and raised. Last year, I worked in an art gallery in Sausalito. I came to Hawaii for a vacation and fell in love with the place and wound up staying ..."

"How'd you end up here? In the Tuxedo Lounge?"

"I saw the help wanted ad in the newspaper. I came in for an interview and got the job."

"How long have you been working here?"

"About a month. My dream is to earn enough money to open my own art gallery here one day. That would be so cool ..."

"Do you like working here?"

"It's never boring. I'll tell you that much."

I don't know how long we sat there talking. I had several more beers and I bought Avis a couple more cranberry juices. We told jokes to each other and, when she laughed, she leaned over and lightly placed her head on my shoulders.

"That's pretty good," I said, watching Avis fold a cocktail napkin into the shape of a bird, like an origami.

"Thanks," Avis said. "I love birds. My name sorta means bird. Did you know that?"

"Avis?"

"Yeah. I wish I could be like a bird. Just fly off to wherever you please. Anytime you want. Sometimes I feel like I'm trapped. With no room to move, no space to grow. That is the worst feeling in the world. Have you ever felt that way, Bret?"

Before I knew it, all of the customers were gone. The waiters were clearing the tables of crumpled cocktail napkins and empty beer bottles.

"It's closing time," Avis said. We were holding hands.

"Can I call you?" I asked.

Avis looked at me for a while and then she smiled.

"Yes," she said, walking me to my car. The air outside of the bar felt thin and fresh. They had already turned off the neon sign above the doorway that said "Tuxedo Lounge."

The next couple of weeks, I saw Avis practically every day. We always met up at the Tuxedo Lounge. Sometimes, as I drove to the bar, I'd ask myself real quick, what the hell I was doing going out with a girl who made a living out of having lonely customers in a bar buy her over-priced drinks. Once or twice, on the freeway, I seriously considered turning around and forgetting about Avis. But somehow, I always made it to the Tuxedo Lounge and Avis would always be sitting on a stool at the bar—one long leg crossed over the other—talking to the other girls. And when she saw me, she'd wave and her eyes would get big and all my doubts'd be forgotten.

It didn't matter much where we went. Avis was the kind of girl who just let things happen to her. We usually just drove around. Once or twice we went to the movies. Sometimes, if we couldn't come up with anything better to do, we'd sit through the same movie twice. Once we went to Kahala Mall and we walked through several women stores and Avis tried on some long gowns and asked me how they looked on her and I said they looked great. I was a little bit worried that she'd ask me to buy the dresses for her but she wound up placing everything on a charge card.

One night, we drove over to the Blow Hole and sat on the stonewall overlooking the ocean. I remember the moon was out and it felt a little cold because the wind blew hard. A light sparkled in the sky. We watched it for a while, trying to figure out what it was. It turned out to be an airplane. A 737.

"So, do you like working at the airport?" Avis asked.

"I do," I said. "Ever since I was a kid, I've always loved airplanes. I wanted to be a pilot. I wanted to fly. Soar in the air."

"Like me. Remember? One day, I'd just like to spread my wings like a bird and fly away."

"Yeah."

I looked up into the sky and Avis did too. It was strange, like we were both looking for something up there but we weren't sure what.

"Being near those big jets now still gives me a kind of rush," I said.

"You remind me of one of my brothers. He always talked about being a pilot. How many brothers and sisters do you have?"

"None. It's just me. I'm a lonely child."

"*Lonely* child? Why do you say that?"

"Because that's what I am. You know, when you don't have brothers or sisters?"

"You mean *only* child, huh?"

"*Only* child? I always thought it was *lonely* child."

"No," Avis said, smiling. The way she smiled at that moment, I'll never forget it. It was like she understood it all. "You're not a lonely child, Bret. You're an *only* child."

"I am? Wow. *Only* child. Well, I'll be damned. *Only* child."

I shook my head and Avis started giggling and I had to laugh too. After a while we kinda ran out of things to say so we just sat and stared out at the dark water. The waves smashed against the coastline and made loud whooshing sounds.

* * *

I wound up going to college in New York City. Julie wrote me every now and then. Not often enough, of course. Maybe once or twice a month. I kept her letters in a shoebox by my bed and when I felt lonely, I'd read them over and over again, hoping to find some secret code where she was trying to tell me she loved me. Sometimes I felt so far away from everything I thought about packing it all up and going home. One night, I had this dream. Julie and I, we were sitting in a garden somewhere. I asked her to marry me and she said yes. We kissed. The feel of her lips, it seemed so real. We were in a garden and there were flowers everywhere. And you know what? When I woke up, there was the smell of flowers in my room.

In late November—Junior year—I got the first telephone call. In the middle of the night. I picked up the phone and the caller hung up. Pretty soon, I started getting these calls several times a week. Always at three, four in the morning. And the caller always hung up. At first, whoever it was hung up as soon as I answered. Then, the caller started staying on the line for a while without saying anything. For some reason, I didn't slam the phone down or yell obscenities in the receiver or anything. I just listened. Sometimes I thought I could hear noises in the background. Talking. Music maybe?

One night, during finals week, four inches of snow fell on New York City. I got the call at four in the morning.

"Hello?" I said.

"Lawrence?" the caller said. A girl.

"Yeah," I said. "Who is this?"

"Lawrence. It's Julie."

"Julie?" I said, elated. "How are you?"

"Lawrence," Julie said. "Help me."

She began crying. And then she hung up.

The next morning, I caught the early plane out of Newark, New Jersey and landed in Honolulu that afternoon. The first thing I did was call Julie. Her dad answered the phone and I couldn't believe what I heard. Dr. Miho broke down and told me Julie had up and disappeared. They hadn't seen her for weeks. They'd hired a private investigator to track her down. Dr. Miho asked me if I'd help him look for his missing daughter. I said I would.

"Have you ever been to a bar called the Tuxedo Lounge?" Dr. Miho said.

"No," I said.

"Check there first."

I figured there had to be some mistake but I drove to the bar, ordered a Coke, and sat in the darkest booth I could find. The Coke was a little flat, like it had been out for a while. All of a sudden, a man and woman walked into the bar, carrying a Christmas tree. I was pretty far away but I could see that the girl wore a bright silver blouse, the color of the bumper of a new Cadillac.

"Hi, Avis," a lady behind the bar said. She smoked a cigarette and read a magazine. "Ooooh, big tree, no?"

"Hello, Mama," Avis said.

Mama disappeared into a back room and came out with a tree stand and several cardboard boxes. One of the boxes was full of Christmas decorations—bulbs, tinsels, and ornaments. Avis and the man stood the tree up and stuck it into the red tree stand.

"This is my favorite," Mama said, handing Avis an ornament. "The first one I bought in my life. A dove with a silver ribbon coming out of its beak. Look what it says. 'Peace on Earth.' Isn't it pretty, Avis?"

Avis tried to place the ornament on the tree. But the ornament fell to the ground and shattered.

"My goodness!" Mama said, pulling her hair out.

"I'm sorry!" Avis said, falling to her knees and gathering the broken pieces.

"Get the broom, clumsy!" Mama said.

It took me a while to realize Avis was actually Julie. Her makeup was heavier and the hairstyle was different but, damn, it looked like Julie. When I was absolutely sure, I walked up to her. She was still on her knees, trembling, trying to collect the shattered pieces of the ornament.

"Julie?" I said, getting down on my knees also. "It's me. Lawrence."

"Lawrence?" she said, hands covering her mouth.

"I'm here to help you. To take you home. Your father is worried sick."

"Lawrence. I ..."

"Let's talk outside."

Julie and I walked outside. We stood in an alley. Her skin looked pale. Her eyes were glazed and watery—the eyes of the horrible catfish Bret had pulled out of Kalihi Stream. Drugs? I didn't want to ask. Not yet, anyway.

"Julie," I said. "What are you doing here? Where did you get the name Avis?"

"Please don't tell my dad, Lawrence."

"Julie."

"Please."

"Okay, okay."

Julie began to cry, tears slicing through her mascara. Painful black lines the color of freeway asphalt ran down her cheeks.

"I had to get away, Lawrence," she said. "I know you wouldn't understand. But my life was just so, I don't know, stifling. I didn't have any room to move. It felt like everything around me was choking me. I didn't have air. I had to ..."

"Julie ..."

"I'm not like you, Lawrence. Maybe you can take the pressure. I can't. All my life. I had to get straight 'A's.' I had to play the piano. I had to take tennis lessons. I had to get into the college of my choice. And that was all okay. For a while. But then something started happening. I started hating the piano. I hated tennis. School was a drag. I hated going to my Dad's office. I hated the patients, their sicknesses. Everyone kept on watching me. Dr. Miho's daughter. Waiting for me to do big things, like my Dad ..."

"Julie ..."

"What they really wanted to see, though, was the doctor's girl fuck up. People like to see other people fuck up. It makes them all feel better. It's a fact of life. I don't know why things are like that, but it's the truth. So, I didn't want to disappoint any of those vultures watching me. And I didn't get into the fucking college of my choice ..."

"Julie. Please."

"You should have seen the look on Dad's face when I had to tell him I didn't get into any of the fucking colleges he wanted me to apply to. I wasn't going to med school. I wasn't going to take over his sorry-ass practice. He gave me the most painful look. It must be the same look he gives his patients when he has bad news to tell them. And then he hugged me. That was the worst. Dad's pity."

"C'mon," I said. "Let's go somewhere and talk about this ..."

"And you should have seen the look on the faces of Dad's bogus friends, neighbors, relatives, country club pals. So full of compassion and understanding. Inside, they were clicking their heels and doing somersaults. The fucking fakers ..."

"Julie. It's not that bad. You'll see ..."

"No," Julie said.

I gently reached for Julie's arm but she moved away from me. I tried again but she pushed me away. All of a sudden, the guy she'd been with earlier stepped between us.

"Lawrence," the guy said. "I think you'd better leave."

I was rocked. The fucker talked like he knew me. It took me a second to realize it was Bret. He had changed. How long had it been since I had last seen him? Ten years? For one thing, he'd grown a moustache. And his hair looked different. Longer, maybe. His body was bigger, too. Like he'd been lifting weights.

"Stay out of this, Bret," I said. "This doesn't involve you."

"You guys know each other?" Julie asked.

"How do you know Avis?" Bret said, looking first at me and then at her. I don't know why. For some reason, I kinda took that as an insult.

"Her name is not Avis," I said, turning to Julie. "Julie and I, we go way back. Our families have known each other for years."

At this point, Julie began crying again. And what killed me is she turned to Bret—not me—for comfort. She cried on his shoulder and Bret wrapped his arms around her.

"Lawrence," he said. "I think you'd better go."

"No, Bret. You don't understand. Julie doesn't belong here. She doesn't ..."

"Please, Lawrence," Bret said. "I think Julie wants you to leave."

That's when, jeez, I lost it. I grabbed Bret's shirt and tried to push him backwards. But he grabbed me, picked me up and threw me to the ground. I got up and went after him again. I had never been in a fight in my life. Yeah, he beat the crap out of me. The next thing I remember, I was on my knees in the Tuxedo Lounge restroom, throwing up in a toilet already filled with somebody else's shit.

I took out the crumpled wedding invitation, the one I had kept in my wallet since I was eleven years old. The paper was so wrinkled now you could hardly read the writing if you didn't already know what it said. For the first time in my life, the invitation seemed pretty silly and I was embarrassed that I had written it and was even more embarrassed to think I had kept it in my wallet all this time. I rolled the paper into a ball and tossed it into the toilet. It floated in the water for a while—bobbing with the pieces of crap—and then sank to the bottom like a rock. As soon as I did it, I regretted it.

* * *

My first punch landed on Lawrence's left cheek. The second punch knocked him out cold. It took a while for me to hear Avis screaming, "Stop it, Bret! Stop it, Bret!" The next thing I knew, Avis was runningforherlife. I left Lawrence lying flat in the parking lot and chased after her.

"Avis!" I yelled.

She ignored me and ran—pushing past pedestrians, crossing roads against red lights, forcing cars to a screeching halt. She kept on running, like a crazy marathon runner. She sprinted all the way to the freeway. I finally caught up to her near the Houghtailing Street overpass, overlooking the Farrington High School tennis courts. She leaned against the metal railing, chest heaving, fighting for breath.

"Avis," I said, reaching out my hand. "C'mon ..."

"My name is not Avis," she said.

"Okay. Julie. Please …"

"And I'm sorry for everything, Bret. I did not come from Sausalito. I've never even been to Sausalito. And …"

"It's okay, Julie."

"I've always wondered what it would be like to fly. Remember me telling you that, Bret?"

"Yeah."

"I wasn't lying then. I was telling you the truth …"

"I know. Please. Let's go …"

"I think it's the only time I ever told you the truth …"

"Julie?"

"Maybe it's the only time I told anybody the truth …"

"Please, Julie …"

"Goodbye, Bret."

I can't remember everything wordforword. But I remember her leaping onto the freeway railing, opening her arms like a diver, and jumping off the overpass. It all happened in less than a second. It wasn't like in the movies. When people fall in the movies, they fall in slow motion. Graceful, dignified, Hollywood deaths. Avis— Julie—fell likearock. Quickly. Straight down. Silent. Hair blowing madly in the wind. Crashing with the sickest

fuck

ing

THUD

onto the hard, asphalt surface of Houghtailing Street. Fifty feet below. Face down, dress up past her thighs, limbs twisted, bones broken.

"NO!" I screamed. It felt like those nightmares where you're yelling your ass off but no sound comes out of your mouth.

By the time I got down to Julie, a crowd had already gathered. Soon an ambulance arrived. One of the first things the paramedics did was cover her with a sheet. The white sheet almost immediately turned a bright, moist red. After a while, they took her away. They did not appear to be in a rush. And when the ambulance left, there was no need for a siren. The cops asked me a few questions. And then everyone went home. After a while, the only evidence left of the whole fucked up night was tiny spots of Avis'—Julie's—blood on the yellow centerline of Houghtailing Street.

Like a handful of quarters. Only red.

* * *

Three months later, Bret, too, was dead. Witnesses say he'd just finished loading some cargo on a plane. Then, for some reason, he became disoriented. Wandering around the tarmac until he was blindsided by a plane pulling away from a jetway. Airport officials classified it as a horrible accident. But, at the funeral, some of Bret's co-workers said he had been very unhappy the past couple months. They say they wouldn't be surprised if Bret had somehow planned the whole thing.

As for me, I graduated from New York University and got my law degree. When I came home, Bret's parents called and said they had something for me. It was a letter Bret had written on the night of Julie's death. I guess his parents decided to share it with me because my name was all over it. This is some of the last stuff Bret put down.

"And that, pretty much, was that," he wrote. "Threeandahalfhoursago. I don't think I'll ever understand what just happened. Maybe if I write all this shit out, it might make things easier for me to understand. Yeah, I'm sounding pretty bad. But I tell you what. I just drank, uh, ~~sixteen seventeen~~ eighteen beers. So fuck it. And damn, what about Lawrence? I hope he's okay. I knocked him stiff pretty good. Maybe I should drive over to his place. His mansion. Apologize, shake hands, talk about the old times. ~~I mean, Lawrence is a good guy in a lot of ways.~~ Maybe I'll tell him how much he really meant to me at one time. How much he stillmeanstome. I'll tell him that, in a way, he's thefuckingbestfriendIeverhad. That'd be something, wouldn't it? Telling him that? I wonder what he'd say?"

I never use the freeway anymore. I'm told that if you drive past the Houghtailing Street onramp on the anniversary of Julie's death, wreaths and pots of flowers line the railing she jumped from. As for Bret, here's one of those things that is always said too late—something I should've told him a long time ago. When it made more sense to say it. But here goes. Bret, wherever you are now, you and me, we were never lonely children. We always had each other.

Take it easy, Bret. Take it easy, brother.

LEAVING KALIHI

"WHATCHO NAME, BRAH?"

"Malcolm."

"Malcolm. Who are you? Where you come from?"

"I'm your son, Pops."

"Oh. No kidding. Whatcho name again?"

I'm not sure when Pops started to smell differently. In the old days, the good days, he carried with him a clean scent of resolve, of hard work, of promise. It was a sweet mixture of aftershave, pomade, freshly-washed clothes. Then, gradually, things changed. Over the years, Pops took on a new smell—a sour chemistry of ointments, stale bed sheets, old bandages, drying sweat, piss.

"Brah, whatcho name?"

"Malcolm. I'm your son."

Tonight, as I do every night, I cook Pops his dinner. I stand barefoot in the kitchen and place three cloves of garlic on a cutting board. I smash the garlic with the flat end of a knife and toss the paste into several drops of vegetable oil bubbling in a hot frying pan. Then I add the aku bone. Smoke fills the air. The fish quickly browns.

Pop understands it is time to eat. He slowly makes his way towards the kitchen table, his back bent, steps tiny and cautious.

"Whatcho name, boy?"

Hot oil spatters on my hand, sharp, the jab of a half dozen needles.

* * *

For almost fifty years, Pops worked ten, twelve-hour shifts on the waterfront as a heavy equipment operator. The sun reflecting off the ocean had burned his skin the color of black coffee. It's a color that has stayed with him. His hands remain gnarled and scarred from moving heavy crates off ships and into warehouses. Every morning, he woke quietly at three—when even the birds slept—stared into the bathroom mirror and rinsed his eyes and face with cold water. Then he packed his lunch—rice, egg and sausage—kissed Mom goodbye, and walked out of the house. He was always careful to close the screen door gently so it wouldn't slam shut.

The day Pops turned seventy, he retired. His buddies threw him a party. Pops' best friend, Humphrey, stood up and made a speech.

Of course, he talked about the rock.

A large boulder—eight feet high—stood in our front yard. As a young boy, I watched men try and move that boulder. They took off their shirts, flexed their muscles, spit and squinted. Then they pushed and pulled until their faces and chests turned a brilliant red. After a while, always unsuccessful, they inevitably gave up. Sometimes, they called on Pops to try and move the rock. Pops always politely declined. He was too old, he said, flashing a smile that caused the skin around his eyes to droop and crinkle. I was always disappointed because I knew Pops could move that boulder.

"What you guys don't know is this," Humphrey said. "I once saw Bruddah here move that damn rock! Yes, sir! He did the impossible! He did what every single bastard in this room tried to do and failed. Tell 'em, brah!"

Pops sat motionless, expressionless. I wasn't sure if he'd heard Humphrey. I was going to tap Pops on the shoulder. Mom shook her head at me.

Soon after the party, Mom complained of sharp stomach pains. She said it felt like she'd swallowed bits of glass. The next morning, I found her kneeling on the bathroom floor, vomiting dark blood into the toilet. The doctors said there was nothing they could do. Three days later, she passed away.

Things went downhill for Pops. My older brother Clay worked on a fishing boat in Hilo. My sister Cindy was a flight attendant in Texas. They asked me if I could stay home for a while and take care of Pops.

I told them they didn't have to ask.

* * *

"Whatcho name, brah?"

"Malcolm."

"Malcolm. Where you come from?"

"I'm your son."

After dinner, I give Pops his bath. He sits cross-legged on the floor of the tub, looking down at the collecting water like a little boy who knows he's done something wrong. I leave the hot water running from the faucet. First, I wash the dirt out of Pops' short, white hair. Then I scrub every inch of his thin, fragile body with a rag foaming with Ivory soap—the back of his neck, his armpits, his chest, his belly with the pink scar from a recent surgery to remove three feet of intestine. Pops' dark skin—once so firm, so sturdy—is now loose, wrinkled, and covered with brown liver spots. Sometimes I'm afraid I'll scrub too hard, that I'll peel away what little skin Pops has left until he is raw and bleeding.

"Whatcho name, brah?"

Months have turned into years. Pops' bank account once held seventy thousand dollars. His life savings. Then came Clay and his hostess bar girlfriends. And Cindy and her three kids. Today, Pops' account has four hundred bucks.

I turn off the bath water. Dirt spills off Pops' withering body, swirling down a drain that houses centipedes.

* * *

Pops' father—Grandpa Zachary—used to own a barbershop on School Street, near the sheet metal factory. As a kid, I often cut my hair there. If he didn't have any customers, Grandpa Zachary read the sports pages or watched the Saturday morning cartoons—the Archies, Bugs Bunny, Scooby Doo—on his tiny black and white television set.

One day, Grandpa told me how Pops was a champion swimmer in high school. Grandpa said Pops had hopes of competing in the Olympics until he was drafted to go to Korea.

"Hell," Grandpa said, smiling and cutting my hair. "They say Duke Kahanamoku himself watched your father swim and marveled at his technique."

"Nah?"

"That's what they say. Hell, your father was the biggest, most arrogant sonuvabitch in all of Kalihi. The buggah had all these medals—gold, silver bronze. And he'd display those things all over the house—on the ice box, the dinner table, even the damn toilet!"

Grandpa laughed. I was amazed. It didn't sound like Pops.

"When his wahines came over—like your mother—they asked to see his medals and trophies and jeez, he was Mr. Bashful. But what the girls didn't know was that the night before, Mr. Bashful stayed up all night polishing those things with a chamois skin rag. I always had to run to the toilet and laugh when one of the girls said, 'Ho, your medals look so clean!'"

Grandpa laughed so hard, he had to bend over and slap his knees. "He even asked me to hang some medals in my shop," he said. "'Would bring in the customers,' he had the nerve to tell me."

I laughed also.

After the haircut, Grandpa closed the shop, bought me a Popsicle at the Ambassador Market, and drove me home. Grandpa took me under the house and opened a trunk covered by a flannel blanket. There were a bunch of medals inside—old and dusty, with the gold and silver dark and faded.

"Your Old Man was a lifeguard," Grandpa said, in a quiet voice so Pops couldn't hear. Pops knelt in the yard, digging weeds. "He was like the hero of the Farrington High School pool. People told me their daughters swam into the middle of the pool and pretended to drown so that my boy—your old man—would pull them out of the drink. Can you believe that? Your father. Jeez. Never been much of a talker except when he talks about himself."

Grandpa and I walked out from underneath the house. It was a hot day and Pops' face was red and drenched with sweat. He looked up at me and nodded to Grandpa. Grandpa started laughing.

"What's so funny?" Pops said.

"Nothing," Grandpa said. "Hot, ain't it?"

"Damn hot," Pops said. "What the hell are you laughing at? I never thought of hot days spent in the yard digging out weeds as being too particularly funny."

Grandpa laughed louder.

"Well, son," he said, barely able to get the words out, "maybe you should go for a swim."

Grandpa winked at me and Pops shook his head and went back to pulling out the weeds.

* * *

"The mother of the universe lives on a mountain peak in Kalihi Valley," he says, sitting up in bed, looking out a window. "She's right there."

"Yes." I say, sitting on the bed, feet on the floor. "You've told me."

"I have?" Pops says. "I'll be damned."

After I give Pops his bath, I brush his teeth, slip him into his gray pajamas, and put him to bed. Of course, Pops has no idea this will be his last night here—in this house he's lived his entire life. 74 years. In fact, this is the last night Pops will ever spend in Kalihi. Tomorrow, me, Clay and Cindy are driving Pops to the Kupuna Care Home for the Elderly in Manoa. It was a tough call. The three of us have wrestled with this for the past several years. Ever since Pops got sick. We figure this will be best for Pops. Especially now. In his condition.

"That's where I wanna go when I die," Pops says, still looking out his bedroom window. "I wanna be with the mother of the universe. Look. She's right out there. Waiting for me. It's only a short trip."

"Don't talk crazy, Pops," I say.

"Whatcho name again?"

It's also my last night in this house. The family has contacted a realtor and put the house up for sale. It's funny. All my life, I've wanted to move out of Kalihi. Ever since the day my bike was stolen by one of the kids from the Kamehameha Housing Projects. At Farrington High School, I watched classmates get beaten up, shot, stabbed. An eighty-year-old lady down the street was tied and robbed of nineteen dollars in her own home. The next-door neighbors grew pots full of pakalolo. And, of course, there were the gangs. I was tired of it all. The smell of the neighbor's dogs, the wail of police sirens, the busy traffic at three in the morning at the crack house next door.

So, I studied hard. It was my only chance to get out of Kalihi. I became a graphics artist designing everything from t-shirts to surf shop logos to computer websites. Finally, I saved enough money to buy a home in Mililani. Two-bedroom, two bath. Tomorrow, I'm leaving Kalihi. Funny. I always thought when the day came, it would feel like a dream come true.

* * *

On the night of Grandpa Zachary's funeral, Mom told Pops that our neighbor Mrs. Shiroma said she knew something bad was going to happen to Grandpa because shortly before he went to the hospital, a black crow constantly sang outside of his window. Pops wore a gray suit that night. I'd never seen him in a suit before. I wore a white shirt, blue pants and black shoes with gold buckles on them. Brand-new. Mom had just bought them at Woolworth's. I must've been about seven years old.

It really didn't hit me until we stepped into the Kalihi Union Church and I saw the candles, wreaths and the white coffin that Grandpa Zachary—Pops' father—had died and jeez, I was at his funeral. My first funeral. There were books on the bench where we sat and Mom picked up one of the books and began to read. It was the first time I'd ever seen grownups cry.

The minister walked out and everyone became quiet. He was an old haole man dressed in black and white. The minister talked for a while and then everyone stood up to walk past Grandpa's coffin. Everyone looked so serious. Mom and Pops stood up. Then Clay and Cindy did.

"C'mon Malcolm," Mom said, softly. "Don't you want to say goodbye to Grandpa?"

I shook my head.

"After how nice he was to you?"

I didn't realize my hands were gripping the bench.

"C'mon, boy," Pops said.

"Please?" I said. "D-do I have to?"

Pops looked me straight in the eye and I stood up.

As we got closer to the coffin, my heart began beating so hard I was sure everyone around me could hear it banging away. An icy chill shot through my spine—worse than the time I was camping at Mokuleia and saw the Seaweed Lady, worse than the time a twelve-foot tiger shark circled me while I was night diving off Kualoa.

Then it was our turn.

There lay Grandpa. His hands were folded in front of him, on his belly, and he wore a dark suit and tie. In a way, he looked like he was sleeping. I mean, he looked the same as he did the day he gave me the skateboard with the stoker wheels for Christmas and the times he cut my hair at his barbershop. But then, in a very important way that I couldn't figure out, he didn't look like he was sleeping. Something about the look on his face, the color of his skin maybe. You knew he wasn't coming back. That it was too late. It was like he was there but he wasn't.

Then I started seeing all these little stars in front of my eyes. My eyes were open but all I could see were stars. Clay whispered something to me but I couldn't make out a word he said. It was like my hands were over my ears or I was underwater or something. Pretty soon everything started getting darker and darker. And then

I couldn't hear anything. Everything went black. The next thing I know, I'm on the floor and everyone is standing around me.

"You all right, boy?" Pops said.

* * *

"Brah," he says, sitting up in bed, under the light from the moon. "I no can sleep tonight."

"Lie down, Pops," I say, adjusting his bed sheets. I need to make sure his feet are covered. His toes always get so cold at night.

"Who are you?"

It scares me. Sometimes I look at Pops and wonder if this is how I'll be thirty, forty years from now. They say it's in the blood. Pops' care home is going to cost five thousand dollars a month. How long can Clay, Cindy and I make those payments?

"I'm hungry," Pops says, trying to get out of bed. "I going cook me some rice and eggs. And some coffee. Black."

"No, Pops," I say. "It's late."

The last time Pops tried to cook, he left a frying pan with three eggs on the stove and walked outside to cut the grass. Fortunately, I came home from work and put out the small fire with an extinguisher. One of the neighbors said there was so much smoke, he almost called the Fire Department.

"I'm hungry," Pops says, placing his thin hand with its curling blue veins on his belly. There is a bandage on his elbow from falling down while trying to collect the mail. There are more bandages on his knees and hips.

"Hungry?" I say, quietly. "You just had a big dinner."

"I didn't eat dinner tonight."

"Yeah, you did. I cooked it for you."

"What did I eat?"

"Aku bone. Rice."

"Hmmm. That's funny. I don't remember."

A gecko is frozen on the screen of Pop's bedroom window, a silhouette backlit by moonlight.

* * *

After Grandpa's funeral, it rained hard. Our house looked very dark. Mom, Pops and Cindy threw Hawaiian salt over their shoulders before they walked through the doorway. For good luck, Cindy explained. Clay looked at me and did the same thing. Then I did.

I brushed my teeth and went straight into the bedroom. My hip was sore. I couldn't sleep. I kept seeing Grandpa Zachary, lying in his coffin. I saw him on the closet door, like it was a movie screen. I shut my eyes but then I saw him more clearly, hands folded, eyes closed. The bedroom door opened. *Aaaugh! Grandpa!*

But no, it was Pops.

He didn't turn on the light or anything. "Malcolm?" he said, speaking very quietly.

"Yes?" I said.

"Malcolm, pal. How you doing?" He sat at the edge of the bed. "How's your head? That was some fall you had tonight."

"I'm okay. I was tired."

"You made me proud tonight, brah. You was a big boy for Grandpa. He was happy." He handed me a box, covered with gold wrapping paper. "Pal, I got you a little, whaddya call, present."

I opened the box. A watch with a leather band. The hands and numbers glowed in the dark. "P-pops."

"Yeah. Pretty soon, you'll be in third grade. Big boy. You'll need a good watch so you know the time of day."

I couldn't say anything.

"But," Pops said, quietly, "you know what the best thing about the watch is? It's a diving watch. You can wear it underwater and see what time it is and figure out how long you been down there."

"Thanks, Pops," I said.

Pops smiled and walked out the door.

* * *

He falls asleep, finally, just after midnight. His hands are folded, resting on his belly. He snores quietly, inhaling through his nose, exhaling through his mouth. In three hours, he'll be up. It's a habit from the old days of waking early to drive to the waterfront.

"Good night, Pops," I whisper.

Then I turn around and walk down the hall to my bedroom. My steps make the wooden floors creak loudly. The house is empty, ready for its next tenants. The furniture is all gone. The closets have been cleared out, except for a few wire hangers. The walls are bare. For some reason, the place now looks so much bigger. I gaze outside the window one more time—towards the moonlit peak where the mother of the universe lives.

In a few short hours, the sun will be rising.

ACKNOWLEDGEMENTS

Some of the stories in this collection first appeared elsewhere, in slightly different forms:

"The House on Alewa Heights" in *Ka Huliau* (1985).

"Benny's Bachelor Cuisine" and "Oz Kalani, Personal Trainer" in *Bamboo Ridge, The Best of Honolulu Fiction* (1999).

"A Hit Man Named Lilikoi" in *Bamboo Ridge* (2002).

"Tending Bar at the Happy Parrot Chinese Restaurant" in *Faultline Journal of Art & Literature* (2003).

"Leaving Kalihi" in *Bamboo Ridge* (2005).

"For Sale" in *Hobart* (2007).

"Something About the Reef, the Tide, the Undertow" in *MacGuffin* (2008).

"The Sincerest Forms of Flattery" in *Bamboo Ridge* (2008).

"What I Have to Tell You" in *Kartika Review* (2009).

"Three Photographs and a Look Back" in *Hawaii Pacific Review* (2011).

"Mortuary Story" in *The Cabinet* (2012).

"Just Like Magic" in *Pacific Review* (2014).

ABOUT THE AUTHOR

CEDRIC YAMANAKA was born and raised in Honolulu, Hawaii. He is the author of *In Good Company*, a collection of short stories. He is a recipient of the Helen Deutsch Fellowship for Creative Writing from Boston University, the Ernest Hemingway Memorial Award for Creative Writing from the University of Hawaii, and the Cades Award for Literature. He is currently working on a novel.